ANGEL, SINNER, MERMAID, SAINT

ANGEL, SINNER, MERMAID, SAINT

ALICE LEE THORNTON

ISBN: 150850993X
ISBN 13: 9781508509936
Library of Congress Control Number: 2015902562
CreateSpace Independent Publishing Platform
North Charleston, South Carolina

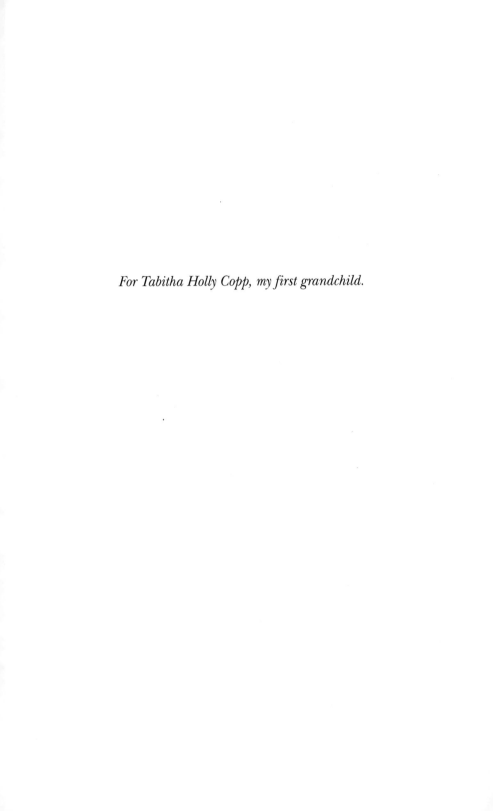

For Tabitha Holly Copp, my first grandchild.

Disclaimers: <u>ANGEL, SINNER, MERMAID, SAINT.</u>
By ALICE LEE THORNTON

All characters in this novel are fictitious. Any resemblance to actual persons living or dead is purely coincidental.

As far as I know, there was no Magdalene Laundry, Home or Asylum in or near Kilburn, London, in the middle of last century; My fictional location was modelled on those institutions such as Bessborough in Ireland itself, which typified the harsh treatment suffered by girls and young women who brought 'shame' on their families by having premarital sexual relationships and illegitimate children.

PROLOGUE

*W*hen the first bright foxgloves stand tall and proud beneath the ancient hawthorn, whose canopy, sculpted by the wind, shelters the secret well; scatter my ashes there, child of my heart, among the flowers his ashes have nurtured, my dust upon the turf his dust has nourished. Then shall we be one again, my love and I, joined in death as we were in life.

The bond that joined us lay deeper than outward things; the rivers of our souls sprang from the same well.' Po-Chü1

ONE

It is hard to determine, as I begin to write in May 2010, whether my writings should be in the form of a memoir, a letter or a diary. Whatever they are, and however random and disjointed, they are dedicated to you, my family and friends; for an account is owed to you and there are questions to be answered even before they are asked. You will make some sort of sense of them, I feel sure, and of the disorder of the museum that is my mind: the memories, the musings, the facts and the fantasies. There is little time left to me now.

I always found it hard to keep a diary, though I was encouraged to do so. Each January 1st I would carefully inscribe my name, *Cecily Rose James*, in my best handwriting, followed by *Cliff Cottage, Porthwenna Cove, PENZANCE, Cornwall, England, British Isles The World, The Universe*. In spite of my resolutions each New Year, I would come across the diary months later, and on finding that the last entry was as long ago as January 16th, make another resolution to do better the following year. One year my aunt gave me a five-year diary, beautifully bound and illustrated, with gold-edged pages like a Bible, and bearing a gilded clasp with a lock. How its blank pages reproached me each time I came across it in later years! I had abandoned it on April 22nd of its first year; and it certainly contained no secrets worth locking up. The last entry stated: *'Billy Trewarren is a cheat and a liar.'*

I suppose one can count on the truth of a diary, both in the recording of daily events and actions and also, perhaps, in the matter of one's emotional response to them. A memoir is coloured by hindsight and is selective in content. It is like a painting in the hands of an artist, a happy memory highlighted in a brighter colour here, a dark thought overlaid with shadow there. Some recollections may be inaccurate in detail, some consciously or unconsciously obscured by the passing of time. It may be that this will turn out to be both memoir and diary – certainly the former and, less frequently, the latter.

I could dabble for a long while in the warm shallows of the sea of childhood, recalling the happy days of endless holiday in Porthwenna; but it is time to summon the courage to go back to 1954 and dig deep into the cold ground: ground which lay undisturbed for so many years; time to unearth that tiny bundle, with its swathing of filthy rags, which for so long was the torment of my nightmares.

They took my child away, my little daughter of the raven hair and the blue-black eyes like her father's – or so I imagined her. Dead, they said, as I emerged from the drugged state they had forced on me in the screaming agony of giving birth. And just as well, my aunt said, for the shame and the sin of it, and the disgrace to my poor parents who had sacrificed so much to bring me up in the right way and to give me a good education. In due course, she said, less unkindly, I would make some man a good wife and bear him other children. My sin might be no less in the eyes of God, but at least the ears of man would not hear of it, except from my own lips. But my heart bled and my body ached with an emptiness I could not understand. My breasts, bound tightly with strips of cotton sheeting, throbbed and burned as their milk was denied outflow, unsought, unwanted.

The smell of the disinfectant which they used to scour the floor and the walls pervaded the room as if to purge my very body and soul of my transgression and wipe away that little life as if it had never been. The nun, Sister Mary Noreen, who hovered like a dark shadow in that forbidding, joyless place, seemed to approve of my tears and thought they told of penitence. But when she was called away one day, the young woman who cleaned my room – my *cell* would better describe it – said quietly:

"Think yourself lucky you're a posh Protestant, girleen. You're no better than I am, but you'll be allowed out in a few days to get on with your life, while I am punished for ever. I had to take the boat and come to England to find work and have my baby, for the shame it would be to my family. Sure, with one a priest and another nun, 'twill be years before I can go back to the ould country – if ever I see it again. I was told that all Protestants go to Hell but I'll be joining ye there too, no doubt."

There was a strict rule of silence in the Home and I had to strain my ears to hear the woman's words as she scrubbed and polished her way round the room, muttering as she went.

"Just remember us in here, so. When you're after marrying and sitting in your smart house with a maid to clean your parlour an' all, remember us 'fallen women' of Magdalene House who have to give away their babies to rich people and stay in this prison for _____."

But the nun had returned; her footsteps, the swish of her black habit and the click of her rosary beads unheard on the cold tiles of the passageway. She grabbed the woman by the ear and marched her out of the room, flinging her bucket and brushes after her and telling her to clean up the mess. I never saw her again. For my remaining days in the home a very young girl came to clean my room. She kept her eyes downcast and her mouth twitched nervously as the same nun stood inside the door, watching her every move. I can still picture the girl's red-raw hands and rough, bare legs, and the way she flattened herself against the wall when the sister swept past her to inspect her work more closely. Were these nuns really called Sisters of *Mercy*, I wondered.

On the eighth day of my confinement my aunt and uncle fetched me in a taxi-cab. As my uncle helped me with my few belongings, my aunt had a brief conversation with the nun in charge, Sister Mary Noreen, and handed her an envelope, which I imagine contained payment or some sort of donation for my stay. My aunt was Chairman of the Benefactors of the institution and as zealous a Catholic as only a convert could be in those days, according to my mother. The nun smiled at her, less than warmly I thought, and then looked sourly in my direction.

"I had a Mass said for the soul of …. for the, er, …infant," my aunt said quietly in the back of the taxi as we passed between high walls, encrusted on top with shards of broken glass, reminiscent of my boarding school, but much higher. Tall iron gates were quickly closed behind us. "Now we shall not mention this sorry business again. There is nothing to stop you going home tomorrow. We have sent a wire to your mother and father who came back to England last week."

Home, I thought. Where is home now?

My uncle, looking in part embarrassed, in part mystified, gave me a rueful smile and patted my hand awkwardly. He was my father's twin, but as different in looks and demeanour as any brother can be from another. An academic of some note, he took refuge from difficult domestic situations by retreating into the mists of classical history and planning his next learned treatise. For all that, however, he was less remote than my own father ever was.

⸺◦◦◦⸺

A s I sat in the train the following day, travelling northwards through the late summer landscape, the sky was leaden and the trees looked dusty and tired of their burden of leaves; the willow-herb had lost its bright colour and the blackened hog-weed and nettles beside the track straggled like unkempt hair. There was still no respite from the desolation I felt as I imagined my little girl, clothed, not in the sickly lemon matinée jacket which was part of the required layette which my aunt had chosen and provided, but in a little smocked dress of purest white silk, lying at my breast and twining tiny fingers in my hair. I would have named her Elowen, since she had started her being in Cornwall and had Cornish blood, at least in part.

Cornwall. Porthwenna, the place I loved best in the world, was denied to me now. There was no going back, either to the place which I thought of as my true home or to the carefree contentment of my childhood. Instead, I was bound for my parents' new house and an awkward welcome which would barely mask their disappointment in their only daughter. No doubt there would be some kind of party very soon – not to welcome me home, certainly not that – but to mark a new beginning for us all: a ceremony to tidy away the immediate past, just as surely as that little child had been put out of sight and mind, buried both literally and metaphorically.

There, I have dealt with that for the time being and can return to the 'before' and 'after'. I spent most of the war years and, later, my school holidays with my grandfather in Porthwenna. My father was in the Diplomatic Service and had postings, sometimes in England but mainly abroad. Being childless, my Uncle Guy and Aunt Dorothea would act *in loco parentis* when my parents were abroad, though on the strict understanding at my mother's insistence, that I should attend the Anglican Church in Hampstead and not go with my aunt to St Joseph's. I stayed at their house some of the time but, probably to their relief, the place where I most wanted to be was with Grandpa Joe in Cornwall.

Grandpa Joe, my mother's father, was a fisherman, though, having been wounded in World War 1, he seldom went fishing now but still owned two boats which he leased to younger, fitter men. He was still referred to as 'The Skipper' and would keep a close eye on what went on in the cove. The lifeboat crew knew that they could always count on him in an emergency. I realised when I was older that my mother was not comfortable about his former occupation. ('My father was in the Royal Navy, actually.' Which he had been, of course, but not quite in the way she implied!) When my parents were in England, my grandfather would never come to stay at our house as my school-friends' grandparents did at theirs.

"I'll never cross the Tamar again, my little mermaid," he'd say in that dark brown, velvet voice of his. "Any road, your mother don't want the likes of me at her fancy cocktail parties. Give me a tankard of good Cornish ale in The Ship any day."

My grandmother had died when I was four years old. I have a vague memory of a kind, smiling face, a comfortable lap and a flowery crossover pinafore which smelt of clean linen and freshly-baked pastry. When she had gone, my grandfather managed well enough with the help of kind neighbours who would cook and clean, wash and sew, in return for a helping hand with the digging or the mending of a leaking roof. In a fishing village there are always widows, alas, and the war was adding to their number. Mrs Pascoe, two doors away, was one such and would have liked to have altered her single status by becoming indispensable to Grandpa Joe, according to the better-informed women of the community. I heard this in the village shop when I was carefully choosing my sweet ration, invisible between a pillar and the high shelf which held the large glass jars of brightly coloured boiled sweets. She was especially indulgent to me, hoping perhaps that I would recommend her to Grandpa Joe as a replacement grandmother.

Cliff Cottage, nestling into the rocks as if it had simply grown there rather than having been built by human hands, with its thick white-washed walls and its warm thatch, was my true home, my safe stronghold. Much as I loved the golden summer evenings and the long afterglow when the sun had dropped into the sea in a final blaze of glory, what I relished most was to sit by the old dog, Duke, on the hearth-rug by the fire on a winter evening, the paraffin lamps lit and the shutters closed tight against the raging of an angry sea, listening to Grandpa Joe's rich, deep voice as he read me stories of fairies and goblins, heroes and princesses, or animals with magical powers; pausing now and then for a puff on his pipe.

JUNE 13, 2010

I am going to interrupt this memoir to say how shocked I am to read in the newspaper today that about 18,000 abortions were carried out last year on girls under eighteen – some as young as fourteen or less. The statistics gave evidence of some women and girls having had up to *eight* terminations. According to a spokeswoman, some of these children – *my* word, for that is all they are - have time for sex and 'can handle it emotionally and physically' but become pregnant because of 'chaotic lifestyles and difficulties in using contraception'. I feel sad about this and, yes, bitter, because of my own experience. Christian doctors are wringing their hands and pointing to the failure of sex education. When I was young, the nearest we came to this kind of knowledge from the spinsters who taught us was the reproduction of the Brussels sprout! As for the so-called Christians who elected to deal with the results of our ignorance, they would punish our 'sins' with worse crimes. In five decades the pendulum has swung too far in the opposite direction. Surely there must be a safe and sensible place for it somewhere in the middle. (Perhaps my analogy is flawed, for a stopped clock is of no use to anyone!)

Actually, we were not as ignorant and innocent as our elders would have wished, but my friends and I took notice of the advice of the agony-aunts in the back pages of women's magazines.

> *'Dear Agony Aunt,*
>   *Please would you explain the difference between petting and <u>heavy</u> petting? ..... My boyfriend wants to ....but I ... etc.'*

> *'Dear Reader,*
>   *....... On no account allow heavy petting. Boys easily lose their self-control and it is up to the girl to stop things going too far. Your boy may sulk because of your refusal, but he will respect you all the more. ....'*

There was a girl in Porthwenna who had, by all accounts, let a boy *go all the way*. I heard Mrs Bossinick in the Post Office say darkly that she was 'no better than she ought to be' and I understood the censure in her remark although I always thought this a rather silly and illogical expression.

The stories in the magazines, and the library books we read, usually ended happily on a moral note, with marriage *suggested* if not actually mentioned – an extension of the fairytales of childhood: '...and they lived happily ever after.' Romance blossomed into love, a wedding followed, sex was then allowable (but seldom mentioned) and children were born.

B ut I will return to my childhood again in an age when most children were still innocents. It is the early summer of 1942 and I am six years old. Grandpa Joe and I are going to church because it's Sunday. (In those days nearly everyone in the village was either 'Church' or 'Chapel') We pass the meeting house in the village with its ominous announcement painted on the end wall: THE WAGES OF SIN IS DEATH, and take the path which winds up the valley with the stream beside it. The long grass in the meadows has been cut and the hay is drying and nearly ready for gathering, its scent mingling with the fragrance of elder blossom and honeysuckle. The foxgloves stand tall and straight along the hedges. I love to linger on the bridge when we reach the road, watching the dippers and the water-wagtails on the stones below in the dappled shade of the over-hanging trees.

"Hurry along, Cecily Rose," says Grandpa Joe as I lean over the bridge. "And you in your Sunday best. You can stay a bit longer on the way home."

There is a large slate-topped bier inside the lych-gate. I would love to climb on it and jump off into Grandpa Joe's arms but he tells me that it is a special resting place for coffins when they are brought to the church for funerals and burials. A little beyond the gate, to the right of the path, is my grandmother's grave, where we pause and lay a few flowers which I have picked along the way. Old Duke has come with us today as he often does, and sniffs around her tomb-stone, looking rather sad, I think. How long would a dog remember his mistress, I wonder? He will sit in the church porch and wait for us until the service is finished.

The church bells have been stopped because of the war. They have been silent for two years now. Grandpa Joe told me that they will only ring again to warn of invasion or celebrate victory. I am quite glad really because the sound used to frighten me rather when I was younger.

We enter the dark hush of the church which, even in summer, smells rather damp and musty. I think this is probably the smell of holiness because, like the stones of the building, God must be very old indeed. The Rector is old too and his cassock smells of mothballs as he greets Grandpa Joe and pats me on the head, as if he has been taken out of a cupboard especially for Sunday. Jesus would not smell like that, I reason, as I sit waiting for the service to start. He was much younger and lived in the open air, sitting on mountains and going fishing a lot. Of course, when he was a baby he might have smelt a little of ox and ass because he lived in a stable, but the frankincense probably helped with the smell.

The singing is good today because there are some soldiers and airmen from the Camp in the back pews. Grandpa Joe sings quite loudly too and I try to match his volume so that I can hear my own voice. I especially like the hymns with lots of 'Alleluias' and think that, when I have children, I will call them Alleluia and Hosanna. (Easter is better for alleluias, really; today it is Whit Sunday and there aren't any, but I sing them all the same because I can't always read the actual words quickly enough). There are prayers for Peace and for the King and Queen and the Princesses and other important people, and a special one for Mrs Lane because her husband is 'reported missing'. There is a long sermon too which I don't listen to because it is hard to understand, though at first my attention is caught by the 'rushing mighty wind and the tongues of fire'. Instead, I find the number of the final hymn in my prayer-book and try to read the words:

> Faith and hope and love we see,
> Joining hand in hand agree,
> But the greatest of the three
> And the best is love

From the overshadowing
Of thy gold and silver wing
Shed on us who to thee sing
Holy, heav'nly love

Then it is time to sing it. I like the tune of this hymn and the words of the last verse stir my imagination. A window opens in my mind and through it I behold a beautiful angel, more beautiful even than the Angel Gabriel or Snow White or Cinderella, spreading love all around like gold. When the churchwarden comes round with the collecting bag, I put in the threepenny bit I've been holding ready in my hand, and then look at the print it has left on my palm. Grandpa Joe puts in half-a-crown. With all these people in church today, I think, the Rector will be very rich indeed.

TWO

In September the previous year I started lessons and walked with the other children of the village to the school next to the church. Unlike the other evacuees from London, I was, to my great joy, allowed to remain in Porthwenna at least until the war ended. I knew that I was to be sent to boarding-school eventually but that day seemed a very long way off. Meanwhile, I loved everything about school, and for the next few years, when lessons were over for the day, I would join in all the games and mischief with the other children on the walk home. We would play in the hay-ricks and harvest fields, paddle in the stream trying to catch tiddlers in jam-jars, steal apples from the Rectory orchard, climb trees and swing on branches. Although I sensed that I was 'different' in some way that I could not define, for those years I was one of them; I belonged. Admittedly, my name was a problem at first.

"What kind of a name is *that?*" one of the older boys asked. All the other girls had more usual names such as Margaret, Mary, Ann and Elizabeth.

"I was called after my daddy's daddy whose name was Cecil," I explained.

"Well, how about 'Cess' – or would you rather we called you 'Silly'?" he asked amidst peals of laughter. "Of course, there's always 'Gingernut' or 'Carrots' …

"My second name is Rose," I said with all the dignity I could muster, although I would not have known what that word meant at that young age. "So you can call me Rosie if you'd rather."

"Well, all right," another boy said, "That'll do: it's *kind* of the right colour, anyway."

So Rosie it was from that day on and even my teacher would call me by that name, except when she was cross with me. I decided to change the name of the 'Rosebud' doll I had been given for Christmas from Rosie to Matilda. I was not a great one for dolls anyway and did not admit to Billy and Johnny and the other boys that I even *owned* one.

I n the spring of 1945 there were changes at the Rectory. The old Rector had retired and a younger man moved in with his wife and family. Our headmistress, Mrs Howard, played the organ in church and decided that some of the school children should form a choir to sing at the Institution and Induction service. The Bishop would be there to perform the ceremony so it was a Very Important Occasion, we were informed. She told me that I was to sing a solo, the first verse of "Brother James's Air", which was to be sung as an anthem. I did wonder if I had been chosen because of my surname but she assured me that it was because I was 'a promising little singer'. (Sure enough, Billy Trewarren, ever the tease, noticed the coincidence too and thereafter the song was known as "*Rosie* James's Hair"!)

Mrs Howard coached and encouraged me, showing me how to control my breathing and open my throat without forcing the tone. Meanwhile the choir learnt the rest of the anthem, the girls singing the descant in the last verse while the boys sang the melody. The day before the service we had a practice in church with the organ. I thought that my voice sounded very small and thin and echo-ey in all that space but the new Rector, Mr Gray, who had come to listen, said that he could hear the words perfectly but suggested that I stand forward from the others, a little nearer to the congregation.

The great day dawned, the Saturday after Easter I remember, because we had some of the 'Alleluia' hymns! We had been told to wear our best clothes and to make sure that our shoes shone 'fit to dazzle the angels'. The Bishop made a grand entrance, looking splendid in his vestments and mitre and carrying his crosier. There were a number of other clergy there too, wearing their best robes.

When it was time for the anthem, the choir moved out of the stalls and arranged themselves on the chancel step. At a nod from Mrs Howard, I stood forward, nearly overwhelmed by the sea of faces before me. I knew that Grandpa Joe's was one of them but was too confused to pick out that reassuring presence.

"Don't worry about all those people," Mrs Howard had said beforehand, "They may well be here because there's a good tea afterwards – and of course they like to see the Bishop. Just take a few deep breaths and give it your best endeavour."

I listened to the few bars of introduction, fastened my eyes steadfastly on a stained glass angel in the west window, took a deep breath and soared up the first arpeggio as if I were bound for Heaven itself.

The Lord's my shepherd, I'll not want, He makes me down to lie / in pastures green; He leadeth me/ the quiet waters by;/ He leadeth me, He leadeth me the quiet waters by.

I stood back again into my place with the others and we sang the remaining verses, our voices rising and falling and blending until at last the threads of descant and melody diverged, the girls flying once more with the angels, the boys left on the earth below.

The rest of the service passed in a kind of mist for me, so moved was I by the performance we had given. Looking back, I realise that this was one of those strangely significant moments which mark the various stages of one's passage through life.

We filed out of the choir stalls and into the church hall where, in spite of wartime shortages, sandwiches and cakes were laid out on tables with cups of tea and lemonade for the children. I had taken only two sips of my drink when Mrs Howard came up to me and said:

"Cecily, the Bishop would like to speak to the little girl who sang so beautifully on her own. Come with me and I will introduce you."

She took my hand and led me to a table where he sat talking with the Rector, Mr Gray, and two other clerics.

"Ah!" he said, "The small angel! God has given you a lovely voice, Cecily, and you must use it to sing His praises and to give pleasure to His people. Well done, my dear; I hope I shall hear you again one day."

And then, a few weeks later, there was another special service in church, one for which there was no time to prepare. Suddenly the bells were ringing again, their joyful peal carrying far out to sea on the off-shore breeze, to celebrate Victory in

Europe. We were given two days' holiday from school, and flags and bunting flew from every building in the village. The Service of Thanksgiving for Peace was held in the evening of the first day, V. E. Day, and the church was full. The whole village seemed to be there, 'Chapel' people as well.

A special committee was formed soon afterwards to plan the Peace Celebrations. In fact, these took place a year later on the first anniversary of V.E Day, when a large marquee was put up on the school field and there was an entertainment and tea for the children and a dance for the adults until late at night.

By this time I was a regular visitor at the Rectory. The Grays had a son called Robert, a year older than I, and a daughter, Sarah, a few months younger. We became firm friends and I would often be invited to tea with them or go with the family on picnics. Meanwhile, Mr and Mrs Gray, having written to my parents for permission and, presumably, payment, encouraged my musical development by arranging for extra tuition in both singing and piano with Mrs Howard. Mr Gray even suggested that I should be sent to a school which specialised in Music, but my parents decided to leave in place the arrangements they had already made. I was to start at All Saints' School in Essex the following January as a boarder. I would have a good all-round education there, they said, and the school had an excellent reputation for both Sport and Music. They were grateful for the Grays' encouragement of me, especially in that they allowed me the use of their piano each day upon which to practise. However, they explained, they were not keen on a specialist education at this stage because of the possibility of my eventually wanting to pursue a musical career, a precarious choice, even if one were exceptionally gifted.

In April 1947, my parents, on a short visit to England between postings, came down to Porthwenna to take me back to London and prepare me for boarding school. I was to have started in January but, as luck would have it as far as I was concerned, owing to a shortage of coal, not to mention the severity of the wintry weather, there were no through trains from Cornwall to London all that winter.

As my father and mother could not comfortably stay at Cliff Cottage, they put up at The Trevelyan Arms at Polburran for four nights.

"More their style there," observed Grandpa Joe. "There's no pasties and apple dumplings for the likes of they, eh little mermaid? 'Tis all fancy cakes and Oat Quiz-een up there!"

Mrs Gray invited them to tea at the Rectory. I could see that my mother approved of my new friends quite as much as she *disapproved* of 'the village children'. We had eaten our bread and butter and home-made strawberry jam and were just starting on the caraway seed cake when she announced:

"Cecily's speech has improved *no end* since the last time we saw her. She was sounding so *Cornish* then – and before that there were overtones of *Cockney*: the influence of all those evacuees from the east end of London, I suppose," she added with a tinkling laugh. "Perhaps there will be no need for special Elocution lessons at her new school, though I believe it is part of the curriculum anyway, according to the Prospectus."

To this day I have always associated the taste and smell of caraway seeds with the feeling of acute embarrassment that overcame me then, manifesting itself as a slow but intense rush of blood to my face. It seemed to go on and on, rising relentlessly until I imagined it bursting through the top of my head and continuing in a scarlet cloud until it hit the ceiling. I thought my hair must surely be standing on end and following in its wake.

"You went as red as a ruddy beetroot," Rob told me when we had been excused from the table. "It really clashed with your hair. I don't know which was redder. Ro-sie, Ro-sie, Ro-see!" he taunted.

"Oh, shut up, stupid," Sarah said, jumping to my defence. "It's a good thing Mrs James didn't hear some of the words *you've* taught her."

"Knew them already," I retorted ungraciously. "Perhaps I should have said them at tea and given Mummy a real shock."

It came to me then that the reason my parents were here at all was that, in only two days' time, they would be taking me away from Porthwenna. It would be months until the summer holidays when I could return. Life would never be the same again. I did not even bother to feign interest in the game of cricket we had started to play before tea.

"Sul-ky Ro-sie," Rob chanted, swiping at a tennis ball bowled by Sarah, which I made no attempt to field. "Just because you were out first ball."

"Oh, go to Hell and Damnation!" I said, though not loudly, for fear of being overheard, especially by Mr Gray. I stamped across the lawn and into the shrubbery, and climbed up a tree in which I sat miserably until it was time for us to leave.

I spent my last day in Porthwenna saying goodbye to my friends. Mrs Howard said how much she would miss my piano lessons and my voice in the school choir and in church. She wished me luck and begged me to work hard, especially with my music. The Greys asked me to write with my school address and to tell them how I was getting on. My school-friends expressed the view that I would be too posh and hoity-toity to speak to them again when I came back in July, which I hotly denied.

The morning we left there seemed to be too little time for goodbyes. Grandpa Joe, seeing the panic in my face, wrapped me in his great arms and whispered:

"Be brave, little mermaid. No tears now, promise me, or you'll upset Duke. In no time at all you'll be home again." (He always said I must be a mermaid because I was never happy to be away from the sea).

My father cleared his throat impatiently as I knelt down to hug Duke and to hide my brimming eyes in his fur.

"Come along now, Cecily," he said briskly, "The car is waiting for us, but the train will *not*."

There was little conversation on the long journey to London. My father spent most of it hidden behind *The Times* or reading Important Papers; my mother and I read our books. We went to the Restaurant Car for lunch. They thought it would be a treat for me but I had little appetite. What I did eat was washed down with fizzy lemonade, which I enjoyed.

When we reached Paddington, we went straight to Daniel Neal's in Oxford Street where I was fitted with my new school uniform. I was not impressed with the nondescript shades of fawn and brown, and the foxy-coloured Harris Tweed coat was scratchy and hot on such a warm afternoon.

"At least it compliments your hair," my mother said approvingly. "What a good thing there's no scarlet in the uniform – but

I suppose there seldom is." She looked inquiringly at the sales assistant.

"No, Madam. Most school uniforms are navy, green or brown, though red and yellow might be used sparingly – on a hat-band for example."

That was another thing, the *hat*: dark brown felt with a fawn band. Though trying not to look, I caught sight of myself in a long looking-glass and thought I looked like a scarecrow with two thick, red pigtails. I made a face at my reflection and looked away quickly.

"Right, if that is all settled," said my father when all the clothes had been tried on, "I need to call into the Foreign and Commonwealth Office if there is still time." He turned to the sales assistant and handed her his card. "Please send the goods and the account to this address."

Why do I remember this day in such detail all these years later? I suppose it was one of those defining moments again, the transition to another stage of my life.

I f anything, boarding school was even worse than I had ex-pected. It was not that I missed my parents as most of the other girls seemed to; I was homesick for Porthwenna and es-pecially for Grandpa Joe and dear old Duke, and I missed all my friends as I looked at the crowd of unfamiliar faces and wondered how I would ever make sense of them all. That I was the only new girl in the school that term did not help my feel-ing of isolation, either.

Being forced to leave the people and places one loves is akin to the separation and grief of mourning. It is loss and loneliness, actual physical pain and mental anguish. Sleep comes as a blessed respite each night but morning brings a return of the sickness that must be carried through the day like a heavy load. There is a verse in one of the Psalms which says: *Weeping may endure for a night, but joy cometh in the morning.* On the contrary, I found that only sorrow came in the morning with the unfamiliar sound of the town's traffic and the noisy chuffing of steam engines at the nearby station, instead of the seagulls' call and the scraping of the night-fishing boats as they were winched up the pebbles in the cove, the men shouting to each other as they unloaded their catch.

I suppose the trains I could hear were what have long been called commuter trains. The irony was that any one of these trains could have taken me to London and thence I could have returned to Cornwall. I had, when the opportunity arose, made a quick circuit of the school grounds which were enclosed by a high wall, topped with broken glass to deter intruders. I had noticed, quite close to the back gates, some kind of service box against the wall which might have made it possible to climb to the top. The real problem, however, was not the broken glass or the fact that I might break a leg as I dropped from the wall on the other side, but that I had no money for the train fare and nowhere to go except to my parents or my uncle and aunt who would only have sent me straight back again.

Eventually, of course, resignation prevailed. I settled down, made friends and began actually to enjoy some subjects, especially English. Music, however, was very disappointing at first. The younger girls were not admitted to the chapel choir and my piano teacher was strict, old-fashioned and uninspiring, which meant that I made very little progress.

M y joy knew no bounds when the term ended at last and I was aboard The Cornish Riviera Express steaming out of Paddington Station on its long journey to Penzance. The grimy red-brick factories and terraces of drab houses, with their small plots of garden littered with broken toys and rusting pipes, slid past slowly at first, then more quickly as they gave way to wood-lined heath-land and a patchwork of fields in all shades of green, with here and there rectangles of gold where the grain ripened in the late July sunshine. Soon we were hurtling along and I exulted in the metallic rhythm of the wheels on the track: 'tiddli-*tum*, tiddli-*tum*, taking me *home*, taking me *home*,'... When we went over points I had to find extra syllables to put in until the rhythm settled down again: 'taking me home, taking me home, taking me home to my grandpa and *Duke.*'

My aunt, who had seen me off at Paddington, had asked a 'suitable-looking woman' if she would kindly keep an eye on me, which she agreed to do until she reached her destination at Plymouth. She offered me a toffee and asked me a few questions, telling me that she had two grandchildren whom she was to join on their summer holiday, but I was not of a mind to share my joy and excitement, hugging it to myself selfishly and unwilling to reveal my thoughts; so she soon gave up the effort to engage me in conversation and read her magazine or nodded off. After an hour or two, she rummaged in her bag and produced her own sandwiches and the packet that my aunt had given her to keep for me, 'in case she eats them straightaway.' Hers were fish-paste by the smell of them; mine were egg, and there was an apple to follow. I hoped that the lady would offer me another toffee after we had finished, but though I looked fixedly at her brown paper carrier bag, she did not produce one again.

Soon after Exeter, which was the first stop in those days, I told her that I was going to stand in the corridor to look at the sea. I pulled on the thick leather strap and lowered the window a little. Too much and the wind would take your breath away; besides, the steam and smuts from the engine would blow in your face as the train snaked round the bends. The longest part of the journey was still to come, I knew, but this wonderful stretch of the line, running beside the sea for several miles, refreshed my excitement and sense of home-coming as I feasted my eyes on the strangely shaped red rocks and the shimmering water beyond. Only here did I wish that the train would slacken its pace a little so that I could marvel for a while longer at this impressive sight; but we sped past the long beach and through Dawlish Warren and Teignmouth stations too quickly even to read their names. Soon afterwards we could see the Tors of Dartmoor and my erstwhile guardian was gathering her belongings and readying herself to disembark.

"Will you be all right now, dearie?" she asked as the train prepared to stop at Plymouth. "Here, have another toffee and see if you can make it last until the next stop."

I thanked her and asked if she would like me to lift her case down from the rack, but a man in the opposite seat got to his feet and handed it down to her, which was just as well because I would have had to stand on the seat and the case looked quite heavy.

"Goodbye then, dear. Have a lovely holiday." And she was gone. I saw her standing on the platform, looking this way and that for her family. A boy of about my age and a younger girl ran up to her shouting: "Here we are, Granny!" Then a man in shorts came striding up and bent to kiss her and pick up her suitcase.

A great hiss of steam and we were off again, with another wonderful moment in store: the bridge over the Tamar. My father had told me that it had been built by the great engineer, Isambard Kingdom Brunel, but though I had thought at the time that 'Kingdom' was a very strange name and 'Isambard' even stranger, I was not to be distracted by admiration of *his* skill at this moment. As I looked eagerly both up and down the great expanse of water, dotted with small craft and sparkling in the afternoon sun, I knew that we were leaving England and were entering my homeland at last. Of course, I had made this crossing many times before and was to make it many times more, but this journey stands out in my memory because of its sense of drama in my fertile imagination: the heroine was at last returning to her beloved *homeland* after her long *incarceration* in a *foreign* country!

In an hour or so we saw the sea again as the train stopped at Par; then there was Truro and the mining country round Redruth. And, at last, the sea again and St Michael's Mount, golden and mysterious, dreaming in the late afternoon sun as we came closer and closer to the end of the line and finally puffed slowly into Penzance station.

I spotted Grandpa Joe at once, standing tall and strong on the platform, his eyes screwed up in his weather-seamed face, scanning the carriages as they passed, and puffing away on his pipe. I picked up my case and hurled myself through the door and into his arms, nearly knocking him over in my delight.

"Steady on, little mermaid," he gasped, laughing and holding his pipe well clear. He pushed me away, holding me tightly by the shoulders. "Let me 'ave a good look at you. My, you'm nearly as tall as me!" He picked up my suitcase and we walked towards the ticket collector.

"That train was spot on time: came in on the dot of five o'clock," he said. "'Tidd'n always as good as that. Let's get on 'ome, then. Old Duke's waiting to see you. He's 'ad itchy feet all day. Must've known you were coming home. There's strawberries for tea," he added as we walked towards the car. "I don't s'pose you've 'ad too many of *those* where you've come from."

Soon we were bowling down the road to Porthwenna. Grandpa Joe put the old Austin into a low gear as we came round the steep bend; and there was the sea – *my* sea - spread out like translucent blue glass below us, dancing with silver light and mottled here and there with tiny cloud-shadows. Here, still looking as dear and familiar as ever, her face white as snow, her eyes and mouth blue with fresh paint and her thatch of brown-gold hair neatly combed, was Cliff Cottage. I was *home!*

Thus I spent my school holidays for the next six years, sometimes bringing back with me a school friend to stay for a week or so, eager to show her the places I loved so much; anxious for her to envy me for living in such a seaside paradise. I suppose it must have rained some of the time but we always seemed to be out of doors, paddling, swimming, and having picnics. I still saw some of my old school-fellows, though they had moved on to secondary schools as well and did tease me for being 'a bit posh nowadays with a snooty accent'. I would laugh this off, however, and put on a good Cornish burr to prove that I hadn't really changed. There were always joyful reunions with my friends at the Rectory, when we would compare notes about school and plan how we would spend our holidays as the days stretched out generously before us. Sometimes Rob and Sarah and I would take our swimming things and cycle to one of the nearest sandy beaches, stopping to shop on the way for food and drink to take with us, a Swiss roll, a tin of condensed milk, a bottle of Corona fizzy lemonade. Usually Rob would cut the Swiss roll with his penknife but I remember one occasion when he had left it behind and had to use a bicycle-clip! On other days we caught the bus into town and went to the Gaumont Cinema, sitting through the main film and supporting programme twice because there was no bus back to Porthwenna till nine o'clock.

I would also visit Mrs Howard at the first opportunity. She would accompany any songs that I brought with me to sing to her and suggest new ones for me to learn. When I was older and had passed my audition for the school choir, she used to take me to choral concerts and to rehearsals of The Byrd Consort who met in a church near Penzance. Grandpa Joe came to a Christmas concert which the group put on in St Breaca Church and told me how proud he was that I should be singing with such a 'highbrow' choir at such an early age. One year in August, when I was fifteen, we joined forces with other choral societies, consorts and choirs to sing Handel's *Messiah* in the Cathedral as part of the annual Summer Festival, under the baton of Bruno Sabra, the renowned choral conductor. Here were Hallelujahs a-plenty, of course, and I recalled my earlier preoccupation with them as we practised the famous chorus for which the great work is largely known. I was spellbound by the whole experience; awe-struck by the dynamism of the conductor and the way in which he could produce the exact effect that he required, the smallest nuance of interpretation, by the barest movement of his little finger. I have sung that work – or excerpts from it – countless times during the ensuing years, as all choral singers and soloists do, sometimes well, sometimes very badly; but those rehearsals and that particular performance remain with me as some of the greatest moments of my musical life, so impressed was I at my young age by the whole experience: the thrill of the music, the massed voices, the orchestra, the grandeur of the majestic pil-lars and the vaulted roof as they made magic of the great sound, taking it up and around and giving it back threefold. But most of all I was impressed by the man on the rostrum, who could direct and control this great stream of wonderful music with no more than the slightest movement of his hands, a hint of a smile, the lift of an eyebrow; or produce a great crescendo like a huge wave, a deluge of resonance, simply by raising his arms as if to lift the roof from the building. Exuberance, solemnity, pathos: whatever the music demanded voices and instruments produced at his command.

Back at school, I continued to spend a great deal of time on Music as I had for the past three years since going into the upper school, learning and practising the piano and the organ (with a much more inspiring teacher now), singing in the Chapel Choir and the Madrigal Group and taking Music examinations; in short, heading for a musical career, which did not please my parents at all. Meanwhile, however, I gained very adequate results in other subjects, particularly English, and left school in the summer of 1953 to make applications to both Music Colleges and Universities for September 1954. (In those days you had to be eighteen before starting advanced education).

In that year between school and university, my parents wanted me to go with them to St Lucia where my father was due to take to take up some important position on the Governor's staff. ('Oh, *do* come with us, darling,' from my mother. 'You'll meet so many *suitable* people out there.' I assumed that she didn't include *the natives* in that category. 'And think of that *glorious* weather all the time – and the *parties* you'd be invited to ....')

But before I could think of a very good reason not to go with them, one presented itself, though how I wished it had been otherwise. My beloved grandfather had a stroke on the very day that I was due to go down to Porthwenna at the end of July. This was followed by another one, more severe, two days later when I was already on my way, willing the train to go faster so that I could rush from the station to the hospital as soon as I arrived. I had no idea what a stroke was and thought that I might be too late. As it was, I did indeed find the sight of him very distressing as he lay in the hospital bed looking pale and grey, his face slightly twisted. I could not hold back my tears as I looked at him. He seemed so withered and diminished as I kissed him hesitantly and too gently, and mourned already the hugs we always exchanged in our normal reunions. But there was still a twinkle in his eyes, I noticed, and he squeezed my hand with one of his and said, sounding as if rather the worse for drink:

"My little mermaid, what's it all about, eh? I s'pose you'll have to stay with me for good, now."

And I knew in that instant that that was exactly what I would do. I would stay here and look after Grandpa Joe, the dear man who had nurtured me all these years.

THREE

The evenings grew cool as August gave way to September. The holiday-makers drifted away and school began again, the sound of the bell ringing down the valley as tiny children, pristine in their new or passed-down uniforms came out of the cottages holding their mothers' hands, some timid and apprehensive, some bold and eager to embrace this long-awaited day. I watched them from my bedroom window and thought of my own first day at school, so long ago it seemed now. I had dressed proudly in my new clothes and my squeaky new shoes. Mrs Pascoe had come in as she did every morning, kind soul that she was, to plait my hair in two thick pigtails, tied with dark green ribbons to match my gym tunic. After breakfast, Grandpa Joe had taken my hand in his, and with Duke lumbering along behind, we had walked down the path into the road to join the little crowd walking up towards the school. The bell would stop ringing at nine o'clock sharp and woe betide anyone who was not inside the building by that time!

I stopped day-dreaming and went downstairs. Having peeped in to check on Grandpa Joe who was still sleeping peacefully, I slipped the lead onto Nimrod's collar and let myself out of the cottage to take him up to the fields where he could have a run. The air was crisp and clear with a light breeze, and heavy dew had drenched the long grass on either side of the path and glossed the leaves of the trees. In spite of my anxiety over Grandpa Joe, it was good to be alive and young on such a day. Nimrod was bounding joyfully in the grass, looking like a sleek grey seal as he rose, sank out of sight and leapt up again. He came back to me and shook himself thoroughly, showering me with ice-cold drops which spangled my clothes like diamonds.

I met two of the mothers on their way back from the school. One of them had been crying, I noticed, and I remember wondering why she should be so upset. One day, I was to understand her tears only too well. Bereavement comes in many guises.

During August my days had taken on a regular pattern. I would get up at seven-thirty and let Nimrod out, taking him for a walk then if the day promised to be very hot. When I had prepared breakfast I would take a cup of tea to my grandfather and sit with him while he drank it - with my help. Sometimes the district nurse would come in and wash him and dress him; otherwise I, sometimes with Mrs Pascoe's help, would give him a quick wash, trim his beard when necessary and help him to dress, after which we would have our breakfast.

"You shouldn' be stuck in 'ere doing this for an old man," he would say in his slurred way. "You should be out in the wide world playing the field or meeting all those 'illegible' bachelors on that island in the sun. But you're a good nurse, I must say, a good little maid."

"I couldn't care less about eligible bachelors," I would assure him, "or illegible, illegitimate or inedible ones. But perhaps I'll find an *in*eligible bachelor one day," I joked.

"Oh, you and your words," he would retaliate. "You swallowed a dictionary or summat?"

If the day was fine and warm, he would sit out in the front garden until lunchtime and 'watch the world go by' – in the form of summer visitors ('emmets', he called them) on the path that climbed past the cottage and up onto the cliff. Some of his old pals, habitués of The Ship Inn, would walk up to greet him and exchange a few yarns about 'the good old days'.

And so the last days of summer passed, but I noticed that Grandpa Joe slept in longer each morning and the day was half gone before he was up and dressed. A day came when he chose not to dress and said he would just sit in his dressing gown until it was time for bed; and soon after that came the day when he would not get up at all. Dr Beswetherick, who had been our doctor for as long as I could remember and had a great regard for my grandfather, said that it would be kinder to all of us if he were to go to a Nursing Home, as he was going downhill so noticeably.

"Your grandfather is a big man," he explained, "too heavy for you and Mrs Pascoe to lift and turn.

It is distressing for him to be dependant on you in this way, and the mental anguish which he cannot express will only hasten his demise. I can make arrangements for him to go into Elm Lodge. It's only about two miles away, so you can visit every day if you wish." He laid a hand on my arm as he saw the tears come into my eyes.

"I know this is hard for you, my dear. You are very young to have to deal with such a decision, and I know that he has been both father and mother to you all these years, but do take my advice. You have looked after him well and will continue to bring him joy and comfort in his last days, but you have your life and career ahead of you and cannot stay here forever, nursing an old man, however much you love him and feel you owe him."

S o the pattern of my days changed again, revolving around my thrice-weekly visits to my grandfather. I would push my bicycle up the hill and ride the mile or two to Elm Lodge Nursing Home where he had a pleasant room overlooking the sea. French windows opened onto a paved terrace, beyond and below which was a well-kept lawn curving round shapely beds filled with autumn-hued flowers. A neat hedge protected the garden from the elements without obscuring the panorama.

"Best room in the place," Grandpa Joe said to me soon after his arrival there. "Lucky the old girl before me snuffed it when she did."

"Only the best for my grandpa," I said, relieved that he had settled in so easily and did not seem to miss his old way of life. "I suppose you get a lot of fuss made of you by the nurses."

"They d' think I'm the best-looking man that ever walked this way," he laughed. "'Cept I can't walk now, I need to be pushed in the wheel-chair. The ladies thought their luck has changed as well when I waltzed into the Day Room. They went all silly and dewy-eyed – those as was awake, that is. There's only one other fellow in the place, and he's gaga."

This chat reassured me greatly, much as I missed him and the familiar routine at home. We had done the right thing for him, which was some comfort. In fact, he seemed to have taken on a new lease of life since he arrived at Elm Lodge, finding a fresh stimulus in his new surroundings.

I had been summoned to call at the offices of Grandpa Joe's solicitor and told that my parents had come up with the wherewithal to pay his Nursing Home expenses. This meant that Cliff Cottage and the two boats, which would be mine when I came of age, he told me, would not have to be sold. Hitherto, I had not even wondered where the money came from for the running of a home and one's daily needs. Now, such matters must be addressed and I had much to learn. The solicitor assured me that my parents had always paid my grandfather an allowance for looking after me and would now pay it directly to me. He would make arrangements with the Bank, he said.

Although because of this regular income I did not have to find work in order to stay in Porthwenna, soon after my visit to the solicitor, work found *me*, in the form of a request from the headmaster of a small Preparatory School for boys, a friend of Dr Beswetherick. The elderly Music mistress had left suddenly, and without explanation, soon after the beginning of term, and a replacement was urgently needed. He did not seem to mind that I had no teaching experience and asked if I would be willing to go into the school on Mondays, Wednesdays and Fridays to play the piano for Morning Assembly and do some class singing with the boys. Trevene Court was only a mile or so further on from Elm Lodge, so I gladly accepted the challenge and started the following week, after consulting Mrs Howard, on the way to our singing rehearsal, for much-needed advice and suggestions as to what songs I should teach. She lent me a large pile of sheet-music, among which was *Brother James's Air.*

"What better than that to begin with?" she said. "And tell them what the other children used to call it. Sing them that first verse and tell them about the Bishop's visit and what he said to you. And that cowboy one, *The Streets of Laredo,* they'll love that. They'll love you too. They always like someone *young* teaching them. That Miss Whatsername is a crabby old thing – far too handy with the ruler, especially if boys are tone-deaf. Apparently she took umbrage at some imagined slight and walked out, never to darken the doors again, or so I heard."

——

M y social life took a turn for the better when I started at Trevene Court in late September. I had been missing the company of people of my own age since Rob had left to do his National Service and Sarah had gone back to her boarding school for the Michaelmas Term. At Trevene Court there were two young masters, one of whom had a car. If they could get time off together, they would sometimes take me and the younger of the two matrons into town to a film, or even on one occasion, a dance.

At home, Nimrod, old Duke's successor, was my constant companion and protector. Duke had died at the good age of fifteen years during term-time in 1949 and Grandpa Joe had made sure there was a wriggly, hairy bundle of puppy to greet me on my return for the holidays, knowing that it might divert me a little from the grief of losing my beloved old friend.

"I don't know how he'll turn out," he had said. "I got him from some gypsies who were camping up on the top road. He's to be *your* dog, Cecily Rose: yours to name, yours to train *and...* yours to clean up after. 'Course, I'll look after him when you're away but otherwise he's your own dog. And don't forget: he'll need to be kept on a lead anywhere near these cliffs or you'll lose him over the edge, sure as eggs is eggs. He'd only have to go after a rabbit and that would be it."

I was delighted with him, much as I mourned the solid comfort and seeming immortality of old Duke. Little did I think then that one of his actions would affect the course of my life so profoundly.

FOUR

There are still places to be found which hold a special magic, an indefinable dimension which is not quite of this world. It may be that it is merely chemistry of some sort which we mistake for enchantment, just as we are attracted to one person in particular rather than another; one taste or scent, colour or musical phrase which is preferred to all others. But I still think that, regardless of scientific explanation, such places do have some spiritual significance or some history, perhaps, that marks them as special to a particular individual.

It was Nimrod who led me to discover such a place on a hazy afternoon in October. We were walking along the cliff path to the west of the village, which is now part of the Coast Path, but in those days was seldom used by anyone except locals. We crossed the old stile of granite steps at the end of the path. Here the ground fell away a little into fields in which hardy cattle grazed the short turf. A path of sorts led to Polburran and thence to the road back to Porthwenna. Here I always let Nimrod off the lead and we would run together towards the houses in the distance. But today for some reason I lingered with my thoughts and memories, sitting for a while on the bottom step of the stile while Nimrod explored the various sights and smells in the vicinity, as dogs do. As I sat there, I had the strange but overwhelming feeling that I was on the brink of something momentous. To my left there was a clump of dense furze, blackthorn and bramble, impenetrable by cattle, humans and dogs alike – or so I had always thought. The blackberries had never really ripened this year and were not worth the effort of gathering. In any case, as Grandpa Joe would have warned, after Michaelmas the Devil spat on 'em and they should be left alone.

I shook off my daydream, got to my feet and looked around for Nimrod, but he was nowhere to be seen. Panicking that he might have slipped past me back over the stile and be chasing rabbits near the cliff, I called and whistled and was about to climb the steps when I heard the sound of him lapping water on the far side of the bushes. Usually the sea was the only sound to be heard up here as it crashed and slapped against the rocks below; but today it lay silken and serene under its veil of mist with only the slightest whisper of sound accompanying the occasional cries of the seabirds. I turned back towards this new, unexplained sound. Somewhere, I thought, Nimrod had found a cattle trough, but however had he reached it? Rounding the end of the thorny bushes, I found the narrowest gap between them and the wall, the bush having been prevented from closing it altogether by a tall standing-stone. Easing myself through sideways, I found myself descending into a grassy depression – a fairy dell I would have termed it in my childhood. Nimrod came to me, his jowls dripping with water, wagging his tail and looking very pleased with himself. In the amphitheatre, among the promise of a myriad of next year's foxgloves, there stood a hawthorn tree, its top chamfered by the wind, standing guard over a low trough of ancient stone which was almost hidden in the long grass. I knelt down and saw my reflection in the cold, clear water as I scooped a handful to my lips. I have found an enchanted well, the voice of romance said. Perhaps I shall turn into a frog, mocked the voice of scepticism, and I looked again at my reflection for reassurance.

Looking up, I saw that the mist from the sea was swirling overhead. Calling Nimrod, I made my way back through the slender gap and found the path across the fields towards the village. It was easy to get lost up here in poor visibility. The gaps in the hedges and banks looked very similar to each other and the scarcely definable path could be confused with others made by the cattle. Eventually, to my relief the dim shapes of the houses of Polburran materialised and, having reached the road, within a few minutes we were back in Cliff Cottage. Inside, on the kitchen table I found a freshly baked fruit-cake with a note from kind Mrs Pascoe: *Thought youd like this for your tea, you could do with building up abit.* But if I had been any wider I would not have passed through that gap and found the well, I thought. I planned to return as soon as possible when the mist had cleared and prove to myself that I had not been dreaming.

Some instinct told me not to share my secret, even with my grandfather, though of course I would have liked to inquire whether he, or indeed, any of the older inhabitants of Porthwenna, knew of the well's existence and, if so, of its history. I knew that there were many wells in Cornwall which had for centuries been visited by people seeking cures for various ailments such as warts, 'tetters', 'stags', heart complaints, - even childlessness. Sometimes people left ribbons or items of clothing tied to nearby trees to mark their visits. A few years earlier I had spent a week with a school friend in Derbyshire and had attended a Well Dressing ceremony, marvelling at the beauty and intricacy of the floral decorations which adorned the spring of precious water. *My* well, my enchanted well, bore no such signs of having been recently visited before Nimrod and I happened upon it. I would tell no-one about our discovery I decided.

———— ∞∞∞ ————

A week passed before I had a chance to return. The early morning held the promise of a glorious autumn day, and Nimrod and I left the cottage long before the sun had mounted the cliff behind us. There was nobody about, apart from a few fishermen in the cove, who wolf-whistled as I passed. I knew most of them well enough to wave and make a mock curtsey before going on my way. One or two of the lads had been my school-fellows only a few years before, though much seemed to have changed in that time and they treated me differently now.

The sun, still low in the sky behind us, lit the path ahead which rose up steep, rocky steps, past gates and gardens and across a paddock with a kissing-gate at either side. Here a donkey grazed contentedly and a floppy-eared nanny-goat inspected us over the half-door of its shed. I always stopped to exchange greetings with both animals, fondling the goat's ears and scratching the top of her head while she tried to nibble my sleeve, and rubbing the donkey's velvety muzzle as his breath warmed my hand. I would rub his long, hairy ears, too, and laugh as he bared his long, yellow teeth in a grotesque donkey-smile.

On the far side of the paddock the path descended again, narrowing into a stony track with grassy banks on the upper side and dense, thorny scrub below, which would break one's fall into the sea but from which one would never be able to regain the path unaided – and even then, punctured by a thousand thorns. The sea was like a great length of silk flung out in all directions, a shimmering silver-blue shot through with graphite, with white feathering at the edges where it lipped the rocks creamily and sucked in and out of the caves in a meringue of foam.

It was with some apprehension that, after winding around the cliff for some minutes, I mounted the steps of the stile, fearing that the well might after all be a figment of my imagination, a dream sequence which could only dissolve into disappointment. I was tempted to sit on the bottom step on the other side to put off that moment. But I walked along beside the blackthorn and found the stone which held the bushes back from the wall, the access to the dell seeming even narrower than it had last time. Followed by Nimrod, I took a deep breath and squeezed through, descending through the dew-soaked grass to the well, where I knelt and washed my face in its ice-cold water.

When the water settled again, Nimrod began to drink, but then an extraordinary thing happened which enhanced for a moment the other-worldly aspect of the place. Suddenly he was on the alert as, hackles raised, he stood perfectly still, his whole attention focused on the may tree, and I realised that we were being observed just as closely by someone or something. Searching the shadows of the tree's still dense foliage, I saw two wide topaz eyes staring down at us. As my eyes became accustomed to the gloom, I realised that they belonged, not to a wild animal but, incongruously, to a black domestic cat. For a moment all three of us were transfixed, and then suddenly it was no longer there: it had simply melted away. Can there be ghost cats, I wondered? The beginning of a poem I had read somewhere came into my head:

> *Cats, no less liquid than their shadows,*
> *Offer no angles to the wind....*

But Nimrod seemed to think that it was substantial enough and took off at great speed, vanishing behind another blackthorn bush on the far side of the tree – and here was another surprise: beyond the bush I found another narrow opening between two pillars of stone. I followed Nimrod along an overgrown path deep between grassy banks of bramble and wild briar, which eventually emerged between laurel bushes onto a lawn, at the far end of which stood a cottage.

Embarrassed to be trespassing, I called Nimrod, who stood staring up at a fence upon which sat the black cat regarding him defiantly, and backed off towards the path again – but too late. A deep, melodious, rather foreign-sounding voice called out: "Maiden with the Titian hair, whom do you call?"

"Oh, I do apologise," I said to the disembodied voice, which seemed to come from an open upstairs window. "My dog, Nimrod, he was chasing a cat – your cat, perhaps – and ran into your garden."

"Oh, Bodkin, you mean; he always moves in when I stay here. It matters not; any diversion is welcome. I take it you will stay for breakfast? Toast, fruit, and cheese – will that suffice? And naturally, coffee. Come to the door at the side. Allow me five minutes and I will reveal myself fully clothed. The reason I am hiding at present is that I have not a stitch on."

A wise virgin would have turned tail and fled, of course, but this foolish virgin was more than a little intrigued – not, I hasten to assure you, at the idea of a naked man, but because I was always attracted by eccentricity and, besides, the voice seemed familiar in some way that I could not identify. This was turning out to be quite an adventure: I would take my chances.

—ↈ—

"WWhy Nimrod?" asked the voice, from behind the door at which I was waiting. "I apologise for keeping you waiting. I was not expecting a visit from a pre-Raphaelite angel, or do I mean mermaid? I have mislaid the key. ... Elgar's Nimrod, or an enigmatic variation? ... Ah, here it is."

"Well no, actually; Christopher Smart: '*Let Nimrod, the mighty hunter,*'" – I heard the key being fitted into the lock.

"'*Bind a leopard to the altar and consecrate his spear to the Lord*'," the deep voice sang as the door opened. "Of course, *Rejoice in the Lamb* – Britten. Great stuff; he was quite mad, - Smart, I mean, not Britten."

But I was awe-struck, speechless, as I came face to face at last with 'the voice': a man of fortyish, I estimated, hardly taller than myself, dressed casually in a black, open-necked shirt and black cords and holding a half-smoked black cigarette to his lips. He was none other than the conductor, Bruno Sabra.

"Come in, come in," he ordered. He held out his hand. "Bob Smith is the name – but I see by your face that you do not for one moment believe me! And you – do you have a name? Have we met before, or are you one of those Cornish Saints, or a mermaid from the sea?"

Recovering my composure a little, I took his hand and replied: "Well, I certainly have very wet feet. Shall I take my shoes off? And my name is Cecily Rose James."

"Ah, *Cecilia*, you mean. Of course – the Patron Saint of Music. My Muse has come to me in person. No, just wipe your shoes; the floor is of slate. And tell Nimrod to wipe his. He can come and make Bodkin's acquaintance instead of terrifying him."

We stepped into a large, warm kitchen with a black-leaded range at one end, on which a kettle was beginning to sing. Nimrod settled himself beside it on a cushion, much too small for his considerable size, which I imagined was Bodkin's bed. Bodkin himself had jumped onto a cupboard, the topaz eyes regarding his pursuer with malevolent intensity, the long tail furiously indicating indignation and displeasure. At the other end of the room there was an old pine dresser with an untidy display of blue and white Cornish-ware cups, plates and jugs; and in the middle of the room a large deal table, stacked with books and manuscript paper which was covered in black notation, written in a bold hand. Beside it a log-basket served as a repository for waste paper, and around that on the floor, lay several balls of screwed-up paper which had missed their target.

"Let us clear a space here," Bruno said, pushing the piles of paper to one end of the table. "I was composing late into the night – deadlines to meet, you know, always deadlines. The inspiration simply was not there, but one must try, try, try. So, you see, I welcome the diversion. I think you were sent to me for a purpose, to relight the fire of my creativity."

As he spoke, he was laying plates, cups and cutlery on the table in a fairly haphazard way and slapping slices of bread onto the hotplate of the range to toast.

"Can I help in any way?" I offered.

"You could look after this toast while I make the coffee but, *en effet*, as the honoured guest, you should be waited upon and not have to lift a finger."

Soon the aroma of coffee filled the room and butter melted on the hot toast, as we sat down at the table to eat the simple meal. I was entranced by his reminiscences and stories, but found at last that my own tongue loosened when he drew me out about my own history, my present and my plans for the future.

I recall every moment of that morning as if it were yesterday: every word that we exchanged, every sight, sound, scent and taste. Much as I would have liked to stay longer, I took my leave after insisting on helping to clear the table and wash the dishes.

"Two requests before I let you go," he said. "First, promise me that you will come back very soon and sing to me. I need your help with the soprano solos in my new work. Secondly, I beg you to tell not a person of my presence here. I am in hiding so that I can work in peace. It must be our secret."

Agreeing gladly to both, I thanked him for breakfast and bade him goodbye, running across the lawn and down the path with Nimrod at my heels, hugging my – *our* - secret to my breast ecstatically. Why should I be tempted to tell a soul? I wanted him all to myself.

FIVE

"You have a lovely young voice, Cecilia: sweet as clear honey and pure as liquid silver. If I dared, I would insist that the part of Nicolette should be sung only by you. But there will be some ageing, bosom-laden prima donna who will claim the part for herself. She will wobble her way through the music which *you* inspired – and wobble all her other parts as well, no doubt, as she masquerades as sweet sixteen when it is plain to see that she is well past child-bearing age."

He handed me a sheet of manuscript paper. "Now try this – to 'lah' if you like, at first. I have tried to write the notation clearly, but manuscript is always harder to read than print. You can add the words later."

I was standing beside a small grand piano in the long, narrow music-room with a spectacular view of the sea, having just sung, to his accompaniment, *The Lark in the Clear Air.* Strangely for me, I was not in the least bit nervous; how could I be when Bruno had made it clear that his 'composer's block' had been swept away by my arrival in the garden four days earlier? He had attributed to me a sort of mystical power, making it easy to play the Muse because of being treated as such.

But the music and the words belonged together. Having 'lah-ed' my way through a few bars, I added the words:

Aucassin, true heart and brave,
Sweet thy love upon me steals,
Urges, clamours, pleads, appeals;
Would to God that peril past
In my arms I held you fast;
Would to God that in this place
We were stayed in one embrace,
Fell your kisses on my face,
My dear, my fere.

There was a moment of utter stillness when I finished. Our eyes met and seemed locked together; then he blinked and shook his head as if to recollect himself. I felt myself blush slightly and the sheet of manuscript paper I had been holding fluttered to the ground. I bent to pick it up, glad of the diversion, while he rearranged the sheets of music on the piano.

"Ten out of ten for reading at sight," he said. "Well, what do you think, Muse?"

How could I answer such a question? My romantic nature was deeply affected by even those few lines: I was mesmerised, enchanted, captivated, - in love. I *was* Nicolette and therefore *he* must be Aucassin.

"It's ... lovely," I said lamely. "I'd like to hear some of the rest of the work ... and know the outline of the story. I'm not familiar with it."

"I have a spare copy of the story which you can take home with you and read. You might be able to inspire me further. *Aucassin et Nicolette* is a translation of a mediæval tale, a *cante-fable* designed for recitation by strolling players, to an accompaniment of pipe and viol. ... Now I will sing you one of Aucassin's songs while you imagine a handsome young knight, hardly more than a boy, sweeping you off your feet. It is written for a counter-tenor, so I shall have to transpose it for myself to sing. My falsetto would make you laugh!"

'Lily-flow'r, so white, so sweet,
Fair the faring of thy feet,
Fair thy laughter, fair thy speech,
Fair our playing, each with each.
Sweet thy kisses, soft thy touch,
All must love thee over much.
'Tis for thee that I am thrown
In this vaulted cell alone;
'Tis for thee that I attend
Death, that comes to make an end,
For thee, sweet friend.'

As I listened, my eyes on his face, the mental picture he had suggested for me was banished immediately. ('Bestride your charger and be gone, Sir Knight,' I might have said, had I not been spellbound once again by the man I had already cast as Aucassin). I felt the blush rising to my face again. This time however there was no lingering glance when he finished singing. After a few words of appraisal, I said that I must be going because I had to visit my grandfather.

"But you are always rushing away," he protested.

"No more often than I am arriving on your doorstep," I retorted.

"Take the copy of the song with you - and the book – and when you have done your homework like a good girl, come back, please do."

I promised that I would. He could not have known the supreme effort it took for me to leave at all.

49

On this second visit I had come on my bicycle on my way back from Trevene Court. The cottage, Foxgloves, as Bruno had pointed out to me on my earlier visit, was to be found at the end of a long, rough drive which I had always imagined to belong to a house called Polwartha, close to the road.

When I arrived in Grandpa Joe's room, he looked at me keenly and gripped my hand tightly as I bent to kiss him. He was having more and more difficulty with his speech but I managed to get the gist of what he was saying, which was that there was a glow about me and a sparkle in my eyes and a spring in my step and was it perhaps one of those young masters at the school who was taking my fancy?

"I shall want to look 'im over," he slurred. "Nobody's gonna be my Rosie's fancy-man without my say-so."

I longed to tell him about my adventures of the past few days but felt that it was too soon – and, if I am honest, I did not want to worry him, nor did I want to be warned off treading a path which might be more dangerous than that which was closest to the cliff's edge. I simply smiled enigmatically and kept up my usual chatter about Nimrod, the village, friends and the boys at school. After half an hour or so his eyes closed and his head nodded and, while he dozed, I took out of my bag the book Bruno had given me and started to read the story of Aucassin and Nicolette.

"Why is it not in the original French?" I asked Bruno a few days later when I returned the book, after what I felt was a decent interval, though it cost me all my patience to stay away for so long.

"Oh well, don't forget it is to be performed first in San Francisco. I find that many Americans are not too fond of the French language – or the French themselves, for that matter. Benjamin Franklin and Noah Webster were, I understand, partly responsible for simplifying English spelling in America and much of the French influence was removed: which explains the appearance of such words as 'center', 'color' and 'program'.

I had 'done my homework' as he had bidden me and we passed the early afternoon in song while he made the odd correction and sketched in suggestions for the accompanying parts.

"Nothing too sophisticated needed here," he said, "just enough to suggest pipe and viol; no symphony orchestra to kill the romance and mediæval flavour."

Too soon the light began to fade and, as I had come by the cliff path with Nimrod, I had to take my leave once again.

"You leave too long between visits, Cecilia," he complained, laying a hand lightly on my arm. "Soon I have to go away – perhaps this month, perhaps next. You have helped me so much. Come tomorrow, come every day."

"I will try," I promised, thinking how hard I had had to try *not* to make my visits too frequent. And as I could scarcely endure the prospect of his leaving the cottage, I began to call on him practically every day after that, sometimes on my way back from school before visiting Grandpa Joe, sometimes on foot with Nimrod.

Anyone who has read my story thus far will have some inkling of what was to come – and yet I find myself almost reluctant to continue. Perhaps it is the thought of confessing to something that, in those days, was considered shameful; perhaps I am ashamed now of being so shame*less* then - or of baring my soul after all this time to those who know me as 'Ma', or 'Grandma' or 'Aunt'. But, as the rest of my life depended upon the events of November 1953, continue I will, and my readers must make of it what *they* will.

One afternoon as the light began to fade, Bruno walked with me down the lane as far as the stone gateway. I had told him about my discovery of the well, and now I teased him that only Nimrod and I were slender enough to pass between the two stones. I ran off, laughing, to the well and bent to scoop up water in my hands to fling towards him. But as I turned, he stood there before me and grasped my wrists, bending his head to drink the remaining drops of water in my cupped hands. Then, raising his head again, he took me in his arms and his lips closed on mine which were still parted in laughter, … which gave way to surprise, disbelief and then the utter joy of the moment.

"Oh, my dear, dear girl," he breathed as he released me, only to draw me close again. "My sweet Cecilia, my Muse, my love."

Feeling the urgency of his desire awakened my own and I knew that his kiss was but the delightful prelude to the fugue, which in all its intricate complexity must inevitably follow. But he groaned and pushed me away gently.

"Go now, sweet girl, quickly, before it is too dark to see. Come, Nimrod, and see your mistress home safely – but bring her back tomorrow: bring her back to me; bring her back again."

I cannot bring to mind a single step of our walk home that afternoon. Did my feet actually make contact with that well-trodden path? Did I greet anyone as we walked through the village, or did my radiant smile brighten someone's day? All I could think of was Bruno's kiss, reliving each second of its duration; feeling that at any moment I might dissolve into thin air. I ran into the cottage, almost forgetting to let Nimrod in behind me. The face which looked back at me from the small mirror in the kitchen had eyes like bright stars, the cheeks were flushed, the hair wild. Once again I was assailed by disbelief. Had I been dreaming after all? But no, I seemed to be wide awake and up and dressed, if not in my right mind!

S ome would have seen me as a brazen hussy as I cycled back towards Polburran later that evening, the full moon lighting my way. I saw myself simply as a girl rushing towards her destiny; impelled to return to the arms of her lover by forces that she had neither the power nor the will to resist. The prelude had been played, the page was being turned and *–segue–* the fugue must now begin.

On our return home earlier, I had made a pot of tea, fed Nimrod, drawn the curtains, lit the fire; in short, I had automatically followed the usual routine of preparing for a winter's evening at home, which would be spent listening to the wireless or reading a book. But the tea remained untouched, the meal unprepared and untasted. The fire, untended after its first promising blaze, smouldered sullenly in the grate. I ran a bath and soaked in it for a while, daydreaming of the events of the afternoon. Had it been a choral rehearsal night, events might have turned out differently: there would have been some other outlet for my euphoric energy. As it was, I paced about the house quite unable to settle, reluctant to face the passing of a long evening, a sleepless night and an interminable morning at school before I could see Bruno again. At last, I snatched up coat and gloves, bade Nimrod keep guard and leapt onto my bicycle, dismounting only to climb the steep, winding hill out of the village. Once on the top road, I flew along in the silvery light, my breath misting around me in the sharp air as I sang the lines from Nicolette's song to Aucassin, the words I had sung on my second visit to Bruno and had sung several times since.

———

Bodkin joined me on the doorstep as I knocked, arching his back and weaving around my legs with tail erect. It seemed an age before the door opened. When it did, he shot in and made for his feeding-bowl, skirting carefully and suspiciously round a large, half-packed suitcase on the slate floor. Bruno had his back to the light so I could not see the expression on his face at first.

"Cecilia!" he exclaimed in a shocked voice. "What are you doing here at this time of night?"

I had imagined that he would hold out his arms and I would run into them while he kicked the door shut behind me. But he did not invite me in.

"Is something wrong? Why are you here?"

"Nothing is wrong," I said in a small voice. "May I come in, please? I thought you might be pleased to see me."

"It would be churlish of me to keep a lady waiting on the doorstep on a frosty night," he said, moving aside so that I could enter. "Actually, I was just writing you a short letter as I must leave for London in the morning." He indicated the typewriter on the kitchen table, while I looked with utter dismay at the suitcase on the floor and hot tears welled in my eyes and ran down my cold cheeks.

"Sit down for a moment," he invited in a formal tone. "You look frozen. I'll pour you a small glass of sloe gin to warm you up. I owe you an explanation – and an apology. I should never have done what I did today. I took advantage of your youth and undoubted attractiveness and it was wrong of me."

He set a small, pretty glass of ruby-coloured liquid on the table beside me and handed me a clean white handkerchief which he had taken from the suitcase.

"Dry your eyes, my dear, and listen to what I have to say." He took a sizeable draught from a tumbler of what I thought was probably whisky, lit a cigarette and took a deep breath before continuing.

"For one thing, I must tell you that I have a wife. True, we are estranged; in fact she threatens to divorce me because I have not been able to give her a child. For another thing, I am old enough to be your father, so am doubly to blame for giving in to my selfish desires without thought of how it would affect you. I thought it would be best to leave before I became even more deeply attached to you. I have finished my work here - and I must acknowledge your considerable help in this – but there is no need for me to stay longer. Believe me; it will be for the best."

I had said nothing since I sat down. My tears had continued to fall unchecked, pooling onto the pale, honey-coloured pine of the table as he spoke, and I made no effort to stop them as I took small sips from the glass. What happened next shocked me as much as it did him, I think. Suddenly, I drained the glass and leapt to my feet.

"How *dare* you say what is best for me?" I shouted. "I am a grown woman who came here tonight because I could not wait until tomorrow for you to hold me in your arms again. Did you think you could sneak away without saying good bye when you must know that I love you so much? Would you just have left a little note pinned to the door? Would you? WOULD YOU?"

He looked profoundly shaken and stood up quickly as I ran at him with clenched fists. For the second time that day he held me by the wrists; for the second time he silenced me with a kiss, longer and deeper than the first, quelling my anger, dispelling my fear, melting my heart, piercing my soul.

Gently he removed my coat and wordlessly led me into the music room and opened the doors of the log-burning fire; tenderly he removed my clothes and laid me down on the hearthrug, spreading cushions under my head; generously he made love to me, taking his own pleasure only after ensuring mine. There was pain when he entered me but it was tempered by yet another paroxysm of exquisite joy, and at last there came the great pulse of his own fulfilment as he cried aloud in release.

Afterwards we lay entwined for a while, our limbs glowing like copper in the firelight. There was silence except for the tick and occasional chime of the clock on the mantelpiece and my little sighs of delight and contentment as he stroked my hair and caressed my body, while I traced the map of his face with closed eyes, like a blind person committing a sculpture to memory. Sometime later, he got up and put more logs on the fire. He fetched a rug from the sofa and spread it over me; then I watched him as he went to the gramophone, put a record on the turntable and gently lowered the needle onto it.

"Listen to this," he whispered as he lay beside me once again. "It expresses so perfectly these moments of our love-making."

The descending scale passage of the second movement of Bach's Double Violin Concerto filled the room, the silken, sensuous beauty of the dialogue causing my tears to well again. He kissed them gently away and we let the poignancy and rapture of the intertwined voices of the instruments bind us even more closely.

How could I have known in those ecstatic hours that, in the space of a few months, the three creatures I held most precious in the world would be lost to me, albeit in different ways? At first it was sustenance enough after Bruno had gone, to relive the events of that remarkable day, joyously examining in minute detail every word and action which had led to its heart-stopping conclusion. But that conclusion was to be an ending that could not also be a beginning; great happiness forever wrapped in the pain of separation.

In the closing bars of the slow movement, Bruno had gently disengaged himself and gone to lift the needle from the record.

"The last movement would break the spell," he had said. "There is too much frenetic energy after that sublime close."

The clock on the mantel chimed midnight and I rose to my feet, the interruption of that Cinderella moment requiring some action.

"I should go home. Nimrod will be waiting…."

"Oh, my sweet girl, my love," he had said softly, taking me in his arms again. "I feel so honoured that you should have given me such a gift – your youth, your innocence. How sad that we should be so in tune and yet so out of time. I am halfway through my life and you are only on the threshold, with the whole adventure before you."

"The only adventure I want is to be with you forever," I declared passionately. "How shall I bear it if you leave me tomorrow—today?"

"I shall return to Cornwall before I leave for the States," he promised. "I have a series of rehearsals and concerts to attend to in London and, of course, meetings with editors and publishers, but after that I shall have a few days before I leave for good."

SIX

Soon there were preparations to be made for Christmas and I was spending more time at school, preparing the boys for their end-of-term Carol Service. Mrs Howard, too, enlisted my help for a musical Nativity Play at the village school. She herself was to retire at the end of the term and planned a long visit to her married daughter in Australia in January. My initial radiance did not go unnoticed.

"Which of those two good-looking young masters has put that sparkle in your eyes?" she asked.

"Well, both of course," I answered. "I just don't know which to choose."

True, I had been out with each of them on occasion, as well as with both in a foursome with the junior matron. Each had the impression that the other was being more successful in his advances. When they went to their homes for Christmas, Rob and Sarah returned to the Rectory and I spent the festival itself either there or at Elm Lodge, where Grandpa Joe was doing his best to be the life and soul of the party in the dayroom.

"We should all be playing Musical Chairs," I remember him saying, sounding as though he'd swallowed half a bottle of whisky instead of two cups of tea. "Trouble is, none of us can leave our chairs, let alone run around. We'll just have to make do with Postman's Knock – though I can't see anyone here I'd want to kiss," he added in a stage whisper. If anything, he seemed to be improving of late, rather than showing signs of his condition worsening, as might be expected.

But one morning in mid-January, I found a note from the school secretary on the piano when I arrived in the school music room. There had been a phone call from Elm Lodge to say that my grandfather had had another serious stroke after breakfast and that I should come as soon as possible.

"Prepare yourself, my dear," Matron said kindly when I arrived less than half-an-hour later. She put her arm round me and ushered me towards his room. "I'm afraid your grandfather is very near his end. It will be a great comfort to him to know that you are there. Even if he seems to be unconscious, it's said that the hearing is the last sense to go."

I was just in time. The man who had been such a massive presence in my life, my guardian, my rock, my mainstay, lay diminished, unaware of my presence and unresponsive to my touch.

"Don't leave me, Grandpa Joe," I pleaded. "Please, please come back from wherever you are."

Then, as my tears fell onto the weather-beaten hands I held in mine, he opened his eyes and looked at me for one long moment and I felt the slightest movement from one of his hands. There was a strange feeling of peace and acceptance in the look we exchanged and I knew that I must give him permission to go.

"I love you, darling Grandpa. Go now if you must. Go to whoever is calling you."

He gave one last gentle sigh and away flew that beloved soul, liberated at last from its frail body. I crossed to the window and opened it, in accordance with the time-honoured custom.

O n a mild, sunny day a week later, my adored Grandfather, Josiah William Trelawney, was laid to rest beside my grandmother. A notice in *The Cornish Guardian* had brought people from all over the county to his funeral. St Petroc's Church had not seen such a crowd since V.E. Day. Mr Gray's sonorous voice recited the solemn words of the Burial Service and a group from the choral society joined the church choir, singing, among other offerings, *Brother James's Air,* by special (prior) request. ('I want you to sing that at my funeral' he had often said, but of course I knew that I should be too choked with emotion to fulfil his request.)

"Your grandfather was a hero and a true gentleman," one old man said to me as we all crowded into the old schoolroom where tables groaned under the weight of sandwiches, fancy cakes and scones spread generously with jam and cream. "I was honoured to serve with him in the Navy and saw him risk his life many a time to save others. There was that time when we were torpedoed......" But my mother drew me away before he could say any more.

"Come and meet Sir George and Lady Barrington-Smythe....." she interrupted, pulling my arm. I looked back regretfully at the old man.

"Excuse me, please. I would love to hear the rest of that story. I'll find you again." But when I looked for him later, he had already left.

My mother had flown home for the funeral two days earlier and, having assumed the role of chief mourner, was graciously accepting condolences from old acquaintances. At the end of our encounter with the aforesaid Barrington-Smythes, I couldn't help being waspishly delighted at her pained expression when an elderly woman accosted her and said:

"Why, *Peggy*, it must be nigh on twenty years since I saw you last ….."

Christened 'Margaret', ever since she met my father at a dance at the Army camp where he was an officer, my mother had liked to be known as Marguerite. Even Grandpa Joe had had to adopt the revision, though, if he used the name at all, it was always with ironic emphasis. (''Fraid we bred a bit of a social climber there,' our *Marguerite*,' I once overheard him say to a friend.)

She and I had fallen out almost as soon as she arrived at Cliff Cottage.

"I don't know why you should be so upset about your grandfather," she had said. "After all, you should be used to being on your own here by now. He had a very good innings and can't have been enjoying these last few months in the Home. Anyway, he was practically doo-lally, wasn't he?"

Then there was the question of what I proposed to wear to the funeral.

"How can you possibly think of going without a *hat*? We must go into town tomorrow and try to find something suitable. You should really get that hair cut, too, you know. It looks so *unruly*; and being that unfortunate colour …… In general, dear, you look rather … *coltish*." (I preferred to believe Bruno, who had told me on that last special evening that I was beautiful.)

Worse still was the insult to Nimrod:

"You cannot *seriously* mean that that scruffy creature – that *lurcher* – is going to come to the *church*?"

Later, as I stood at the graveside, hatless, in my navy blue suit, with Nimrod (my *Irish Wolfhound cross*) sitting tall and dignified by my side, I could imagine Grandpa Joe's mischievous grin as *Marguerite* stood stony-faced under her chic, black-veiled hat, and I heard his deep voice in my head:

"You won *that* round, Rosie girl! And whatever's that on 'er 'ead – a bit of old seaweed caught in a scrap of fishing net?"

....I heard a voice from heaven, saying unto me, Write, From henceforth blessed are the dead which die in the Lord; even so saith the spirit: for they rest from their labours.

Thus were the solemn, valedictory sentences and the inexorability of the coffin making its slow descent into the grave mercifully tempered with a touch of humour.

The grief that had been to some degree kept at bay by the irritation of my mother's presence at Cliff Cottage, crept in like a dense fog immediately after her departure. On its heels came an unrelenting wave of agony as I realised that I was mourning the loss of Bruno as well as that of my grandfather. Life could not go back to normal: there was no 'normal' anymore. Daily visits to one or both of them had shaped my days; now there was only school, where I put in a lacklustre appearance three times a week.

Nimrod sensed my utter desolation and looked at me with sad eyes. His walks were shorter now, and without fun. We kept away from the path which would lead us past the well and on to Foxgloves. The sight of its shuttered windows was more than I could bear. Bodkin would be back with his owner, Mrs Burrows, who acted as caretaker for Foxgloves and 'did' for Bruno's aunt who actually owned it, living there most of the summer and spending the winter in South Africa for her health.

My friends and neighbours were full of kind concern. Mrs Pascoe showered me with culinary treats.

"You're as lean as Nimrod here, dearie," she would say, putting a plump arm round me. "Where's that bonny little girl who used to come and lick out my mixing bowl and spread brown sugar on her bread and butter? Here, these will put a bit of fat on those bones and some colour into your cheeks."

But the rich pasties and sticky cakes made me nauseous, and the gulls who stood in a watchful row on the roof each morning were the grateful beneficiaries of her kindly offerings, though sometimes I thought of those ever-hungry boys at Trevene Court and smuggled some into school for a break-time treat.

The Rector and Mrs Gray were clearly worried about how long I was taking to recover after Grandpa Joe's death. They tried to involve me as much as possible in the activities of church and village when I was not teaching. I had already taken over as church organist when Mrs Howard had left for Australia and spent some time practising in the cold building, huddled into a warm coat with a hot-water-bottle on my lap, leaving Nimrod lying by the Aga in the Rectory kitchen.

My eighteenth birthday fell during the school half-term holiday in February 1954 and the Gray family made a great fuss of me. Sarah was home from school and Rob contrived to have leave of absence from the Army for a couple of days. Although in those days one did not 'come of age' until twenty-one, eighteen was, as Mr Gray pointed out, a significant age.

"It's time to look to your future now, Rosie," he said as we sat over coffee after a lunch prepared in my honour. "You should leave Porthwenna very soon, much as we shall miss you. Go to London, have some fun, apply to music colleges or universities. September will come soon enough and you need to have arrangements in place. You have all the qualifications you require at present."

"But what can I do about Nimrod?" I said. "I know you're right, but my aunt would never agree to have him there. And Cliff Cottage – how can I leave it unoccupied?"

"That isn't an insurmountable problem. A tenant could easily be found, I'm sure, if you were willing to let it. As for Nimrod, we would willingly look after him until you're settled. Just look at him! He thinks he owns the place already. Big dog needs big house – and *vice versa*."

Nimrod was lying at full stretch in front of the dining room fire. Sensing that we were talking about him, he thumped his spiky tail in agreement.

<hr>

When I returned home, Mrs Pascoe came out of her house, all a-twitch with excitement, carrying a package in her hand.

"A gentleman called when you were out, about 12 o'clock. Came in a taxi, he did. Rather foreign- looking, he was, sounded foreign, too – sort of Frenchy. Good-looking man in early middle age, I'd say. I've never seen him before. Anyway, I heard him knocking at your door and came out to tell him you were out to a birthday dinner at the Rectory and had walked up there with the dog."

She handed me the package, her eyes bright with curiosity. "He had this to give to you. I expect it's a birthday present, don't you? Although, come to think of it, he didn't seem to know it was your birthday or that your dear Grandpa had passed away. He seemed disappointed not to give it to you himself, but said he had a train to catch."

It took every ounce of my self-control not to snatch it from her and tear at the brown paper wrapping there and then.

"Oh, I know what it is," I lied. "It's some music I was expecting," I said quickly, in what I hoped was a level voice, though my heart was beating like a drum which must have been audible all over the village. "Thanks so much for taking it in, anyway."

As soon as I politely could, I went inside and opened the parcel with trembling fingers. It was indeed 'some music': a bound choral score of *Aucassin and Nicolette* – an operetta by Bruno Sabra.

I cannot adequately describe my emotion when I saw the printed dedication therein, which stated simply:

For Cecilia, who breathed life into this work.

Under this, in his flourishing, bold, black handwriting, Bruno had added: *Not the saint, but the angel mermaid,* with his signature beneath it.

There was another book, separately wrapped: Bruno's original copy of French mediaeval tales, the cover and frontispiece beautifully illustrated in Art Nouveau style. I opened it and found the inscription: *Á mon fils, Bruno Maximilian Sabra, de la part de sa mere, avec affection; le 17 juillet, 1930. In the centre of the book, to my great joy, was a letter.*

Foxgloves. February 20, 1954

My dear Cecilia,

I would like you to accept this book with my deep regard. Also, at last in print, the copy of our little opera which as you will see is dedicated to you, though all who see it will think I mean the Patron Saint of Music!

I regret that my visit to Foxgloves must be a flying one only. I have to pick up the rest of my luggage before flying to New York on the 24th. I have been hoping you might pass by with Nimrod, but perhaps you do not come this way so often now. I will try to deliver this to you before I leave and catch at least a glimpse of you.

Meanwhile, my dear, I cherish always the memories and wish you the happy life you deserve.

Ever yours,
Bruno.

How different it would have been nowadays with mobile phones! There was not even a telephone at Cliff Cottage. Overwhelmed though I was by the contents of Bruno's parcel, I wondered desperately how I could catch up with him before he left for America, but realised that even if I caught the next train to London, I had no idea where he would be; if I waited at the airport, I would probably miss him - and in any case he might be with his wife, for whom I felt a burning resentment.

It was, strangely, almost with a sense of relief that, two evenings later, I realised that Bruno must be out of reach now on the other side of the world. Every day, every month now, I reasoned, I would be nearer to seeing him again. Meanwhile, I had the three precious gifts he had given me to sustain me, as well as the memories of our time together. Slowly but noticeably, I started to climb out of the despondency and apathy of the past weeks.

SEVEN

A week after my birthday, I went to the public telephone box and put through a trunk call to Aunt Dorothea and Uncle Guy, asking if I might come and stay with them while I made arrangements for my future education. As I expected, my aunt agreed - but on one condition.

"I'm afraid we cannot have that dog here, Cecily."

"Well actually, Nimrod has been offered a very good temporary home at the Rectory here," I reassured her. "Anyway, I don't think he'd think much of London. He likes wide open spaces to run in."

"Hmm, that's all right then," said Aunt Dorothea, disapprovingly. "We'll see you on Wednesday then, Cecily. Uncle Guy will meet your train."

"I have to go away for a while," I whispered to Nimrod, burying my face in his wiry fur. "But I'll be back as soon as I can, I promise." Did I imagine the reproachful look in his eyes? By this time, he already knew what the packing of trunks and suitcases foretold.

We went for one last walk along the cliff path and to St Elowen's Well. It was the first time that I had touched its water since that last day with Bruno. One peep at Foxgloves from the end of the lane was enough to assure me that Bruno's aunt had not yet returned from South Africa. With its whitewashed walls and the dark blue shutters closed across its windows, it had the air of one asleep, wearing dark glasses and basking in the afternoon sun.

"Oh Bruno," I said aloud. "Where are you now and what are you doing at this moment? Can my love and my thoughts reach you across the ocean?"

There were primroses along the path and in the dell, and bluebells nearly in bloom. The hawthorn was beginning to open its buds.

"I will return when you are in flower," I told it. "And you," I said to the foxgloves, which as yet showed only their leaves, "Stand tall and guard this sacred, secret place, like good sentries."

L ess than a month later, having had an audition and an interview, I was offered a place at the Royal College of Music in the autumn, the offer being subject to my passing a medical examination which could be carried out by my own doctor.

"You had better register with Dr McNamara," said my aunt. "We should have done that as soon as you arrived."

At the appointed time I walked the half-mile or so to the surgery. In the park, tulips were opening their petals to the warm April sunshine and the leaves of the plane trees were unfurling in the balmy air. I felt, for the first time for many weeks, a sense of well-being. The Grays had been right: a change of scenery and some positive action on my part had been good for me. I had regained my appetite and put on weight and had enjoyed going to art galleries and films and the odd concert with one of Uncle Guy's research students. William Tyler had introduced me to a group of his friends, all of whom had given me advice and guidance in my various applications and had suggestions for student accommodation for September. William's nickname was 'Wat'; his circle of friends being, naturally, known as 'The Peasants'. He, himself, was warm and witty and very good company with his keen, self-deprecating sense of humour.

I felt fortunate that I would have this nucleus of young people with whom to socialise and exchange ideas when I began my studies. Meanwhile, after this medical there was no reason why I should not return to Porthwenna, to Nimrod, to Cliff Cottage, and to Trevene Court for the summer term.

Dr McNamara was tall, thin and stooping, with sparse, greying hair. After the routine tests for sight, hearing, colour blindness and reflexes, recording of height and weight and soundings of heart and lungs, he asked:

"Is menstruation normal?"

"Well, usually," I replied, embarrassed, "Though for the last few months there hasn't really been anything - only a few spots, really."

"Hmm; you are a little anaemic I suspect. I shall have to look further into this. Please take off your lower garments behind the screen and get up on the couch."

After more soundings and uncomfortable poking and prodding, he straightened up and told me to get dressed.

"Miss James," he said when I emerged from behind the screen, his voice stiff with disapproval, "Had you really no idea that you might be ... expecting a baby?"

I sat in the park for a long time, considering the implications of my situation, a deluge of conflicting thoughts breaking upon my mind like the waves and cross currents of the turning tide. My eyes were blind now to the colours of the flowers and the trees, my ears deaf to the birdsong around me. An elderly man came to sit on the bench beside me and tried to make conversation about the fine spring weather. When I made no response he shrugged and tutted and moved further away.

A baby! The result of that magical evening with Bruno; Bruno's baby! But had he not told me that he was unable to father a child? He had had tests in Switzerland he had told me, at his wife's insistence and had been told that it was almost impossible for him to give her children because, as a young man, he had had a disease which could render him sterile. So it was *almost* impossible, but clearly not entirely so, I thought. I felt at once privileged, honoured, delighted – and *appalled* at the prospect of what lay ahead. I began to rehearse what I would say on my return to Charlton Walk.

"You must tell your aunt as soon as possible – immediately would be best," the doctor had said, distaste plainly evident in his austere features. "Arrangements will have to be made. And I cannot, you understand, return this document, confirming that you have a clean medical record."

Clean: the opposite of which is – dirty, blemished, besmirched or impure. That is certainly how the world would judge me, particularly my aunt and her ilk. Young people nowadays can have little idea of the attitude towards pre-marital sex which prevailed in the 1950s. Sexual morality had tightened its grip again after a lapse during the war years, now glamorously portrayed in films as all bright red lipstick, bouncy curls, fetching uniforms and dangerous flying missions. You could be forgiven for a little illicit sex on what might be, literally, your last night on earth – but then, men have always been forgiven for 'sowing their wild oats', while women have borne the consequences, the disgrace and the censure.

As I write this nearly sixty years later, I realise that I am postponing the recounting of my confession to Aunt D. just as I postponed it on that day in April. I rose from the bench to make my way to the café where I sometimes met Wat and one of his friends. On my way to the park gate I passed a little girl skipping happily beside a large baby-carriage pushed by a nanny, a uniformed Norland nurse.

"Did that lady *paint* her hair to make it that colour?" the child asked in a piping voice.

"Hush, Wendy," said the nanny. "It's not polite to make personal remarks about people."

"What's pers'nal mean?" asked the little voice, but I didn't hear the reply. Babies, prams, children, I thought with a shudder, though not, strangely, one of horror. I had to come to terms with the change of direction which my life had suddenly taken.

The juke-box in the café was playing, appropriately, *Bewitched, bothered and bewildered.* I sat over my coffee, still rehearsing my announcement to my aunt, to a background of *They try to tell us we're too young* and *Do not forsake me, O my darling.*

"All alone today, then?" asked the girl behind the counter.

"Yes, I seem to be," I replied, thinking how alone I really was now – except for that little creature inside me. The music stopped and the couple who had been feeding coins into the machine got up and left. I finished my coffee and now it was time for me to go back and face a very different kind of music. Perhaps it would help me to believe the momentous news when I told another person, however much I dreaded the disclosure.

⚒️

There was a note from my aunt on the hall table: *Forgot to tell you that I'm out to lunch with a friend. We have a Meeting afterwards. Back about 4. There is soup and bread in kitchen. Aunt D.*

So the dreaded moment was postponed again. Having dragged unwilling feet from the café, past the parade of local shops, along tree-lined avenues and into Charlton Walk, its front gardens festooned with sugar-pink almond blossom, I had turned into Number 11 and put my key in the lock resolutely, determined to deliver my news as succinctly as possible and get it over with. Now I sat at the kitchen table eating my lunch, though quite oblivious of taste or texture, trying once again to make sense of the turmoil in my head. How could I go back to Porthwenna now? And Nimrod: how were we to be reunited – and where? When the baby was born, where could all three of us live if not at Cliff Cottage? One by one the questions dropped like the components in a cement mixer, churning around until they formed a dense mass whose separate properties could never again exist in their original state. I was still sitting there when I heard my aunt's key in the front door.

"Why Cecily," she said, taking off her serviceable blue hat and shaking her greying, permed hair as she came into the kitchen, "Whatever are you doing? I thought you'd have the kettle on for tea. Were you very late back? How did you get on with Dr McNamara?"

"I think you'd better sit down Aunt D." I said in a tremulous voice. "I have something to tell you."

"Oh dear! I hope it's not bad news – some ailment or disease. You didn't look at all well when you came here, but you've seemed so much better of late."

"Aunt, the doctor told me I'm going to have a baby." I blurted.

"Cecily! Don't joke with me; that is in very poor taste. If it's something serious you really should be straight with me."

"I know you'll be shocked but that really is what he said – about four months into pregnancy, he said."

"But surely there must be some mistake. You've been mourning your grandfather ….. You cannot mean …." Her eyes darted round the room as she searched desperately for the right words. … "That you – that some *youth* took advantage of you – or forced you against your will."

"It was not against my will, Aunt D. I fell in love – am still very much in love with the baby's father. I shall love him forever."

"In *love*, Cecily! What can you know about that kind of love at your age? It is nothing but animal lust. Does the boy know? Is he willing to make an honest woman of you – though you are far too young to marry in any case."

"He is not a boy, Aunt: he's a man, married at present, but his wife wants a divorce."

"A *divorce*! This gets worse and worse. He has ruined your life, that's what he has done. I assume he is not a Catholic or he would not contemplate divorce."

"Actually, he's Jewish – or rather his father was a Russian Jewish refugee and his mother was Austrian, I think. He was brought up mostly in France."

Her eyes were bright with angry tears and my own responded in sympathy. "Oh, the shame of it all! Go away now, child, and leave me to decide what can be done. Whatever are Uncle Guy and your poor parents going to think?"

"I will go upstairs and leave you for a bit," I said, clearing away my lunch plates. "I need to think about it all myself."

"I should think so too, you silly, silly girl. Get down on your knees and ask God's forgiveness for your sin."

As it happened, I did get down on my knees – but to thank God for giving me this tiny seedling of Bruno's to nurture and cherish, and to ask for strength and guidance as I trod what was sure to be a difficult path ahead.

———

Once my aunt's practical and organisational ability reasserted itself, my immediate future was mapped out for me within days. An advertisement in *The Lady* magazine was answered on my behalf. I was to be dispatched to Surrey the following week to act as tutor to a French child for the summer term. I was to pose as a young, expectant mother whose husband was stationed in Cyprus, and to return to London three weeks before the due date to enter the Magdalen Home of which my aunt was Chairman of the Trustees. As a Protestant, by special arrangement with Mother Superior I was to be treated differently from the – mostly Irish - Catholic girls and women who were the Home's temporary - or permanent – residents, being confined to my room except when they were all at Mass. At such times I would be permitted to walk round the gardens for exercise. Communication with the other girls would be strictly forbidden. When the baby was born it would be removed immediately and sent to the convent's orphanage for adoption. Because of my aunt's position in relation to the Home, I would be spared the penances demanded of the other women and the risk of becoming attached to the child by having to nurse it for three weeks.

"But I want to keep my baby," I protested, though I had not any clear idea of how this could be achieved.

"Don't be ridiculous, Cecily. It would completely ruin your life – if it has not done so already. It is so like you to entertain romantic notions like that before you've thought of the consequences."

"Also, I need to go back to Porthwenna and collect Nimrod and fetch things from Cliff Cottage."

"That will have to wait until after all this is over. You can hardly take a dog with you, either to your new job or to the home. Write and tell the – Whatsernames …"

"Grays."

"Grays – that you have a summer job and ask them to look after the dog for a good while longer."

A week later, wearing a loose shift dress under a light, voluminous duster-coat and self-consciously twisting a narrow gold ring round her finger, *Mrs* Cecily Rose James was on her way to Richmond to meet her new charge.

Mercifully, there were few demands on me at the large apartment in Richmond. My employer was a Frenchwoman who spoke very little English. Her husband, a businessman, was seldom at home. Their ten-year-old daughter, Simone, was recovering from Scarlet Fever and my duties included teaching her English, encouraging her musical studies and taking her for walks in Richmond Park. The language teaching was of mutual benefit. Simone would laugh at my schoolgirl French and correct my attempts to converse with Mme. Blanchet at table. My aunt had told them all they needed to know about my situation and they had not the vocabulary to ask further questions.

Letters replying to those I had written before my departure from Hampstead were forwarded to me, my aunt having taken care to change 'Miss' to 'Mrs' on the envelopes. There was one from Mrs Gray assuring me that Nimrod was fine, though still missing me. They were happy to keep him for the time being and were sure that I would be back before they left for their summer holiday in mid-September. Another was from Grandpa Joe's solicitor. The Will was simple to execute, he said. My grandfather had left everything to me, though it would have to remain in trust until I came of age. In my absence, he had already had enquiries as to whether I would be willing to sell the two fishing vessels. He thought that this would be a good move; the money could be used for some necessary repairs to Cliff Cottage, such as re-thatching, and the rest could be invested to give me a small income. Mrs Pascoe wrote to say that I seemed to be a long time away. She was keeping an eye on the cottage for me and was sure I would be back before starting college. Summer holidays in Porthwenna wouldn't be at all the same without Cecily Rose and her dog. She had seen Nimrod only a couple of times, she told me, and he had looked very sad without me.

Reading this in the privacy of my own room, I cried copiously when I pictured his large, brown eyes. If only I could tell him to be patient; that soon we should be reunited, even if we could not be at Cliff Cottage; that there would be another little person for him to look after – an energetic little person by the feel of it! I was determined to find a way to keep my baby: there must be some degree of control, even for an unmarried mother, I reasoned. I was better off financially than most, even if I could not count on the support of my family. I would find a way, somehow. The fidgety little creature inside me gave me courage with every kick.

I longed for Bruno and wished with all my heart that I could tell him that I was expecting his baby. I thought of trying to reach him through his publishers but decided against it. I had no idea how long divorce proceedings took but had read enough in novels to be aware of the scandal attached to being named as a co-respondent. Instead, I scoured musical publications for a mention of his name, which might give me a clue as to his whereabouts, but to no avail. No doubt he was still in America.

The long weeks passed eventually and at the end of July I took my leave of *la famille Blanchet* and travelled back to London with my aunt, who came to fetch me in a taxi. I need hardly record that I was delivered straight to the Home, rather than run the risk of being observed by the residents of Charlton Walk. Aunt D. took home the wedding ring and my surplus luggage, in return for a parcel containing two ugly maternity smocks, three pairs of outsize interlock knickers (passion-killers, we used to call them at school) and a layette for the baby.

How confidently I walked into that convent with my aunt and with what great hopes and plans for the future. How brokenhearted and desolated I emerged a month later. But I dealt with that earlier in this narrative, if not in detail, and it distresses me, even after all these years, to visit that time again.

EIGHT

Today I will return to the present for a while; a present enriched by the love of my family, by my lovely home and by some glorious spring weather.

For my 70th birthday the family gave me a computer, one of the miracles of modern technology, which I have embraced with surprising aptitude for one who has lived for nearly three quarters of a century! I started straight away to use it for this memoir, but today I prefer to sit in the sun to write, enjoying the sight and scent of each moment as it passes. At my side, the faithful Labrador, Bo' sun lies contentedly spread-eagled, half in sun, half in my shade. On the lawn there are primroses and violets still, yet in the sheltered part of the garden, amongst the last of the daffodils, the foxgloves stand proud and tall already, their tight, grey-green buds ready to burst into bells of brilliant magenta. And beyond them is the sea, serene today as it reclines in its silver-blue mantle; the sea of holidays and childhood memories. Oh, I shall return to those other, later days of storm and tempest, for the whole story must be told; but not today; not today.

The house in Shropshire which my parents had bought in advance of their retirement was much pleasanter than I had expected, though I was hardly of a mind when I first arrived there to find any joy or pleasure in anything or anybody. It was situated on the edge of a small, busy market town: an old, stone-built house set in a large, pretty garden which backed onto hilly pasture, grazed by flocks of Kerry Hill and Clun Forest sheep.

As I had predicted, the whole subject of my 'unfortunate mistake' was aired only briefly and then firmly closed. In those days it was a matter of 'if we don't talk about it, it didn't happen'.) My mother was much more inclined to talk about my hair.

"You've had it cut at last!" she exclaimed when she first saw me. "Not *well* cut, I have to say, but I've found a reasonably good hairdresser in town and he'll soon put that right."

The new style had not been of my choosing, in fact I had protested strongly. As soon as I had arrived in Magdalene House, I had been told that my long hair was unsuitable and unhygienic, even if tied back or put up. Watched closely by a nun, one of the pregnant girls, a hairdresser by trade, had cut it straight across at the level of my ear-lobes, as instructed. The swathe of hair was handed to the girl who had originally shown me round on my arrival, the only person in that desolate place who had shown me any kindness. On that occasion, with tears in her eyes, she too had protested at the 'haircut' and was punished for her impudence. She was told to bind the hair with ribbon. No doubt it was sold, just as the babies in the orphanage were, to raise money for the convent.

By agreeing to go with my mother to have my hair restyled I felt that I could safely broach the subject of reclaiming Nimrod from the Grays. There was little time left before they were due to leave for their holiday; in any case, I was desperate to be reunited with him. My mother was more reasonable than I had dared to hope.

"I suppose you'll have to have him here if you've promised to collect him," she said. "I don't know what your long-term plans are now, but we have to return to St Lucia at the end of September."

The fact was that now I had no long-term plans; also I was very reluctant to return to Porthwenna.

"Well, I need to go there myself to check that your grandparents' headstone has been re-engraved, for one thing," my mother said. "And for another, I must see Trethewy and Co about the Will. It's all very well for you to have been left nearly everything, but there are practical matters to sort out between now and when you come of age."

It was decided that I should look after the house while my father went to London and my mother went on to Cornwall by train. She would find some excuse for my not accompanying her, she said, and would bring 'the dog' back. He would have to travel in the guard's van, though, and I would have to come to London to fetch him. They could not be expected to cope with him in the car.

On reflection, Paddington Station was not the ideal place for a large dog and his owner to be re-united after several months of separation. The joyful meeting caused quite a stir on the platform when Nimrod was handed over by the guard, and even merited a few lines in next morning's *Standard*. Wat sent me the cutting which I still have somewhere. WELL I'LL BE DOGGONED was the headline, and below it:

This is a shaggy dog story with a difference – in fact I thought it was a shaggy pony trotting up the platform at Paddington Station, having alighted from the guard's van of the Cornish

Riviera Express. Said his attractive red-haired owner, Miss James: "Yes, Nimrod [Nimrod?? I thought dogs were usually called Rover or Shep] is on his way from Cornwall to Shropshire…" Just as if large shaggy dogs travelled to London by train every day. The white-faced guard was not available for comment.

⚭

A s I walked with Nimrod in those green hills in the weeks that ensued, and rustled through the rich copper coinage of late autumn as the beeches shed their leaves at the edge of the wood, my wounds began slowly to heal. The neighbouring farmer and his wife were welcoming and helpful. If they thought it odd that a girl of my age should be living alone and without a job, they kept it to themselves. Their two sons invited me to various social functions run by the Young Farmers, and although I did not relish any amatory advances from either them or their friends, I knew that it was important that I should not sit at home and brood. I met the organist of the parish church and was recruited to join the choir as they prepared for Christmas services. Paul Davies taught Music and Drama at the local Grammar School and conducted a small group of singers which he invited me to join. It was good to be singing again. It was Paul who persuaded me to re-apply for a place at Music College the following year. His wife, Judy, was a singing teacher, so I resumed my studies with her and widened my repertoire as well as working on my technique.

The anniversary of that last, momentous encounter with Bruno had come and gone – not unnoticed by me, of course: I thought of him every day and imagined how we might meet again one day, though at the same time mourning him as keenly as I did our little girl. Judy Davies was such a kind and sympathetic teacher that I was tempted to break my long silence and mention his name, at least. One day she said to me: "There is a sadness in you and a depth of feeling that is unusual in one so young. You choose sad songs and reject the lighter, happier ones." She laid a hand on my arm. "I don't mean to intrude in any way at all. It was just an observation."

There was a knock on the door. "Time for my next pupil already," she said, handing me a book. "Choose something jolly from this collection for next time."

She must have noticed that my eyes brimmed with tears, but tactfully ignored the fact, though her expression was one of kind concern.

At the beginning of my next lesson the subject of the Three Choirs Festival came up and it seemed a natural progression to tell Judy how enthralling I had found it at the age of fifteen to sing *Messiah* in the cathedral, especially with Bruno Sabra conducting.

"Oh yes," she said. "Isn't he wonderful? I had the same sort of experience in Durham Cathedral singing in *The Dream of Gerontius* when I was a girl – not as young as you were, though. I remember the excitement: Chorus, semi-chorus, full symphony orchestra with two harps ... *and* – Bruno Sabra. You don't get much better than that. We all fell madly in love with him of course. Actually, it's funny you should mention him," she went on. "Only a day or two ago I read something - in *The Times*, I think it was ..."

I waited with bated breath for her to continue. "Oh yes, it was actually about Maria Scholtz, the American opera singer, coming to England to sing at the Royal Opera House. The article said that she is married to the conductor, Bruno Sabra and they have a six month old daughter. I had no idea they were a married couple, had you? Of course professional women keep their own names nowadays – not like the olden days of Mrs Henry Irving and co., is it? In those days she'd have been Mrs Bruno Sabra. ... But I'm prattling on; let's do a few loosening-up exercises first." She turned back to the piano and played a chord of D major.

It was an odd constricted sound that issued next from my mouth: a spasm of shock and grief. But then, mercifully, there came a wave of anger which loosened my throat and lent a strange energy to my voice. I even managed my 'happy' song. It was not until I arrived home after the lesson that I threw myself onto my bed and gave way to the racking sobs that had been clamouring to be released ever since I heard the news. Nimrod was so concerned at my distress that he climbed onto the bed and stretched out beside me, licking my tears now and then and gazing at me with his big, brown, intelligent eyes.

Dusk fell early on that dismal February afternoon. At length I dried my eyes, washed my face and took Nimrod for a short walk in the fields behind the house. *My* baby too, I thought, would have been six months old in a few days' time. And tomorrow, I realised, it would be my nineteenth birthday and there was nobody with whom to celebrate it – if indeed there *was* anything to celebrate. I can honestly say that if it had not been for Nimrod, I would have found a way to 'end it all' that very day.

NINE

T he arrival of the lambs that spring lifted my spirits, in spite
of the sorrow and anger that I suffered in equal measure.
I volunteered my services as unofficial shepherdess, helping
Ben Probert, the elder of the farmer's sons, with the birthing,
and adopting an orphan lamb after he was rejected by his foster
mother, even though he wore the fleece of her own dead lamb. I
would rise at 5.30 each morning to give him his Ostermilk from
a baby's bottle. By the end of the day I was physically exhausted
enough to long for the moment when my head hit the pillow.
Sleep came immediately and there was no time for the mael-
strom of doubts and unanswered questions that had accompanied every wakeful moment hitherto.

Nimrod was gentle and fatherly towards Lambert, who clearly concluded that he too was a dog, joining us on our long walks,
following us around the house and sleeping next to Nimrod in
the kitchen at night. What my parents would have thought of the
strange little family living in their house, I cannot imagine!

In return for my assistance with the lambing, Ben gave me
driving lessons in the farm's Landrover. In the early summer
I passed my Test, admittedly not before the second attempt.
Using some of the money from the sale of Grandpa Joe's boats, I
bought the old Landrover from the Proberts when they acquired

a new one. Nimrod and Lambert appeared to be quite happy to be bowling along the leafy lanes in their respective 'nests' in the back.

As for reapplying to the Royal College of Music, a perverse sense of independence asserted itself. In view of the revelations about Bruno, I no longer wanted to pursue a musical career. Instead, I applied to St Katherine's Hall in Cambridge, a city in which I knew there would be music a-plenty. I was accepted and went up to read English and Philosophy at the end of September 1955. I had many offers from among my new acquaintance to look after Nimrod for the relatively short periods while I would be away; as one such offer was from Ben and his parents I felt more inclined to leave him with people he knew well. By now he knew that I would always return to him. Lambert, by then a burly six-month-old and too big for the house, grazed the paddock or rejoined his flock. He could easily be identified as being the one who ran *towards* humans and dogs instead of away from them.

The next three years flew past. In no time at all it seemed, I was processing to the Senate House one sunny Saturday afternoon, in gown, hood and mortar-board, to receive my degree. Paul and Judy Davies were present, at my invitation, to witness this important day in my life. Afterwards we had a picnic tea by the river and went to a mainly choral concert in King's Chapel in the evening. Paul, being an alumnus of the college, had booked tickets for it.

It had to happen one day, I supposed: one of the instrumental items was the slow movement of the Bach Double Violin Concerto. All these years I had studiously avoided hearing it; now I was forced to listen to that sinuous entwining of the two violins again; relive, against my will, those moments I had once thought so precious and exquisite, those memories so painful and shameful now.

We emerged into the green and gold evening during the interval, my equilibrium somewhat restored by that time, and stood about talking to friends. I introduced one of my fellow graduates, a handsome, well-known charmer, to Judy and Paul.

"Cecily has agreed to marry me tomorrow," he told them. "I hope you can stay for the wedding."

"I don't remember any proposal," I joked.

Holding my hand, he went down on one knee and began a flowery speech.

"Forgive my interruption, sir," said a voice behind me, a voice which made my heart stop beating and turned my legs to jelly. "But *Cecilia* is mine."

I took two seconds to compose myself before turning round; two seconds to realise that I must put on the most convincing act of my life. In my high-heeled shoes I was an inch or so taller than the man I faced. I noticed that the raven-black hair which sprang so vigorously from his head was peppered here and there with white.

"Why, Dr Sabra!" I said, with all the *sang froid* that I could muster. "What a surprise!" I held out my hand. "What brings you to Cambridge?" I must have sounded like a character in a Jane Austen novel. Worse, I heard echoes of my mother's 'social' voice.

"Judy, Paul, you'll remember Bruno Sabra," I announced, without waiting for his reply. "Judy and Paul Davies from my home town in Shropshire. And Mike Lester, who was just in the middle of proposing to me. I have to refuse, I'm afraid, Mike: I couldn't possibly be called Cecily Lester – too difficult to say, even when sober." I heard myself give my mother's tinkling laugh.

Hands were shaken, words exchanged politely and it was time to go back into the Chapel. Our seats were near the front. Bruno had arrived late and without a ticket, he said, and had persuaded a steward to squeeze him in at the back.

"I have to rush back to Ely afterwards," he said to me quietly, "But I shall be in the Fitzwilliam Museum on Monday morning and would be overjoyed if you would meet me there at 11 o'clock."

"I will do my best, though it may be difficult," I replied stiffly, knowing full well that, even if the Queen herself ordered my attendance at Court, I should have to decline.

When I took my seat again, Judy regarded me with a quizzical look.

"Am I right in thinking that there's some history there? I shall expect to hear all afterwards."

I cannot now remember what I told her, - except that it was certainly not 'all'.

—◦◦◦—

I was deliberately a little late, grimly enjoying the fact that it was in my power to keep the great man waiting. He was standing on the half-landing of the stairs, looking at the bust of Alexander Pope.

"*A little learning is a dangerous thing*," I quoted – and caught my breath, in spite of myself, as he turned to greet me, his gaze so intense that it almost weakened my resolve.

"Cecilia! It has been such a long, long time."

"We both seem to have survived, however," I observed, haughtily.

"You seem angry with me, Cecilia – coldly angry, I think. Where is the fiery angel I used to know; and the happy, laughing girl?"

"Grown up," I replied. "No longer the impressionable ingé-nue she used to be."

"You must tell me about your life, my dear. Is there perhaps somewhere away from here where we can go for coffee or lunch? I have to be back in Ely for a rehearsal in the Cathedral, but not until seven o'clock. Have you time to spare?"

"I changed my plans in order to come here, so yes, I have. I have my car parked not far away, so we can get out of town for a while, if you wish."

My parents had bought me the green MG sports car for my twenty-first birthday the previous year. 'You'll never catch an eligible bachelor in that dreadful old bone-shaker of a Landrover,' my mother had said, as if that were my sole objective in life. I was thrilled with it, of course, and it gave me considerable cachet with my fellow students, although most of the time I used my bicycle to get around. I should have been the happiest young woman in the world that day to be sitting in an open-topped car, driving the love of my life into the countryside on a balmy summer's day.

Once out of the city, I drove fast along the Newmarket road, where sunlight dappled through the leafy green canopy onto our heads. I was glad of my large sunglasses for more reasons than one.

"There's another pair in the cubbyhole if you need them," I said, glancing at Bruno.

"Kept there for your lover, perhaps?"

"I have no lover," I replied shortly, "Many good male friends, but no-one special. There was only ever one."

"And what became of him?"

I took a right turn down a narrow road overhung with trees, which led to a village where I had heard of an inn, reputedly good for its beer and food.

"He took what he wanted and left me," I said, regretting the tremor in my voice.

"Oh my dear girl, how can you say such a thing? You came to me of your own free will; we met as equals and I treasure the memory."

By now I could hardly see the road for tears. I swung the car into a field gateway, switched off the engine and turned to face him.

"I had a *baby*!" I shouted. "Yours. *Your* baby, your parting gift to me. It was all I had of you - but she died, so I didn't have a baby anymore."

There was a stunned silence for several seconds, broken only by my sobs.

"Oh, dear God!" he said at last. "But that is impossible."

"On the contrary; you seemed to produce another one at about the same time, - a *live* one, by all accounts."

"Let me explain, Cecilia." He reached to take my hands in his but I pushed him away.

"I can save you the trouble: you lied to me, that's all the ex-plan _____"

"The child is my *wife's*, not mine," he broke in quickly. "She admitted to me that she was … with child … when I returned to the States that time. You must believe me, Cecilia. I would never lie to you."

It was my turn to be silent. He looked at me pleadingly, his dark eyes glistening. In them I saw hurt and, yes, love, which softened my heart and made my anger evaporate; anger which

I realised had become a habitual emotion where thoughts of Bruno were concerned. Now I was left without its support and knew that I would have to believe and trust him.

"Tell me your story, my dear," he said gently "and I will tell you mine. But first, I suggest that we eat and drink to fortify us for these revelations."

We found a quiet corner in the pleasant old pub on the village green. Most of the customers were outside enjoying the sunshine, so we were unremarked and undisturbed. I cannot recall what we ate, but remember that we both drank Pimms No. 1, which dissolved my tension and loosened my tongue, so that we fell into the kind of easy exchange which had flowed at our very first meeting, five long years ago. For the time being, we navigated round the subject that loomed like a huge rock in the sea of our conversation; that was for later. Instead we spoke of Nimrod, my time as an apprentice shepherdess and the antics of Lambert, the orphan lamb who thought he was a dog; of my decision not to pursue a musical career but to keep my singing as an interest apart from my academic studies; of my years at Cambridge, my involvement in 'Ban the Bomb' marches, of mad student antics, including the amazing spectacle, just recently, of a *car* straddling the roof of the Senate House, the manner of its appearance there a complete mystery to all who saw it. I was curious to know how he came to be in Cambridge on the very day that I received my Degree. He hung his head in mock embarrassment.

"It was not entirely by accident," he admitted. "I had to be in Ely for a concert yesterday and another on Thursday. My host, an old friend and colleague, told me that it would be busy in Cambridge on Saturday because of the Degree ceremony, so it would be better to go on Monday – today. I decided to do both, hoping that I might catch at least a glimpse of you."

"But how did you know I was in Cambridge?"

"I went to look for you in your village. Your good neighbour, Mrs Pascoe, told me that you hadn't been back for years – that she thought you'd never got over the death of your grandfather - and that's why you stayed away. She kindly asked me in for a cup of tea and gave me your address in Shropshire, but said that you were studying in Cambridge."

"An account of that visit will be all over the village by now," I said, laughing. "When was it?"

"Only about two weeks ago," he replied.

After lunch, we walked up a lane towards the church, through an avenue of ancient beech trees, standing like the massive pillars of a great cathedral, supporting a vaulted roof of green fan-tracery. Having admired the church, noted for its magnificent stained-glass windows and fine brasses, we sat on a bench in a shady corner of the churchyard. Bruno took my hand in his and said:

"Now tell me, if you can bear to. Tell me everything that happened to you after – that day: the day I had to leave you. But first – may I take the pins out of your hair and let it down? Then you will look like the girl you were when I loved you first."

I turned my head away from him and he took out the hairpins from my French pleat slowly, one by one, and handed them to me.

"It is lovely as ever," he said, fanning it around my shoulders, "but not as long as it used to be."

"I will explain that later," I said grimly.

Then I poured out my heart and soul to him, holding nothing back, and it was the first time that I had done so to any human creature. There were tears at times but no recriminations now. He heard me out without interruption, regarding me with that intense and luminous gaze of his and registering in his own expressive features all the emotions that my words evoked. When I told of my enforced haircut, he winced and touched my hair almost reverently. Only when I fell silent did he speak.

"Oh my love, I would not have had you suffer all this for the world. You are too young to have known such distress." He took me in his arms then and stroked my hair with a repeated motion, as if I were a small animal needing reassurance.

"I understand your anger now," he said at length. "Can you bear to hear my excuses after such an account?"

"I believe you and I trust you," I replied. "Tell me, if you feel the need – but spare me too many details. I know your wife's name but I don't want to hear it from your lips. Can you understand that?"

He nodded. "Of course I can. I will make it brief. When I returned to the States after those unforgettable weeks in Cornwall, *she* wanted a rapprochement. She had had an affair, she said, and was expecting her lover's child. Divorce would harm her reputation and her successful career, she pointed out, and mine, too. Nobody need know that the child was not mine, she said. So we stayed together – except that we are usually apart because of our work. She has had another lover since, I think."

"And you?" I asked. "No, please don't tell me." I held up a hand as if to fend off a blow.

"There is nothing to tell," he said simply.

"And the child ... your step-daughter?"

"Heloise. She is a healthy, normal little girl. A typical American four-year-old, I imagine."

"But do you love her as your own?" I was driven by the memory of my own loss.

"She is an - endearing child – but she is not *mine*, Cecilia. In looks, she is like her mother, but not in temperament, for which I am truly thankful."

"Would you have loved *our* baby, Bruno?"

"Of course I would, my darling." He kissed away the tears which were filling my eyes again. "But you are tormenting yourself by such questions, so no more now, please."

He gathered me close and kissed my mouth; a kiss that was balm to my re-opened wounds; a kiss more of love and comfort than of desire.

A song thrush started to sing evensong somewhere high above our heads, pouring forth a stream of melody, as if to call the 'rude forefathers of the hamlet' to evening prayer; but they slept on, unheeding in their graves and it was time for us to leave.

———

I drove him back to Ely, the great cathedral, 'the ship of the Fens', visible for miles ahead of us, rising majestically from the flat Cambridgeshire landscape in the golden light of early evening. I stopped a discreet distance from the Canonry house in which he was staying with his friend, and with one swift kiss on my cheek, he was gone, having promised to reserve a seat for me at Thursday's concert.

"It would be so good to know that you were there," he had said. "The music will be more *alive* with you there to inspire me."

I felt proud, yet humbled, as I drove back to Cambridge, that this great man should say such a thing to me. After our day together, I felt cleansed and purified by the disclosures that we had exchanged, every vestige of anger and bitterness washed away.

The nave of the Cathedral was packed already when I arrived, but when I gave my name to one of the stewards, he ushered me to a reserved seat: a chair at the end of a row, from which I would have an excellent view of Bruno. I knew that tonight I would have to share him with hundreds of people but knew also that my presence there would be of special importance to him. I looked around at the magnificence of the ancient building. I had sung in the Lady Chapel once or twice during my years at Cambridge, but tonight I envied the choir, up there on their tiered staging; envied them the privilege of having Bruno to conduct them, remembering how it had been that first time in Truro. The orchestra was tuning up – that magical confusion of sound in response to the oboe's A, which heralds, after a few seconds, the equally magical silence immediately before the arrival of the leader of the orchestra, the soloists and finally, the conductor.

The chorus stood, and here they came, that small procession, and arranged themselves in their places; but I had eyes only for my beloved man as he mounted the rostrum. Still in silence, (there was no applause in sacred buildings in those days) he turned, bowed low to the audience and turned again to command the choir and the orchestra, his baton raised and every eye upon him.

This concert was being presented as a memorial to a one-time Organist and Choirmaster of the Cathedral and consisted of Parry's *Blest Pair of Sirens,* followed by a Handel Organ Concerto and, after the interval, Mozart's Requiem Mass. (I still have the programme among my memorabilia. How could I ever throw it away?) As I watched every gesture of Bruno's and listened to its response from the musicians, there was a strange sense of reversal in my mind, almost as if I were proudly watching my own child's performance. It lasted for a fleeting moment and was gone, leaving only the invisible thread which seemed to join us. Sublime music will always weave its spell in the spirit of the listener but, on this occasion, the Requiem transcended all I have ever heard, before or since, because of that thread, which bound us more closely than any physical union.

———

Bruno had told me that there would be little chance for us to meet after the concert. He had to leave for London in the afternoon of the following day and had suggested that we spent as much time together as possible. We arranged that I should meet his train from Ely.

With heart racing, I stood on the platform as the train pulled in, but there was no Bruno. I sat in the car for a while and met the next train, but still there was no sign of him. After making enquiries at the ticket office as to the time of the next train's arrival, and having been assured that there was no message for me, I sat in the car, worried and despairing, watching our precious time slipping away.

I was just leaving the car for the third time when a taxi drew up, and to my huge relief, out got Bruno.

"My dearest girl," he said as he came towards me, "How good of you to wait. I was so afraid you would be gone by now. I was unavoidably detained by a well-meaning person who insisted that she should drive me back to London. I had to tell her that I had an appointment at the Fitzwilliam."

"Oh Bruno," I said, "you are here now and I'm so very relieved and happy to see you. I imagined all sorts of horrible scenes: accidents, injuries, – even death."

"But not attempted abduction," he said, laughing. "Drive me away quickly in case she saw me hail that taxi outside the Fitzwilliam. I want to take you in my arms again. Can we find somewhere quiet?"

We stowed his suitcase in the back of the car and I drove towards a place near the river where I had picnicked with friends once or twice. It was far enough out of Cambridge to be quiet on a Friday in the middle of the day. On the way we spoke of the previous night's concert.

"I cannot tell you what it meant to me that you were there," he said simply.

"But how did you *know* that I was there?" I asked. "Could you see me?"

"Not at first – not in fact until the final bows did I catch sight of you. No, it was simply a strong awareness of your presence: a sixth sense awareness, if you like."

I was too overcome to speak, but reached out my hand to touch his. He kissed it gently and held it until I needed to change gear, then held it again.

"You see," he explained, "after each performance, wherever you are in the world, people require more of you. You are exhausted but still they demand your attention, personally. They are infatuated with you; they clamour to be noticed by you; they want to *own* you, performers and audience alike."

"I suppose it must be like that for film-stars, and pop-singers like Elvis Presley – fans mobbing them and screaming."

"Yes – but they actively *seek* the adulation they crave. Mar – my wife - is the same: she thrives on it. I suppose it is gratifying at first but after a while it becomes a burden."

"All the same, I do understand them," I said. "Don't forget that *I* fell in love with you when I was fifteen, at just such a performance as last night's".

"But that infatuation turned into love – into the pain and suffering of love also, alas. You have *given* and never taken, and last night I could feel the power and radiance of your love like a current of electricity. You are Muse, enchantress and lover all at once."

There was no one else at the picnic place. I backed the car a little way down the grassy lane and tucked it carefully into the side, sensing that we would leave it until the last possible minute before leaving for Bruno's train.

"There is a practical side to my nature," I said, laughing, "One must try to balance the romantic dreamer on the other side." I took a rug and a picnic basket from the back of the car. "*Et voila! Nous avons des aliments et du vin, pour faire pique-nique.*"

"*Tres bien, ma cherie,*" he said, "*Mais attends un moment.*" And he removed the basket and the rug from my hand, put them on the ground and took me in his arms, kissing me until I trembled as if an earthquake had struck beneath my feet. When he released me, he too was trembling.

"Treasure these moments, my love," he said, "They are all that we have."

"But now we have found each other again, we can have so many more of such moments – a whole lifetime of them," I said, my voice still shaking.

"We will talk of that a little later," he said. "Shall we find a place for our picnic?"

So we walked a little way and spread the rug on the long, lush grass near a backwater of the river, cooling the wine in the water while we ate our simple picnic of bread and fruit and cheese. I had even remembered to bring glasses, and a corkscrew which Bruno managed deftly. It was an idyllic scene, but our time there was so short that we would hardly leave an imprint on the grass. How relentless time is when one wants to hold it back, rushing on like an impatient tide, claiming the present and leaving only the past in its wake. We sat very close, sipping our wine with linked arms, or each offering the glass to the other's lips, both painfully aware that the hour we had left was diminishing to half-an-hour and that soon it would be time to leave.

When we got back to the car, Bruno opened his suitcase and took out a book which he handed to me.

"Another parting gift," he said. "Or rather, a gift to mark another parting."

"Oh Bruno!" was all I could say. It was entitled THE SONGS OF LOVE, and turning to the first page, I saw that he had written:

For dear Cecilia, with my love always, Bruno.

Underneath, he had added:
Littore quot conchae, tot sunt in amore dolores. OVID: ARS AMATORIA.
(There are as many pains in love as there are shells upon the seashore.)

"One day perhaps, you will sing the songs to me," he said gently as, unable to speak, I buried my face in his jacket.

We hardly spoke in the car. He held my hand or stroked the back of my head, running his fingers through my hair. In the end, we had little time to say good bye, standing on the platform in that awkward way that people do, waiting for the final, cruel moment when the train would take him far away. I had begged him again to take me with him – to London, to Paris – anywhere in the world as long as we were together.

"One day, God willing," he had said, "We shall be together, but now cannot be that time."

Now he said: "There was so much I had planned to say to you, Cecilia. I will write you a letter when I get to Paris. When do you go home?"

"Very soon," I replied. "I have to play the organ for my neighbour's wedding next week. Shall I be able to write back to you?"

"I will give you an address when I write," he assured me. "Good bye, my love, and thank you for all you are and all you have given me. I shall hold you in my heart forever."

And the train came in like a great monster and swallowed him, and I, enchantress though I might be, could do nothing to save him.

TEN

L ooking back through this memoir, I realise that, like an artist who cannot tell when a painting is finished, adding a brush-stroke here and a shadow there, I have gone into minute detail about certain episodes in my early life and left little time to deal with what came after those events: namely, half a century! If I skim over the next few years, it is not because they are of no importance; that the friends and family who peopled those years are of no account, the events not worthy of recording.

Some live their lives on an even keel, content to inhabit a flat landscape; for others like me there are mountain ranges rising out of that flat landscape and, before and beyond those peaks, there are deep valleys. I found myself in one such valley when, a few days after my return to Shropshire, and another joyful re-union with Nimrod, there was a letter from Bruno in the morning post. My heart leapt at the sight of his handwriting on the envelope, which carried a French stamp and postmark – but my spirits plummeted as I read his words:

My dear Cecilia,

Between engagements and rehearsals here, I find I have a little time to write to you of matters that I could not bring myself to utter at our last meeting, although I had resolved to do so.

Self-denial is one of the hardest disciplines to endure, but I feel that I must impose it upon myself and therefore, upon both of us. Please be assured that this decision is born not only of my deep love for you, but of a profound concern for your own future happiness.

For one consideration, I think that you have a strong maternal instinct and need, when the time is right, to have children to love and nurture; for another, you have a fine intellect and need to use it for both your own benefit and that of others; for a third, you have a lovely singing voice and need to express yourself through it, giving pleasure to others and receiving praise and recognition for it.

I am going to depict an alternative course for you – though I am not offering it. I shall enumerate it thus:

1. *We scandalise the world by setting up home together.*
2. *We live in the utmost bliss of love but the miracle of conception is not repeated and we remain childless.*
3. *My peripatetic life seems appealing to you at first but does not suit your need for a home in which you can put down roots and live happily with your dog(s) and other animals.*
4. *As I grow old and gray, you are still in the full bloom and beauty of womanhood and are tempted to take a young lover.*

Oh Cecilia, I do not need to paint more of this picture. I know you will protest against my decision, even be angry with me again, but consider it well. My own mind is made up. I realise (and it pains me to think of it) that this will necessitate marriage on your part to a person as yet unknown – or even known, perhaps: that pleasant young friend of yours, Lester, for example. I beg you not to invite me to the ceremony, but entreat you to tell me of the births of your children: dates, weights, names, - and whether they look like you or show signs of being musical.

Lastly, I enclose the address of a good friend of mine who can be trusted to pass on any communication, and to whom I will give your present address.

Be assured always of my love, as I am of yours. God bless you and keep you.

Bruno.

I read the letter over and over again, each time, irrationally, willing its content to have some other meaning: that he could not live without me; that he was calling to me, just as Mr Rochester called for Jane Eyre; but the message was always the same.

On the half-sheet of paper which Bruno had enclosed was the name of 'the trusted friend' – the go-between – with an address in London:

Fr. Michal Wieniawski,
St Augustine's Presbytery, Victoria Road, Fulham.

I slipped deeper into the pit of despair. A Roman priest – Polish, probably. Was he Bruno's adviser, - confessor, perhaps? Any hopes I might have entertained that this friend might be approachable, - even susceptible to my feminine wiles – were dashed at once.

I kept to the house for several days, feigning a mystery illness when necessary. (In very truth, it was heart-sickness.) I walked with Nimrod only in the very early morning or after dusk. Several times I wrote letters to Bruno – and then tore them up or burnt them. The astringency of anger was no longer there to brace me; all that remained was the inertia of hurt and hopelessness.

In the end, my natural optimism prevailed and I climbed out of the pit, setting my sights on the range of mountains that might lie beyond the vast plain which stretched before me. I could dismiss the years it took me to reach those distant peaks in one sentence, but will probably permit myself a little more space.

I was offered a post as a teacher of English at a Boys' Preparatory school near my home town, accepting it only on condition that Nimrod could accompany me each day. (Permission granted; welcomed, even.)

With the help of Paul and Judy Davies, I made a recording of some of *The Songs of Love*, - the saddest ones, naturally - and sent a copy to Bruno. I heard nothing in return.

I married a widower, the (clerical) father of one of my pupils, and became a fond stepmother to Edmund Knight and his two younger sisters. I had two early miscarriages but no live children of my own.

I lived an exemplary life as the wife of a village clergyman, teaching the Sunday school, training the choir, playing the organ, cooking for harvest suppers, hosting the Church Fête and acting as unofficial welfare worker in the community, as good clergy wives did in those days.

By condensing those years in this way, I can save myself – and my readers – the grief occasioned by the demise of my beloved Nimrod, who died at the age of thirteen years and four months.

As the days turned into weeks, then months and years, I be-gan to congratulate myself on my stoicism. Looking back, I saw that the sentence of penance and servitude had not all been hard – even enjoyable at times. The mountains must be getting closer by now, I thought, and on one of them Bruno would be waiting for me; the ensuing reunion would be my eventual re-ward for my 'pilgrim's progress' across the plain, and my exile in the wilderness would be over.

And then a day came, an amazing, life-changing day, when I was so busy straining my eyes for the first glimpse of those moun-tains, that I failed to see the great chasm at my feet.

PART 2

ONE

(Narrated by M.G. Manning)

LIMERICK, REPUBLIC OF IRELAND: 1964

Doctor Cornelius Manning and his wife are sitting in their fine drawing-room discussing their children's education. Up until now there has been a resident tutor, but the boys will be ten in the summer and they plan to send them away to school in September.

It is a dreary, damp afternoon in late February. Outside in the street people hurry through the drizzle, their collars turned up against the east wind. Inside the elegantly proportioned town house, coals burn evenly in the handsome Adam fireplace, their amber glow reflected in the leaf of a polished mahogany Pembroke table upon which a maid carefully places a tea tray. Two large table lamps shed warm radiance into the swiftly fading light of late afternoon.

"Will I close the shutters and draw the curtains now, Ma'am?" the girl asks.

"Thank you, Cathleen," replies Una Manning. "Oh, - and would you ask Master Dominic and Master Donal to join us in here at six o'clock?"

"I will of course, Ma'am."

Cathleen is one of a succession of maids the Mannings have had in the past few years. Some have left to be married; one or two have been unsuitable in some way. They have great hopes for this new girl: she is respectful, knows her job well, and furthermore, she is rather plain and dumpy – homely is perhaps the best description - and there does not seem to be a 'young man' in the offing.

"As I was saying, my dear," says the Doctor when Cathleen has closed the doors quietly behind her. "The boys may be inseparable, as you pointed out, but for that very reason I think they should go to different schools so that each can develop independently of the other. Donal is more wilful and in need of discipline than Dominic, for example. The Benedictine Brothers at Barrageen Abbey will lead him in the right direction. "Dominic, on the other hand, needs to learn to stand on his own two feet without always looking to Donal for protection. How do you think St Patrick's College would suit him? 'Give me a boy before he is seven and I will give you the man.' Isn't that what the Jesuits say? Except of course that the boys are a few years past the seven year deadline," he adds with a smile.

"Well, he is certainly the more *religious* of the two," his wife answers, "And more musically inclined, though Donal does sing well. Who knows, Dominic may be a candidate for the priesthood. The girls will go to St Philomena's together, of course. They both show signs of being musical too, which needs to be encouraged - as well as the need for a sound education in the main subjects."

The conversation continues in the same vein until the boys present themselves in the drawing- room at the appointed hour to hear how their immediate - and possibly long-term - future has been mapped out for them.

Upstairs in the day-nursery, while Nanny sits knitting by a fire of glowing coals, Katharine and Theresa play happily, one at her dolls' house, the other on the rocking-horse, giving never a thought to their future, but content simply to exist in the eternal present.

THE LIMERICK EXAMINER: THURSDAY, OCTOBER 10, 1968.

Couple's Tragic Death

The eminent anthropologist and philanthropist, Dr Cornelius Manning, was killed in a road accident in Belfast yesterday. His wife died later in hospital and the driver of the taxi-cab in which they were travelling was critically injured. Dr Manning had been giving a series of lectures at Queen's University in the city and, accompanied by his wife, Una, was on his way to the railway station to catch the train back to Limerick. A spokesman said that all road traffic had been diverted because of an attempted Student Demonstration and March to City Hall to protest against the extreme brutality used by RUC Police in the Derry Civil Rights March last week. Road blocks had been set up in advance to stop the Student March and, in the resulting chaos and an absence of effective diversion signs, the Mannings' cab was hit by a lorry carrying concrete blocks to the site of the disturbance.

Dr and Mrs Manning were well known in the city and farther afield for their good works and espousal of charitable causes and will be sadly missed in the community. The couple are mourned by four children, twin sons and two daughters.

A Requiem Mass will take place on Monday,14th at S. John's Cathedral at 10.30 am...

In another drawing room in Limerick a week or so later, Mrs William Leahy is receiving the family's solicitor.

"I am sorry to intrude on your grief at this saddest of all times, Mrs Leahy," he says, "But as your daughter and son-in-law left no specific indications for the guardianship of their children, I wondered if I might ask what your thoughts are on this matter."

"Please sit down, Mr O'Dowd," the lady bids, her halo of newly-coiffed silver hair contrasting elegantly with her black mourning dress. One manicured and heavily be-ringed hand indicates a leather chair. "I must confess that this – untimely – event has put me, as both a parent and a widow, in a very difficult position indeed."

"Quite so; quite so. I assure you that matters can rest as they are, at least until after Christmas. The school fees are paid until the two boys break up on the 19th and 20th of December, respectively. The housekeeper and the maid will not seek employment elsewhere until the New Year, after which, of course, both this and the Glengariff house will need to be sold. They are willing - and perfectly capable –to hold the fort until the children's respective futures are determined."

"I must say that at present I cannot envisage having any of the children here, even on a temporary basis," says Patricia Leahy. "My health is not good and my Church work is much too demanding. I am waiting to hear from my son-in-law's parents in New York. They too must be feeling horribly shocked, but I do feel that they should make some contribution when it comes to considering the children's future."

"Then I will come and see you again in due course when you have heard from them, and await your joint instructions," says O'Dowd, rising from his seat. Mrs Leahy reaches for the bell-pull.

"My maid will show you out. ... Oh, Mr O'Dowd," she says as he walks towards the door. "As you know, I was always very much against these adoptions in the first place, - and one of the – er – fallen women a Protestant at that!"

"Indeed, Mrs Leahy. How these good works can come back to haunt one," observes the solicitor as, with a small inclination of the head, he leaves the room.

I f that fateful day in early October 1968 marked the beginning of the renewal of Ulster's Troubles, it surely marks a momentous change in the fortunes of the Manning orphans.

It falls to the lot of Mr Sean O'Dowd of O'Dowd, Lawless and McBride, Solicitors at Law, to divulge to the children at the beginning of the school holidays the secrets which they have never been told. Their grandmother elects not to be present as he faces them across the long Heppelwhite dining-table in the handsome, spacious house which has been their home for as long as any of them can remember. He sits with his back to one of the tall sash windows, his face in shadow but the pale December light emphasising the sparseness of his wispy hair. He lowers his glasses and looks over the top of them at the row of faces opposite him: the two girls with their fair curls, the boys black-haired and fresh-faced.

"It may come as a shock to all four of you," he begins, "to learn that only the girls are actually the children by birth of your parents, God rest their souls. You, Donal and Dominic, were adopted by them immediately after your birth. Furthermore, you are not twins, not even brothers, in fact."

He pauses to allow his words to acquire meaning in four different minds. Four half-formed questions tumble all at once into the stunned silence:

"But when ....?"

"How did.....?"

"Who was ...?"

"How long ago ...?"

"Let me continue, if you will," says the lawyer, holding up his hand to silence them. "There will be time for questions when I have said what I came to say."

He straightens the sheaf of papers in front of him on the table, aligning it precisely in the angle between the edge and the transverse joint of the table-leaf. He unscrews the gold-banded cap from a maroon fountain-pen and replaces it carefully. He looks at the two boys. "There were irregularities with your adoption, I fear," he goes on. "You were both born in an – er - Institution – a Convent in London, to mothers who were not married."

"You mean to say we're *bastards?*" breaks in Donal.

O'Dowd looks shocked. "That is not a word to be bandied about in front of your sist ... – the young ladies," he says reprovingly. "Perhaps we should leave your comments and queries until they have left the room." He turns to the girls. Tears are streaming down Theresa's face and Katharine, all colour gone from her face and biting her lip at the complexity of this revelation, puts a protective arm about her younger sister's shoulder.

"May I suggest that you two find Mrs O'Leary and wait with her until I send for you again? Say nothing at all of what I have told you," he adds, as Katharine pulls her sister gently towards the door. The girls find the housekeeper in the hall, a good deal farther from the dining room door than she has been a few seconds earlier.

"To return to what I was saying." O'Dowd moves the sheaf of documents a few inches to the left and realigns it with the edge of the table. He uncaps and caps the pen two or three times. "The women in question: one was an English Protestant of good family, the other an Irish servant girl. I know very little more than that."

"And who was my – were our – fathers?"

"Fathers unknown," O'Dowd replies firmly. "This is usually the case with such - um – women."

"But why London?" asks Donal.

"Adoption was not legal in this country when you were born," replies O'Dowd, "Although, actually, it became legally available later in that same year, 1954. However, your father – *adoptive* father, was working at an English university at the time, which is why they decided to adopt over there."

"But why did Father and Mother need to adopt us?" asks Dominic. "Why would they break the law?"

"They had waited a long time for children. Your father was fifty years of age and your mother in her late thirties. It was not until you boys were two years old that the miracle happened: God answered their prayers and sent them two children of their own. Being the good people that they were, they treated you all alike and determined that they would not favour their own children."

"But a *Protestant* mother!" groans Dominic, "And by the way, which one of us *is* that one's son, because that means that one of us is sure to go to Hell?"

"I cannot answer that question," O'Dowd replies. "Nobody actually knows which of you is which, and perhaps that is just as well. Now, I suggest that you go out of the room for a short while and discuss this between yourselves. Kindly ask the girls to come back to me – and please tell Mrs O'Leary that some liquid refreshment – preferably from a whiskey bottle - would be very welcome."

Christmas was a sad affair that year. Mrs O'Leary and Cathleen did their best to encourage the Manning children to decorate the house as they had done so joyfully in past years. The boxes of decorations were fetched from the attic; holly and greenery were ordered and delivered and presents bought and wrapped. On Christmas Day a fine goose was cooked and a plum pudding, made as usual some weeks before, was put on to boil. But none of them had the heart to pretend that this was just an ordinary Christmas, following the pattern of those that had gone before. In the absence of their parents, and Grandmother Leahy and Father O'Keefe who always celebrated with them, it was agreed that they should all have their Christmas Dinner in the kitchen, rather than the children sitting sadly spaced around the large dining table, waited on by the staff.

It was not so much the loss of their parents that grieved the children; although they had had the greatest respect for them, they had always seemed somewhat remote. Consequently, it was the thought of separation from each other which caused them to grieve in advance of the dreaded day when the girls would be separated from their brothers – as they still thought of them. They had all talked of little else since the lawyer's visits, trying to imagine what the future held for them all in the light of his revelations, but unable to see any resolution of the difficulties that lay ahead.

Mrs Leahy had pleaded extreme shock and grief as an excuse not to have any contact with them – except to exhort them, through Mrs O'Leary, to go to Mass on Christmas Day itself and on the following Holy Days. They were therefore unable to ask her any further questions about either their past, or the future which had been decided for them.

The children had learned of their fate on a second visit from O'Dowd. Donal and Dominic had been told that there were serious irregularities with their adoption in England which, as had been suspected, had broken the laws of both countries. It should be remembered also, O'Dowd said, that it was against English law for adopted children to be told anything that would identify their natural parents, nor should they themselves ever try to trace them. In spite of the terms of the Will, he informed them, neither boy had any claim whatsoever to the assets of their adoptive parents. Any share they might have had of the Estate would go to the Church, whilst the girls would benefit from the bulk of the inheritance, to be held in Trust until they came of age. Meanwhile, they were to go to their paternal grandparents in America, escorted by a cousin, a nun who had returned to Ireland for the festival. When the Limerick and Glengarriff houses were sold, he assured them, much of the furniture, pictures and heirlooms from both would be retained in storage until they came of age or married.

As for the boys, he said, Father O'Keefe, out of the goodness of his heart and real regard for their moral welfare, had contacted a Christian Brothers' School in Dublin. The school, O'Dowd said, would accept both boys, in spite of their very regrettable origins, until they were old enough to leave and make their way in the world.

———

"I do fear for those boys," Maeve O'Leary says. She and Cathleen are clearing the house after their departure for Dublin and are working in the boys' bedroom.

"And them so mannerly and well brought-up," Cathleen agrees. "I've heard those Brothers are terrible hard and strict. 'Tis not what the good Doctor and Mrs Manning would have wanted for them, God rest their souls." She crosses herself quickly. "Whatever the rights and wrongs of the boys' adoption, they meant the best for them, the very best. Protestant hoors their mothers might 'a been but they're after being brought up in the Faith, the both o' them."

"Poor motherless creatures, *all* of them," says the other, folding the linen from one of the beds and stacking it in a neat pile. "The two girls have their grandparents, I suppose, but over the water in a strange land. I wonder shall we ever see them again."

"Mother of God! To hear the two of them weep at the parting from their brothers," exclaims Cathleen from the top of a step ladder, where she is unhooking a curtain from the rail above the tall sash window. "And who do those boys have but each other now?"

The two women folded one of the heavy curtains between them.

"Sure, 'tis a tragedy all right; two young gentlemen disowned by the woman they thought to be their grandmother."

"That Leahy woman was always hard on them; now we know why. Her with all her churchy ways: 'Father O'Keefe this, Father O'Keefe that; here's some money for the church, Father; three bags full, Father.' "

"*Cathleen*, will ye have a care! The walls have ears round here. And she and that lawyer have seen *us* all right: you with a place at the Presbytery when Annie is wed - and myself only a bus-ride away at the McCausland house."

"Still an' all," says Cathleen, "she's a disgrace altogether. I'll not say any different, so I won't."

"Didn't I ask her for an address for them?" Maeve whispers, fearful now that, by some chance, they might be overheard. "The boys had no idea where they were going, except it was to Dublin. Mrs Leahy said that any correspondence, birthday cards and the like, should be sent to the solicitor first. I feel there's no certainty that they'd ever receive any mail that way."

"I'd agree wid ye, so." Cathleen descends the ladder with the other curtain, and hands two corners to Maeve. "But when you say *birthday cards* – what *about* their birthday? I wonder do they even have the same birthday if they're not a twin?"

"Well, only God in Heaven would know that, it seems. At any rate, *they* know where *we* are and I hope they'll keep in touch somehow. They both used to write home from school every week."

"Sure, you told them where you would be in a week or two and they can send to me at the Presbytery."

"Now we've the curtains folded and ready for the cleaners, we'll take this lot downstairs," says Maeve O'Leary. "After that we'll start on the press: it's still full of the boys' belongings and God alone knows what we do with *those*."

"And He'll not be telling us, to be sure," observes Cathleen.

TWO

DOMINIC'S NOTEBOOK.

<u>*Feb 27 1969*</u>

My hands are so cold and sore with chilblains that I can hardly write but as I have had no answers to my letters after 6 weeks here I think it's important to write about what it is like in this school though I don't think anyone outside would believe it. How I'm going to keep this notebook safe from prying eyes I don't quite know, but I shall find a way somehow.

This is a list of the people I have written to:

Katie and Tess c/o Mr O'Dowd

Grandmother Leahy

Fr O'Keefe

Cathleen Shea & Mrs O'Leary c/o Fr O'Keefe.

Fr Vincent SJ (Superior of St Patrick's)

I have not heard back from one of them.

My old school was strict and old-fashioned, I suppose, but the teachers were fair and as long as you worked well and behaved yourself you didn't get punished. But this is <u>PRISON</u> – in fact I think it might be worse than prison. Two of the Brothers are monsters. They bless themselves with one hand and lash out with the strap in the other, never minding where it lands – hands, legs, backs, heads – and then walk about saying *their rosaries or reading their breviaries, and seem to think that they are doing God's work – but how can it be right? There are even worse things going on too, but I cannot write about them here.*

March 2ⁿᵈ

The most awful thing is being separated from Don. Br. Rourke, The Disciplinarian, soon saw how he could punish us both and 'bring us down'.

"Let us see how REFINED and CULTURED ye are after ye're finished here," he sneered. "Yes indeed, ye could call this a FINISHING school. We'll have the both o' ye finished altogether."

This happened only a day or two after we arrived, in front of an assembly of dirty, snotty, shivering, hungry, grey-looking boys. One of them, a kid no more than 10 I should think, but looking more like 7, laughed – just nerves I suppose – and Br. Rourke grabbed him by the ear-lobe and sent him spinning out of the line and across the yard.

March 7ᵗʰ

This is called an Industrial school. We have to work at trades as well as having some lessons. There is a farm where some boys work and there are workshops for Carpentry and Tailoring and Shoe-making. There is also a Bakery and a Laundry. Some boys work in the kitchens and we all have to do a lot of cleaning. I am lucky I suppose because I can write well and was picked out to work in the outer office, replacing a boy who has just left. I am responsible for cleaning the office every day as well.

When I was younger I wanted to be a priest but now I want to be a writer or a journalist, which is why I'm keeping this notebook. It is an exercise book like any other and I have started to write towards the back, where nobody would look if they found it. In the front are meaningless notes and drawings, things like in a rough notebook. There are even some games of Hangman and other word-games that Don and I played in the train on the way here. Mostly I hide it between two cupboards in the office but sometimes I slip it behind the books on the top shelf of the tall bookcase.

March 10th

Someone has left an old newspaper in the office. It is dated Jan. 5th and I see that there has been bad trouble again in the North between Catholics and Protestants. Why does that last word always mean trouble? I still worry about either Don or me having a Protestant mother and wonder if being sent to this place is to prepare us for the Hell we shall end up in.

March 20th

I have not seen Don at all for over 2 weeks now. No one seems to know where he is – even the kinder brothers when I ask them tell me nothing. He and I have hardly had a chance to speak to each other since we came here. After the incident in the playground, Rourke said to us: "If ye so much as <u>look</u> at each other from now on ye'll not sit down for another year, such a clattering I'll be givin' yez, spawn of Satan that ye are."

I usually see him, Don I mean, at mass each morning. He has a way of lifting one eyebrow. (We always used to laugh about this because however hard I tried I couldn't do it.) All we can do now is let our eyes sweep over each other while he lifts his left eyebrow and I scratch my right ear. That has to be our conversation for the day!

March 25th

I am getting really worried about Don now. It is three weeks now since he was last at Mass. I'm thinking of the day we came here. We were almost glad to be going to this unknown school because at least we were going together. A Garda came for us in a car and came with us on the train to Dublin where we had to attend Court. It was something to do with being orphans with no one willing to 'exercise proper Guardianship'. We were committed to *The Sacred Heart Industrial School* until we were 16 years of age, by which time, the magistrate said, we would have learned a trade which would equip us to make our way in the world when we left. A Brother came for us in a car and drove us and the Garda a few miles to the outskirts of the city where we turned in through some big iron gates and saw at the end of a long drive a huge white house. The Brother showed us through a tall black door and through a hall and into the Superior's room which has a big picture of the Sacred Heart in a gold frame. The Superior's name is Br. Heaney and he's quite old really, about 70 I'd say. He greeted us in quite a friendly way and said he had had good reports of our progress at school. He was pleased to know that Donal had a good singing voice and that I played the clarinet. (I brought mine with me.)

"We've a great Band here and a good Choir," he said. "Ad majorem Dei gloriam is the Jesuit motto, is it not?" He looked at me inquiringly. "I expect both of you know your Latin so I do not need to translate it for you. It would be fitting for us, too, as we offer our music for the glory of our Lord. Now, Brother McMahon will show you what to do next. Meanwhile, I daresay this gentleman might welcome a cup of tea." (The Garda)

We soon discovered that the white front of the building is like a clean and smiling face hiding a cruel black heart inside. After leaving Br Superior's warm room we were led along a passage of cold, grey slate flagstones between sweating walls of a seasick green colour. We were taken into a gloomy room and told to remove the good clothes we had on as we would not be needing them any more. A pile of brownish-grey clothes was produced for each of us: a collarless tunic of rough material, a coarse, hairy jacket and itchy, baggy trousers which are too short. Mine have patches on both knees. Don's jacket is torn at the back.. For footwear we have hob-nail boots.

"But those were new suits," Don protested. *"We've only worn them a few times. We can't wear these old clothes – they're not even clean."*

"Ye've a great deal to learn about what ye can and cannot do here," said Br McMahon, rather sadly, I thought. *"For one thing we're not made of money as ye appear to be. A rude awakening's to be had for the likes o'ye. 'Twill be the worse altogether if ye argue with Brother Rourke. Get changed quickly, now. Ye'll have better clothes for special occasions and a smart uniform if ye play in the Band. C'mon, away now and have something to eat."*

<u>April 1<u>st</u></u>

At last I know where Don is! Yesterday I had to take a message to the Infirmary to the new Sister who has only just come to be in charge there. It is a long way from the main house and I think I found the wrong door. Well, it was the <u>right</u> door actually. I walked along a passage but as there was no one about downstairs I went upstairs and wandered about calling, "Hallo, is anyone there?" Imagine my joy – and his - when I poked my head round a door and saw <u>Don</u>! He was alone in the room and was sitting in a chair near a window, reading the Beano comic. One arm was in a sling and he had a cut above his eye and another on his chin. He put his finger to his lips warningly and nodded towards a door at the end of the room.

"Whatever happened to you?" I whispered. "I've been out of my mind with worry."

"I can't tell it now," he muttered. "Listen; I've been in hospital but soon I'm being sent to Artane. We <u>have</u> to get away somehow. Write to someone – Cathleen maybe or Mrs O'Leary – and ask for help. Don't trust <u>anyone</u> else. Just do what you can. Now GO quickly before the black banshee gets you."

I got out just in time and ran back down the stairs. A black–robed, sharp-nosed nun came down a few seconds after me and saw me waiting there. I handed her the envelope and said, "I'm sorry, Sister, I couldn't find anyone." She just grunted and asked who I was. "Number 192," I replied, glad for the first time to be identified only by a number. "Br. McMahon told me to bring you this letter."

April 5<u>th</u>

It is Holy Saturday today so there has been no time for anything besides religious things this week – extra services, masses, confessions, kissing the Cross and so on. <u>But</u> on Monday there is to be a special Band parade in the park. We have been practising for some time. I might have a chance to post a letter when we are walking there so will write to Cathleen now and take a stamp from the office. (I wonder does that count as a sin. Anyway I've my Easter confession already made!)

April 6<u>th</u>

A boy called P. B. told me yesterday he'd heard that St Joseph's Artane is a really terrible, place, far worse than this. I don't understand why Don is being sent there. A Br. came along just as we were talking and started giving out about silence being observed especially on the holy vigil of Easter. I've the letter written to Cathleen and <u>must</u> find a way to post it tomorrow. How would she ever believe that this could happen to us? It's like something out of a book – a horror or spy story. Please God she will think of some way to help us – <u>rescue</u> us.

April 8<u>th</u>

I have failed Don who is relying on me to save him – save us both. It could not be done yesterday, the posting of the letter. It was the first time I have been outside these walls in the three months since we came here. We passed two green pillar-boxes and a post office on the long walk to the park but we were marching in the middle of the road playing our instruments, national songs and the like. I'd the letter in my pocket but *there was no chance of breaking the line and slipping onto the pavement. The Bandmaster was leading us and Br Freel was bringing up the rear. He had a friendly smile plastered to his face for the parade but he is well-known for his skill with the strip of rubber bicycle-tyre which he likes to use on the bare skin of his victims and there is never a smile to be seen on his lips at any other time. When we got to the Park we stopped playing for a while and assembled in and around the Bandstand. We seemed to give a good performance and there were a lot of people watching and clapping us. It was good to be out in the fresh air and the sun and see the new green leaves on the trees after the cold, bare greyness of the school yard, but all I could think of was how to post the letter. It is hard to know that I <u>must </u>do it soon and yet realise that if I take too much of a risk I may get it <u>wrong.</u>*

April 15<u>th</u>

In the end it was easy! Br. McM. (the manager) said he would be away for 2 days for a funeral and told me to type some lists for him for the Brother Provincial's visit next week. He showed me how to use the typewriter and told me to make sure that the lists were neatly done. So once I was alone I was able to type another envelope for the letter, though I must say that my heart was thumping away all right in case one of the Bros came in before I finished it. When it was ready it looked much more professional than my hand-written envelope and I found a stamp and slipped it in with all the other stuff waiting for the mail van to collect. (We boys are only allowed to write to parents or relations once a month and they are left open for the Bros. to read.)

Now it is nearly the end of Tuesday and so far thank God no-one has come raging to find me, waving the letter and saying: "What in God's name is this?" I know that a great beating with the strap or rubber whip would follow and I would be banished from the office for ever if I was found out.

April 28ᵗʰ

P.B. told me today that some of the boys think I am a 'spy' because I work in the office. They don't trust me it seems. More important, he told me that he heard from a boy who works in the carpentry workshop that Don got into a fight with a boy called Murphy who was bullying one of the younger ones and got his arm broken. Br. Freel caught them and Murphy is his pet. He also told me that he heard the Carpentry teacher (he's a lay teacher) tell Br. Rourke that the Artane school is soon to close. What will happen to Don then? Oh how I wish I knew what is happening to him and how we can keep in touch with each other. I keep waiting for some sign that C. received the letter. We have had a Visitation from the Brother Provincial and an Inspector who stayed for 6 days and there was hardly any beating while he was here. Also we had better food and wore our best clothes. I've noticed that when there are special visits a great show is put on such as ware cups and plates instead of tin, and knives and forks which are kept for best. Now things will be back to normal again I suppose.

THREE

Cathleen has caught the bus outside the Presbytery and is sitting in Maeve O'Leary's little sitting room in the McCausland house. Maeve's eyes widen with horror as she reads the letter which Cathleen has handed to her. Her hand flies to her mouth.

"Jesus, Mary and St Joseph! Would you ever believe such a terrible thing?" she exclaims. "What in the name of the good Lord and his Holy Mother are we going to do for the poor loves?"

"Sure, haven't I been praying all this long time that we'd one day get a letter from them, and in all this time we've only heard this once and look what the boy tells us."

"And now the two of them are after being separated and Donal gone without a trace. I wonder, should we tell Fr O'Keefe at all? Wouldn't he be horrified altogether at such a tale?"

"No!" Cathleen shakes her head vigorously. "Master Dominic says to tell nobody, trust nobody. Father has asked me once or twice whether I've heard anything from the boys and I've quite truthfully said I have not. 'I know you were fond of that family, Cathleen,' says he, 'but I would advise you to put all that sorry business behind you now you've a place in the Presbytery.' He did say once though that he'd heard from the school that the boys were doing just fine, so where's the truth and the rightness in all of this?"

"Well, men of the cloth these Brothers may be and we know well Fr O'Keefe's views on those who are not of the Faith," says Maeve, "but I would believe Dominic before *anyone*, I have to say, priest or no priest, God forgive me."

"I'd believe him too all right, and I'd have anyone *slaughtered* who harmed a hair of their heads," declares Cathleen vehemently.

Maeve O'Leary looks down at the letter again. "He says that it'd be no good to answer this letter – that there's never a letter been received since the two of them left home. Some boys have visitors, he says, parents, aunts and uncles sometimes come to see their children, though 'under the watchful eyes and ears of one of the Brothers' – and a good strapping to be had afterwards if any one of them speaks out of turn, he says."

"But just supposing you or I, or the both of us, went up there, who would we say we were? If I'd an untruth spoken I'd never be able to look your man in the eye."

"I have another idea." Maeve holds up a hand in warning. "Don't shoot me down in flames now, Cathleen. Listen while I tell you what is in my mind. I think we have to trust *somebody* to help us, help them. Mr McCausland has friends in high places. His sister's husband is a T.D. and there is some connection with Mr Erskine Childers who is a highly thought-of man in the Dáil, a minister, I believe, even though he is a Protestant. Himself here is a Protestant too I think – at any rate he doesn't attend church with his wife. How about if I showed him this letter and *begged* him to do something for the boys?"

"Sure, I've no better idea myself," concedes Cathleen. "It's like you say: we need another to help in any plan we make; some person of the quality, as Mam would say, might be the right choice. Will you speak to himself, so?"

"I will all right, this evening as ever was," promises Maeve.

———◦◦◦———

May 15ᵗʰ

I am to have a visitor! Br. M told me to be ready to see a lady called Mrs Harrington on Saturday afternoon at 3 o'clock. Cathleen, good Cathleen, you have answered my prayer. Please God let this be true; let nothing happen between now and Sat. – and let that day come <u>soon.</u> I wonder will it be Cathleen herself or Mrs O'Leary using a different name.

May 9ᵗʰ

It is Friday and of all things to go wrong I have a black eye. I was playing handball on Tuesday and a fellow from the other side of the wall (in a different unit, the one Don was in) came and challenged me to a fight. He's a well-known bully who everybody tries to avoid. They say he's Br. Freel's right hand man. Anyway he shouted at me: 'Spy, spy, here's a black eye', and he landed me one on the cheek.. 'Think yerself lucky I didn't break yer arm,' says he, and now I know for sure that it was Murphy, the one who beat up Don that time. I didn't fight back or argue with him and didn't "turn the other cheek" either because I knew I would come off worst and would miss my visitor on Saturday – <u>tomorrow</u>.

And now Br. M. has noticed it. He said, 'Now Manning, ye're after having a fight are ye not? Ye'll not be able to see yer visitor with an eye that's all colours o' the rainbow – glorious Technicolor ye might say.'

'No, Brother, I was not fighting, I was playing Handball,' I replied truthfully, 'and the ball came flying back and hit me in the eye,' I lied.

(Actually a lie "is the intention to deceive" we were always taught. But then, I'm going to Hell anyway amn't I?)

'We shall have to see how it looks tomorrow,' he said. 'At any rate that is certainly a reasonable explanation.' He is not an unkind man and seems to like me although I do <u>not</u> want to be seen as his pet or spy. I wish I could scrub away the bruise with soap and water. I wish I could scrub away many things that go on in this place, like the cruelty, the poverty, the disgusting things I can't mention – and the disappearance of my brother – not my brother. Who is he? Who am I? I am not yet 15 and have not the words or the understanding to describe what life is really like here. I try to remember what Father O'Brien at St Patrick's told us: when life is at its most difficult, he said, try to keep a quiet, calm place at the centre of your being, your inner sanctum. Listen for "the still small voice"- (God I suppose he meant.) 'No enemy can reach you there; neither man nor Satan himself can assail you. Your body may be broken but your spirit will never be.' He was a good man, you could ask him anything. There is nobody here who would say such things. The parish priest does not seem to be a holy man at all. One boy told me that when he was an altar boy Fr. W. had made him ...... (No, I cannot write it.)

<u>May 16th</u>

I have not had a chance to add to this until now because of extra Band practices for Ascension Day – yesterday - when there was a special visit by a Monsignor and we had to wear our best clothes (<u>better</u> clothes I should say) and there was a parade in the yard, which was cleaned specially for the occasion. Some younger boys had to scrub it on their hands and knees as a punishment.

I am pleased to report that my bruises did not stop me from seeing Mrs H. on Saturday and at last there is some hope, in spite of Br R. hanging around nearly all the time she was there. He was pretending to be very friendly to her and patted me on the shoulder and said what an asset I was to the school, especially with my "expertise on the clarinet." She, Mrs H., is a lady of about 40 I should think, not fat, not thin, with dark, curly hair and a nice, kind face. She has asked the Superior if she may take me out for the afternoon on Monday week when there is a holiday (Whit Monday). There is an old lady who wants to meet me because she is a relative of some sort. He has given his permission for me to go with her after we have given a band performance in the park in the morning. I must try to hide my excitement or Br R. will try to stop me. We talked about this and that while he was lurking around, but when he turned away to speak to another Brother, she touched my hand quickly and said, 'Dominic, help is at hand, never fear. More when we meet next if you can be patient. People are working on your behalf. We're trying to find where your brother is, too. … Now, tell me about the Band. How long have you been learning the clarinet? I have a daughter who used to learn the violin, but it always sounded a bit scratchy…'

This is the first conversation I've had with a real, normal person from the outside since I came here four months ago now. I can't believe it really and wonder if I'm dreaming. When she said goodbye she said that she would come to the park on Whit Monday to listen to the Band. It is hard to be patient with another 9 ½ days to wait but I'm trying to make myself invisible especially to Br R. who will try to stop me going out if he gets any chance at all, I know it. He would hit you for nothing, just for existing. Strap, Hurley stick, rubber tube, chair leg – anything he can lay hands on he'll lay on you. I've seen boys with bleeding fingers and bruised legs. And the parts you can't see are worse. Some boys have been beaten on the soles of their feet. I've been hit nearly everywhere except my hands. He and Br Freel dare not hit me there in case I wouldn't be able to play my clarinet. Then there would be questions asked.

May 21ˢᵗ

It is good practice for me to write this diary because there are no proper lessons here. In fact, because I can read and write well I have to try and teach some of the other boys. I am doing this instead of having lessons myself. Although they are beaten and ridiculed for not being able to read, they don't seem able to improve at all. Then they are beaten again and if I have failed to help them I am punished as well. There is one boy of about 11, who told me that his name is Eoin, who is really "making progress" as they used to say on my old school reports. But he has a bad stutter or stammer and when he has to read in front of the class he is frozen in a kind of fright and cannot say the words, even if he knows what they are. Also they do not allow boys to be left-handed here so he can hardly write either. If the teacher sees him with the pen in the left hand he has to put those fingers on the desk to be lashed. Before this happens I am usually sent for and have to witness this, which is punishment enough for me. Today Freel was teaching instead of the lay teacher and I had to bend over and receive "six of the best" with his strap: one for being alive at all; one for being a bastard; one for being a Protestant bastard; one for being devil's spawn; one for not being able to teach this "bleddy eejit" how to read and the last one for not crying and letting the devil out of me while I was being clattered. Only the thought of Monday keeps me from going wild and running into the yard and shouting and screaming.

Sat. May 24th

The very worst has happened, which somehow I knew it would. I am quite certain that I shall not be allowed out on Monday. Although we live in constant fear of Bros R. & F., on Saturdays when the staff – teachers etc. – are not here, we are usually left alone while the Bros take time off or are out with the football team or at Croke Park. This is a time when you can play handball or other games in the yard and, as long as you are watchful, maybe have talks with other boys. Friendships are forbidden here and even boys of the same family are split up in different units and not allowed to speak to each other, as happened with Don and me. This afternoon as I was coming out of the outside bogs,

I met Eoin in the passage coming in. He told me (without stuttering) that he was sorry to have got me into trouble on Wed. and that he felt he had let me down etc. etc. Then he burst into tears and sort of threw himself at me. Just as I was recovering my balance, Murphy with 2 of his "gang" came round the corner. 'Oh-ho-ho!' he said, 'just wait till Br Rourke hears about this. Ye're in deep shit now, all right.' Sure enough, at teatime R. called Eoin and me out to stand in the middle of the room. 'What we have here,' he said, 'is 2 disgusting bastards, two filthy sodomites, a big one and a little one, caught doing all kinds of wickedness to each other in the toilets. What d'ye t'ink we should do with them at all?' He took E. by the earlobe and swung him around. 'What have ye to say for yerself, Devil's child?' Of course, E. could only stammer: ' I d-d-don't know w-w-what you m-m-mean, Sir.'

'Well, get out of me sight and get to yer bed without tea,' R. roared, giving him a punch on the ear. ' John Wayne or whoever it is will have to do without yer company this evening.' (There is to be a film in half an hour). 'And as for you, high and mighty bastard,' he said, 'evil Protestant sodomite, I t'ink I know just the punishment for ye.' He kicked me hard on the ankle and sent me back to my place. I think he is determined to stop me going out on Monday – but I am equally determined to go; for Don's sake I <u>must</u>. Whatever I am suffering here, his life must be even more unbearable.

⊸⧫⊸

"I am very sorry to have to tell you, Mrs Harrington, that young Manning has not been able to play in the Band today and cannot accept yer kind invitation for the rest of today's holiday."

Brother Freel is wearing his best soutane and the smile that he keeps for special occasions such as the Whit Monday parade – his *public* smile. He has seen her scanning the band as they perform in the park and has walked over to her as some of the boys disperse with their parents and family friends. She stands out from the crowd, not from any flamboyance of dress but rather from an understated elegance which sets her apart from the motley gathering of spectators.

"Oh, how very disappointing," says Dominic's would-be bene-factress. "This explains his absence in the parade – a notable absence, since he is such a talented clarinettist. But whatever has happened? Is he ill, perhaps?"

Br. Freel adopts a look of grave concern. "No indeed, ma'am. I wish it were so simple an explanation. I fear that he is after be-having very badly and has had to be confined and punished as a result. I will spare ye the details, being a lady."

"I am surprised and dismayed to hear this, Brother. He seems such an exceptionally well-behaved and polite boy – a well brought-up young man."

"I fear he has let the school, and particularly the band, down very badly, in spite of that. It was necessary to reprimand him severe-ly on a serious matter and he responded by smashing his clarinet. In fact he said: 'See how the band gets on without me on Monday.'"

Mrs Harrington's eyes widen in disbelief. "But he is such a good player and spoke lovingly of the instrument, a precious gift, he told me, with an interesting history, given to him by his par-ents. Surely he could not bear to damage it."

"There's no accounting for the lack of self-control that some of our boys display when disciplined. No doubt he was spoilt and indulged in his earlier life."

"My elderly friend, a connection of Dominic's adoptive par-ents, was so looking forward to meeting him today. She *will* be disappointed." Feeling nothing but disgust and loathing for the man before her, Mrs Harrington tries to inject some warmth into her voice. "Perhaps it will be permitted for me to take him out after the ceremonial Mass at Corpus Christi. I trust he will have fulfilled the terms of his penance by then? I will be in touch with the Superior shortly."

Br. Freel wipes sweaty hands on the skirt of his black soutane and re-arranges his expression, restoring his smile with repulsive ob-sequiousness. "I am sure that might be arranged, Mrs Harrington, and now, if you'll excuse me, I must get back to the boys."

"Indeed, Brother.   Oh … just one thing before you go. Perhaps you would suggest to Dominic that he writes a letter of explanation or apology for his absence today. Would that not be good social training for him? Brother Superior has my address so perhaps you would suggest it to him."

"I will all right, ma'am. 'Twill be good for the boy to give ye an account of his behaviour. I do apologise that ye and yer friend have been put to this inconvenience by it. Good day to ye now."

He strides back to the group of boys waiting near the bandstand. Mrs Harrington remains for a few seconds staring after the tall figure thoughtfully. He and Br Rourke are a force to be reckoned with, she concludes.

⸺∞∞∞⸺

Sacred Heart Industrial School,
Dublin.

May 27th 1969

Dear Mrs Harrington,
*   I am writing with sincere apologise for not being able to come out with you on monday last due to some*

very bad behavior and a delibrate damage to my clari-
net so that I was not aloud to take part in the parade
and band concert in the park. Br Freel told me you
were after asking if you could take me out on Corpus
Christi but I shall still be on punishment then because of
the clarinett. So I cant play in the band again.

I am very ashamed of my badness and sorry to cause
your inconvenance. And your friend I would of liked to
meet her.
I remain,
Your respectful servant,

D.C. Manning.

Moira Harrington reads the letter with mounting incredu-
lity and anger.

"This has clearly been dictated by that monstrous brother,"
she says. "You can see that Dominic has not only taken it down
verbatim but has added a few grammatical and spelling mistakes
of his own. How clever of him! A boy as articulate as he is would
never have written such a letter of his own accord. The Superior
probably knows nothing of this." She hands it to her husband
across the breakfast table. He puts the newspaper he has been
reading to one side.

"This is one for Mrs Justice Kennedy's Report," observes her
husband when he has read it. "There is a good deal here between
the lines, so to speak, after what you've already told me."

"And of course her committee have the original letter that
Dominic managed to write to the family's former maid. I saw a
copy of it and remember being impressed at the way he expressed
himself. He's very advanced for his age. Oh, it's so *frustrating* not
to be able to take him away from that dreadful place. There is

definitely a message there. What else could he have done with that tyrant standing over him?"

"We must move very cautiously now for the boy's sake. You are upset and angry, my darling, but I advise you not to do anything hasty, such as making phone calls to the Superior. Perhaps a more prudent and subtle approach might be the delivery of another clarinet." Gerald Harrington folded *The Irish Times*, drank the last of his coffee and rose from the table. "I must rush, my love," he said, planting a quick kiss on her cheek and leaving the room. "Come on, Frances," he called up the stairs. "If you're late for school, I shall be late for the office. Think about what I've suggested, Moira," he said, putting his head round the door again. "Think, but don't do anything - yet. We'll discuss a plan of action this evening when I come home."

There was a clatter of feet on the stairs and the front door slammed behind father and daughter.

—✦—

Friday May 30th

It is nearly a week since I wrote in this book. It seems like a year! It is like being reunited with an old friend, finding it undiscovered in its usual hiding place. All day on Monday I was in a room (cell) on my own with only bread and water, brought to me by a very fat boy who works in the kitchens. It was great gas for him to tell me what he had enjoyed – a long list of tasty left-overs from the Brothers' dining-room, which made my mouth water and my tummy rumble and clench. 'Br Freel said to tell ya that ye'd have had an even <u>better</u> *lunch if ye'd behaved yourself and gone out with Mrs ... somebody – can't remember her name. He told me to tell ya to pray for the poor souls in Purgatory. 'Twill help ye to digest yer stale bread,' he said smugly. I said nothing, though I wanted to shake him till he wobbled even more.*

Anyway, the next day I had to write to Mrs H. and apologise – at least I wrote what Br F. <u>dictated</u> to me. Although I used my neatest writing there were lots of mistakes: bad grammar from him (Teacher??!!) and a few spelling mistakes from me, a crafty touch which I hope told Mrs H. that I was on a trumped-up charge. I was always taught to read a letter through before putting it in the envelope but luckily he just glanced over my shoulder and gave me an envelope and a scrap of paper with her name and address for me to copy. He seemed in a hurry so I sealed it quickly and wrote the address. When I had finished he snatched it away and went to find a stamp. I wonder will she ever receive it and what she can be thinking. She would surely know that I would never damage my precious clarinet. I've spent every moment since I discovered it thinking what I will do to whoever broke it. It is quite beyond repair – and so will <u>he</u> be when I find out. And because of all this another opportunity to help Don has been missed.

<u>Saturday evening.</u>

An odd thing happened this afternoon – a good thing I should say. Br Heaney (Superior) sent for me and when I got to his room I was surprised to see Mrs Harrington sitting there with him. She put out her hand for me to shake (mine was rather sweaty and dirty because I'd been playing handball). She said, 'Hello Dominic,' giving my hand an extra squeeze. 'Thank you for your letter. I was so sorry to miss you on Whit Monday. I understand that your clarinet was broken so I have brought another one. It may seem a poor substitute for your own but it belonged to an experienced player so should have a good tone. Br Heaney has accepted it on your behalf with the proviso that it remains the property of the school when you leave next year. He knows nothing of the disaster that befell yours.' She looked inquiringly at Br H. and he nodded back. 'I understand that there's a grand Procession on Thursday for Corpus Christi and that boys will have an exeat for the rest of the day. (That's a word I've not heard since I left Barrageen)Br Superior has kindly given permission for me to take you to lunch at my house afterwards.' I wanted to run across the room and hug her but I just thanked her politely and said that I looked forward to it very much. Please God nothing will go wrong this time. When she had gone, BrSup said a strange thing: 'You'd do well to keep that out of harm's way. Why not put it in the office out of sight for the time being? Keep it safe for Thursday, eh? I will explain to Br McMahon, but nobody else need know.'

As there was nobody about when I left the room, I took the clarinet out of its case and examined it. Everything I need is there – and there is a separate compartment for music. Perhaps that would be a safer place for this book.

There was nothing more written in Dominic's notebook.

FOUR

(M.G. Manning)

As neither my father nor my uncle would tell me much about their incarceration in their respective Industrial Schools. I have had to piece together the various details of their story from others: my mother, my grandmothers, my aunts and, of course, Dominic's notebook and later writings. I have tried to assemble their early history as a weaver prepares fabric: threading the loom with historical facts and weaving in their various contributions. As the family archivist, I will therefore continue their story as best I can.

The feast of Corpus Christi, Thursday, June 11th, dawned bright and clear. It was Sacred Heart's turn to host the celebrations that year. The avenue and the processional path had been decked with bunting, flags and banners. The front gates, manned by two tidily dressed boys, stood open as cars arrived, bearing civic and religious dignitaries and invited visitors.

Brothers, teachers and children from other schools and parents and relations of the boys arrived at the back gates, which were similarly attended by a group of boys directing all arrivals to take their places along the processional route.

The Band assembled on the parade ground, arrayed in their green uniforms, the sun glinting off the silver and brass of their instruments. All eyes were on the Bandmaster as he raised his baton. The drums and percussion rolled as he beat two bars to indicate the tempo. On the next beat the cymbals clashed to usher in the rest of the band with the march from Handel's *Judas Maccabeus,* the company moving off after sixteen bars, in well-rehearsed formation, to march out of the parade ground, past the workshops and round to the chapel where the rest of the boys joined it, followed by the Brothers and the priests. Last of all came the Host, reverently carried under a richly embroidered canopy to the hymn *Tantum Ergo,* sung by the choir and accompanied by the Band.

When all were assembled, Dominic soon spotted Mrs Harrington seated amongst the group of dignitaries, which included the Bishop and specially invited visitors. He caught her eye and acknowledged her with a smile and a slight bow. Sitting next to her was a fair-haired girl in a flowered frock, whom he supposed to be her daughter, Frances. He saw her mother nudge her and whisper something, nodding in his direction and felt proud and pleased that they were *his* visitors. During the long celebration of the High Mass, he anticipated with excitement his visit to their house when the service was over.

At last the final hymn had been sung and the visitors gathered on the freshly mown lawns to one side of the main house to greet each other and the Brothers as they were offered refreshments and were further entertained by the band and the choir. Mrs Harrington detached herself from the gathering as the members of the band prepared to go and change out of their uniforms and came across the grass towards Dominic, introducing Frances and arranging to meet him where the cars were parked after a quarter of an hour or so, to give him time to change out of his uniform.

As he was making his way back to the back of the main building with a group of other boys, the younger of two visiting Christian Brothers, standing near the edge of the parade ground, stepped towards them and inquired: "Which of you is Manning, 192?"

One of the cornet players pushed him towards the Brother, who held out his hand and took Dominic's in a vice-like grip, introducing himself as Br O'Neill, while the other boys, only momentarily curious, went on their way. The man retained his friendly expression and ushered him over to his companion who also shook his hand with painful pressure. Br Geraghty's words were at odds with his smile:

"Do exactly as we say and ye'll not be harmed. We have your brother, Donal. If you want to see him alive ye'll come with us at once. We've a car waiting."

Dominic was almost too stunned to protest.

"B-but my unif…," he started his mind in utter confusion at such an unexpected turn of events.

"No time for 'buts'," said the first man. "Walk with us to the gate just as y'are and pretend to give us directions to the city. Bring the sax with ye – ye're going to need it to earn yer keep. I have a gun, so ye'd do well t'obey – NOW!"

Thus it was that for a second time the Harringtons sat down to lunch without their specially invited guest.

"So where is our young man, then?" Gerald Harrington asked as his wife and daughter came through the front door, looking dismayed and flustered. "He's not gone missing yet again, surely?"

"Well yes, I'm afraid he has," replied Moira. "It's all very mysterious. Just let me take these shoes off and pour me a stiff G&T – and I'll try to explain what happened – or, rather, what didn't happen."

She took off the smart high-heeled shoes she had been wearing and stood in her stockinged feet on the polished floor of the hall, looking for something more comfortable, hanging the jacket of her elegant blue-and-white outfit on the newel-post.

"Don't tell Dada without me," Frances said, rushing up the stairs. "I'm going to change out of this frock now, as that great-looking boy is not here to impress."

"So what went wrong this time? Those wretched Brothers again?" Gerald asked, as the three of them sat with their drinks on the terrace outside the dining-room, where lunch awaited them on the table, which was laid with four places.

"I wish I knew," answered Moira. "Dominic was playing the new clarinet in the Band, both in the procession and the short recital afterwards. He spoke to us briefly and excused himself to go and change out of his uniform, and we arranged to meet in the car-park in fifteen minutes or so."

"Yes, and he said how pleased he was with the clarinet and that he would bring it with him and play his exam pieces to us," Frances added. "But we waited and waited and he never came back."

"Do you think that dreadful man, Freel, prevented him?" Gerald asked. "Locked him up somewhere, perhaps; or maybe Freel and Rourke together cooked up some plot."

"Somehow, I don't think that's the explanation. They were both in the crowd in the front gardens, being unctuously polite to the guests and fawning round the Bishop and other bigwigs. In the end there was quite a hue and cry when nearly everyone but ourselves had left. Brother Superior sent them and Br McMahon to look for Dominic."

"But he seemed to have vanished without trace," Frances put in. "Oh Mam, do you think I frightened him off? Maybe he's terrified of girls."

"Don't talk nonsense, Frances," said her father. "The boy has sisters – in America now, I believe. He must be used to girls. Anyway he's far too young to be put off by you."

"Perhaps we'd better start lunch without him, anyway," Moira suggested. "Dominic knows where we live. There may have been some misunderstanding." She looked doubtful. "Perhaps he was given a lift by someone else."

But the fourth place at the table remained unoccupied as the three of them ate, without enthusiasm, the lunch which had been specially prepared with their guest in mind.

"That poor boy will not have seen the like of this for many a month," said Moira. "And that would seem like years in that place. By all accounts, they have to survive on very little – except for the Brothers themselves. They don't stint themselves."

"I'd like to feed him this trifle mouthful by mouthful," Frances said, "from a large silver table spoon. He looks so thin and pale – but handsome and poetic-looking, don't you think, Mam? Oh, it's so disappointing he's not here."

It was not until after seven o'clock that the Harringtons received a telephone call from Brother McMahon. The boys who had been out with parents or relations had been back for an hour or more and there was still no sign of Dominic, he told them. The Gardai had been informed and were looking for him. If he had run away, he should be easy to spot because his band uniform and the clarinet were missing.

"Of course," Br McMahon continued, "There is a policy of severe punishment for running away from school – usually solitary confinement for several days. It is very unlikely that the boy would ever be permitted either to receive visitors or to be allowed out again. I do sincerely apologise on the school's behalf for the trouble he has put ye to. We try to inculcate good manners into our pupils but they do not always reward our efforts, I fear, although I would have expected better of young Manning, I must say."

Six days later, two letters addressed to Mrs Gerald Harrington arrived by the afternoon post: The first, with a local postmark, was from Br Heaney C.B., Superior of The Sacred Heart School and read as follows:

Dear Mrs Harrington,

It is with great regret that I have to inform you that your erstwhile protégée, Dominic Manning, having absconded from our guardianship, has not so far been traced by either the Gardai or the Department of Education since your visit to the school. I gather from the former that you yourself have had no word from him to date. On questioning the boys, all we know is that he was last seen in his Band uniform, walking out of the back gates with two visiting Christian Brothers soon after 12.30pm last Thursday, Corpus Christi.

This morning there comes the news that the other Manning boy, his adoptive brother, has also escaped from custody while being transferred from St Joseph's, Artane to Letterfrack reformatory in Co. Galway. (The school at Artane is shortly to close owing to falling numbers).

I should be most grateful if you would tell me immediately if the boys try to contact you. Meanwhile, I reiterate BrMcMahon's apology on behalf of the school, not only for the reprehensible abuse of your hospitality but also for the theft of your generous donation of a clarinet to the School Band.

With kindest regards, I remain
Yours in Christ,

Patrick K. Heaney.

The second letter, addressed in a familiar handwriting, bore the postmark, LONDONDERRY, 12.15 pm, 10. 6. 1969.

Dear Mrs Harrington,

If you ever receive this letter and the notebook I am hoping to send with it, you may just want to throw it away in disgust at my sudden disappearance last Thursday. However, I do hope you will forgive me a second time when I try to explain.

I was so busy trying to figure out a way to rescue my brother that it did not occur to me that he would plan to rescue me. When I left you that day to go and change out of my band uniform I was approached by two Christian Brothers– not from our school – who said they knew where Donal was and I was to go with them immediately. They said they had a gun so I did not argue with them.

We only have a chance to write one letter and I felt that it should be to you, for all the trouble I have caused you. I cannot tell you where we are but beg you 3 things: 1. Not to tell the Gardai or the school that you have heard from us. 2. To keep the notebook safe and please read it so that you - and others - know what it is really like in that place. (Don had a much worse time in Artane). 3. Please tell Cathleen Shea and Mrs O'Leary that we are safe at the moment and that we will be in touch as soon as we are able, though it may be some time. And please ask them to tell our sisters.

I do thank you very much indeed for all you have done for me and hope that I can return your kindness one day.

   Yours sincerely,

      Dominic C. Manning.

P.S. I have the clarinet safe and sound. Luckily the notebook was hidden in the case, but it will be safer with you.

"I am so relieved to have heard from him at last," said Moira Harrington as Gerald finished reading the second of the two letters. "I just hope those boys haven't gone from the frying pan into the fire. Presumably they're outside Irish jurisdiction if they are in the Six Counties?"

Gerald took an appreciative sip of the whiskey which his wife had brought him with the letters. "Yes, I suppose they are. I don't know how much co-operation there is these days between the Gardai and the R.U.C. – not much, I imagine, with relations getting sourer by the day. There is real trouble brewing up there in the North again."

"Anyway, we're not going to comply with Br Heaney's request to tell him and the Gardai about this letter, are we?"

Gerald raised his eyebrows and pursed his lips. "Well, strictly speaking, we shall be breaking the law if we do not. Withholding information is an offence, of course."

"Well then, we shall have to be law-breakers," Moira said firmly. "I've had all afternoon to study Dominic's notebook. When you've read it yourself, you'll see what those poor boys have had to endure. That is criminal in itself – and seems to go on with the blessing of both the Department of Education *and* the Law."

"And the Church, too, I fear," Gerald admitted. "I'm afraid that, by all accounts, two of the Religious who have condoned the behaviour of the Christian Brothers – and certain other brotherhoods and sisterhoods for that matter – are actually sitting on the Kennedy Committee."

"Then there is bound to be a cover-up and we should have no part in it," said his wife. "Look, I'll leave you to read that notebook while I get the supper. Shall we eat on the terrace as it's such a lovely evening?"

"That'll be grand," Gerald said. "This spell of weather can't last forever."

"By the way, I think we should say nothing to Frances about all this at present," Moira said. "If she read that notebook, she would start a one-woman crusade and the whole city would know about it – especially as she found Dominic so 'delectable', as she put it."

Gerald picked up the notebook. "You're right; if she comes home while I'm reading this, I'll tuck it under the chair cushion. It's her play rehearsal night, isn't it? Yes, I agree about not saying anything until we know the outcome of all this."

FIVE

Geraghty and O'Neill had plans for 'The Toffs', as they referred to Donal and Dominic. It would soon be pay-back time, they said. They could not lie low for ever, gorging themselves on Bernadette's boiled bacon and champ followed by apple dumplings and ice-cream; they must get out into the bars and clubs and do their double act for clarinet and voice. None of that classical rubbish, mind you: they must get up to date on the pop scene.

Later there would be some military training. They were used to marching, weren't they? And brutality. Well, they'd be dishing it out for a change: it was called Proddie-bashing. This year there would be WAR in August when those Orange eejits marched through the streets of Derry – *Catholic* streets – flaunting their history with flags and standards in their silly uniforms.

"Ye'll be in on the action, boys. That's what ye're here for: to lay yer lives on the line for your country – see *Catholic* Ireland united once more. Send the feckin' Prods back where they came from." (that might be difficult, Dominic thought: it was all something to do with a battle between William of Orange and James 11 in 1688).

Bernadette Geraghty was not happy with this kind of talk either, but if she protested, she received a clout for her boldness.

Her best friend was a Protestant, she told the boys, but she was no longer allowed to see her, and their kids couldn't play with each other anymore. It was Bernadette who had posted Dominic's package for him when Geraghty and his cousin were out all day.

"I'd be killed entirely if he found out," she had said. "But I doubt the two o' you were after having such a terrible time of it and you deserve much better. It takes a mother to understand; the Blessed Mother herself would say no different."

She was from Galway, slight of figure and still youthful-looking with her black hair and dark blue, dancing eyes and fair skin. She had a warm and welcoming manner and the two boys had been absorbed into the family of four younger children with remarkable ease. There was no such warmth in her husband and Bernadette and the children were wary and subdued when he was at home. Paddy Geraghty owned a new and second-hand car business which he ran with the help of a cousin, Kevin O'Neill. It was the latter's younger brother, Dan, who had arranged with them for the boys' 'rescue', when he himself left Artane School on his sixteenth birthday in early May.

Dominic found Donal much changed by his time at Artane. Their reunion had not been the happy event he had dreamed of. Donal seemed taciturn and rather aloof, unwilling to share his experiences with his brother; and yet he seemed oddly excited at the idea of the impending trouble forecast by Geraghty and O'Neill, eager to begin training for the planned attacks during the Orange Order's marching season in August. Dominic shrank from the idea of violence and tried to divert his brother's attention towards forming a musical duo, not least because they needed to contribute to their board and lodging. They listened to the latest Irish, English and American hits on radio and record-player and watched *Top of the Pops* on the small television set in the front room, catching up on being normal teenagers after their months of incarceration in monastic establishments. Their short hair had been the cause of unwelcome attention from other young people but at last it was beginning to grow as long as that of their peers.

"Forget about the Beatles and the lovey-dovey stuff," Geraghty told them one day when he heard them rehearsing. "The old rebel songs are the ones they'll be wanting to hear in the bars: *The Rising of the Moon* and the like. Ye'll have played that in the school band. *The Rifles of the I.R.A.* …. *The Sea Around us*" He sang in a gravelly voice: *'The sea, oh the sea is the grá geal mo croi / Long may it roll between England and me / 'Tis a sure guarantee that some hour we'll be free / Thank God we're surrounded by water.'"*

Eventually they built up an appreciable repertoire and the O'Neill brothers procured them engagements in various bars and dance-halls, where they went by the name of 'The Toffs'. At the end of June they were approached by the manager of a dance–band called The Derry Planets, who was looking for a new vocalist and was more than happy to welcome Dominic with his clarinet, with the suggestion that he should learn to play the saxophone as well. Soon they had several week-end engagements lined up and were able to hand over a good proportion of their earnings to Bernadette, who was delighted by their success. The O'Neills, however, wanted their cut as well: an agents' fee, they called it, so the boys were left with practically nothing. Meanwhile, in any case, they had to lie low during the daytime for fear of being 'noticed' by officialdom. As it was, although they had assumed the surname of Maloney, Bernadette's maiden name, for the time being, posing as cousins of hers from Co Galway, they had no real identity and 'officially' did not exist at all.

It soon became clear why the band manager wanted changes. After Hammy, the saxophonist, had given Dominic lessons for a few weeks, he and the vocalist were sent packing.

"There's no place for Presbies in our band," Kelly told the others. "Surely to God, there's trouble ahead for the likes of them. 'Tis 'them or us' time now all right."

The band was renamed 'The Moon Rockets', in honour of the recent moon landings, and was much in demand in the city's dance-halls. In that twilit world of dim lights and loud music, many a plot was hatched amongst the groups of young men standing in clusters on one dark side of the hall, while the girls on the other side in their short skirts danced with each other or surveyed the lads hopefully from under heavily made-up lashes.

While Dominic felt very uneasy at the prospect of the planned demonstrations and attacks during the marching season, Donal was fired with enthusiasm and impatience to play his part.

"You're such a sissy, Domino," he said. "Have you forgotten already who it was killed our parents – well, indirectly anyway? They died because the RUC decided to stop a *peaceful* Civil Rights march with baton charges and road blocks. Then, only six months ago, the same police *stood by* and watched the bloody Prods ambush another protest march at Burntollet Bridge only five miles away. No wonder there were riots here when the marchers arrived – all the way from Belfast – some really badly injured. Aren't the politicians and police meant to represent and protect *all* the citizens?"

Dominic sighed. "Yes, of course they are. D'you know, one of the few times I saw a newspaper in that hell-hole, there was a report on the front page of that trouble at the bridge. But you know me: I just hate violence, though God knows I saw enough of it in that place – and you won't talk about what you went through, but it *has* changed you. Maybe you want revenge for what happened there – but remember, it was not the politicians or the RUC *or* the Protestants who put us away, it was our *own* people."

"I s'pose it was, all right, but it is 'our own people' here who are suffering injustice and I feel it's right to avenge Father's and Mother's death as well. August the Twelfth, here I come. Just watch me!"

Dominic groaned. "For God's sake – and mine – *please* be careful, Don. I don't want to lose you again, having only just found you. And remember, whatever you say about 'our own people', don't forget that *one* of us is probably a hundred percent English – and Protestant as well. What about that?"

"Bugger that," Donal said angrily. "I know perfectly well it's not me – I feel it in my bones. I'm a hundred percent Irish and Catholic. So be a Protestant coward, why don't you. Stay skulking indoors with Bernadette and the kiddos and miss the action, 'cos action there will be, believe you me. Play baby word games with them or something, while I go out to *fight*. Those Apprentice Boys are going to be sorry they ever set foot on *our* streets, and so are the RUC for letting 'em."

On the 30th of July a meeting of the Derry Citizens' Defence was convened. Geraghty came home with the light of battle in his eyes, bringing the O'Neill brothers with him. Street committees had been formed, he told them all, as they crowded into the small front room. Bernadette shooed the children outside to play in the back yard.

"They should stay," said Geraghty roughly. "Derry's future citizens they are. They must learn to fight."

"They must also be protected while they're so young," Bernadette said firmly, though she knew she risked a black eye later for voicing it.

There was no sign that the Government was going to ban the annual Apprentice Boys' march, Geraghty continued, so barricades were to be erected to deny access into the Bogside by marchers and police. There would be no dances on the weekend before Tuesday, August 12th, so the boys must get down there and muck in and get their hands dirty like everyone else. They would receive instruction on making petrol bombs, which might be needed, especially if the 'B Specials' were drafted in. They were known to play dirty and they would get 'dirty' back again.

"Six months ago, after the *massacre* at Burntollett Bridge," he reminded them, "There was a sign painted on the end of a house at the corner of Lecky Road and Fahan Street, saying: 'YOU ARE NOW ENTERING FREE DERRY'. The RUC had it painted out but it will always be known as Free Derry Corner. Let's see that slogan put back again. History will be made that day."

Donal spent the intervening days in keen anticipation, anxious to win approval from Geraghty by helping in the preparations for battle with fanatical zeal. Dominic, however, was increasingly reluctant at the prospect of violence. He shared his misgivings with Bernadette, who understood only too well.

"Perhaps you should ask the advice of Fr McDonald," she said thoughtfully. "He's old and wise, retired from St Gregory's now but works for the Peace Movement. Surely to God, Dominic, you're not alone, you know: there are plenty here who want to sort out all this trouble without bombs and bullets. Go and talk with him privately. Himself is from Glasgow and very distressed by the tension caused by these sectarian divisions."

So it was that, soon afterwards, Dominic attended a pre-arranged meeting with Tom Fahy, the old priest's nephew, a photographer on *The Derry Record,* who said he would take him on as an unpaid observer and right-hand-man when he covered the events of August the Twelfth. If he seriously wanted to be a journalist, Fahy said, it would be a revealing, though tough, experience for him.

"History will indeed be made, all right," he confirmed. "You will be another pair of eyes and ears to witness it. 'The pen is mightier than the sword', don't forget. In the finish it will be a far more effective weapon than stones and bottles of petrol in the fight for the rights of us all."

SIX

**The Battle of the Bogside: an eye-witness account
by D. C. Manning.**

I t is twenty years since those three days of rioting in August
1969. At school, the battles we learnt about in History lessons
were all neatly packaged, with dates, sites marked by crossed
axes on maps, uniforms and plumed helmets, war-horses, pikes
and staffs, swords and muskets, strategies and generals directing
brave fighting men. Afterwards, hundreds of dead lay strewn in
muddy, bloodstained fields; (it was always fields, wasn't it?)

Until it is put into the context of history, any battle is probably
just as horrible a mess as this one was. Look at the old newsreels –
records of those black-and-white days when the camera could
not lie. In that momentous year when Man had travelled
through space, stepped into another world and picked up dust
and rocks of a substance unknown on Earth, the mean streets
of the Bogside were littered with stones, metal bars and broken glass, thrown in anger with intent to wound or kill. (It was
strange to reflect that the same action would not have been
possible on the Moon because of zero gravity!)

The festering ulcers of the past burst on those three days in
August 1969; the simmering fires of hundreds of years of racial

and religious division and provocation erupted from a volcano that was to discharge the toxic lava of sectarian hatred for years to come. Where was God that day? Perhaps only in the hearts of those from both sides who had painted 'GIVE PEACE A CHANCE' on the road, only to have it expunged by those bent on confrontation.

My brother, (for I still think of him as such) and I were nearly fifteen at the time. We parted company that day in the city centre, he to join his fellow Nationalists at Free Derry Corner, I to meet Tom Fahy, a photographer on THE DERRY RECORD, who had invited me to join him as an observer, further back along the marchers' route by the city wall. And here they came, the men in their best suits and white gloves, embroidered bands and chains of office on their chests, faces proud and defiant under well-brushed bowler hats, the Apprentice Boys, banners held high and proud, drums beating, pipes skirling, in a demonstration that could – and should – have been banned by the Government of Northern Ireland.

The first stones were thrown at the marchers in Waterloo Place, from behind the barricades erected on the previous day. The police, equipped at first only with small shields, in a vain effort to protect the marchers and allow them access into the Bogside, became the focus of the angry mob of nationalist youths determined to keep them out. As the stones bounced off their shields, the police bent to pick them up and threw them back. From our vantage point, the first floor window above a shop overlooking the entrance to Rossville Street, we watched the RUC, backed up by jeering loyalist civilians, break through the barrier with armoured cars and drive the Bogsiders back down the street. The stand-off that ensued was broken when the roof of the high flats was occupied by a crowd of young people waving the tricolour and throwing petrol bombs which exploded in flames amongst the RUC's ranks and their vehicles, driving them back up the street once more.

Following the action when it was safe to do so, Tom and I changed to new observation points several times on that first day. At around midnight, the police fired shells of CS gas into a crowd of youths, dispersing them in all directions, as they ran with streaming eyes into nearby houses to seek relief and treatment. By the light of several small fires still burning in the street, we saw another armoured car driven at high speed, smashing through the barriers of metal bars, paving stones and planks of wood gathered from a building site. As the young people reassembled and older residents, furious at this invasion of their territory, turned out of their houses in indignation, more tear gas was fired into the crowd surrounding the police vehicle. At this point we were on the street ourselves and witnessed at first hand the intense pain and discomfort caused by this attack.

"This could go on all night," said Tom, as we rushed blindly down a side street with our eyes streaming as we fought for breath. "I'm taking you home." We sped along the labyrinth of small streets until we came to the house in which Don and I had been staying for the last three months.

"Some introduction to being a reporter," he gasped as he knocked on the door. "This is not a day you'll be forgetting in a hurry. I shall be at the City Hotel at ten o'clock tomorrow morning if you want more of the same."

Bernadette, our erstwhile landlady, opened the door and let me in to a roomful of women and children.

"Holy Mother of God, will you look at yourself!" she exclaimed, hugging me tightly. "Let me bathe your poor eyes and get you something to eat and drink. We've a houseful of refu-gees, as you can see."

There was no sign of my brother or Bernadette's husband all night. Upstairs there were children sleeping everywhere. I lay on one side of Bernadette's bed with two little ones fidget-ing and whimpering between us, but slept little, the events of the day replaying in my mind. Had Donal been one of those silhouetted on the roof of the Rossville Street high flats, I won-dered? The thought obsessed me until daylight filtered through the curtains.

The City Hotel had become the Headquarters of the Press and the Civil Rights workers. Among the latter was that other Bernadette, Miss Devlin, who seemed to be taking charge and di-recting the battle which still raged on the streets, addressing the rioters with her loud-hailer. She and others were also broadcasting on Radio Free Derry (200m. Medium wavelength), appealing to all Nationalists in the Six Counties, especially those in Belfast, to join in the campaign of civil disobedience, thus putting extra pressure on the RUC and provoking the arrival of the dreaded B-Specials.

A pall of tear-gas and smoke from burning cars still hung about the streets which were littered with stones, pieces of twist-ed metal and broken glass. Some residents wore old gas-masks, relics of the last war; others had soaked handkerchiefs in vinegar for protection, and children appeared in doorways, their faces smeared with baking powder, sometimes used as a protection against possible attacks of mustard gas during the war. The front rooms of some houses were turned into First Aid posts super-vised by the Knights of Malta, though most found that they could not cope adequately with the large number of casualties.

Rumours abounded. As evening approached, there was talk of a planned attack by police and auxiliary forces on St Eugene's

Cathedral. This turned out to be mere gossip but so enraged the residents, particularly the older members of the congregation that the violence and damage increased still further. Fires raged as darkness fell, with the bakery alight and a disused factory in Great James Street sending flames high into the sky. Police, many wounded and as yet unrelieved after over thirty hours of confrontation, fired live rounds into the crowd and at the doors and windows of houses, many of which had fortunately already been evacuated. Firebombs were thrown into the City Hotel only moments after Tom and I had left.

On the third day we made our way towards the border with other journalists in a rough-looking van, protected only by the word PRESS on each side. The previous evening Jack Lynch, the Taoiseach of the Republic, had made a broadcast in which he implied that there would be military intervention from the Irish Army on the nationalists' behalf. In fact, the soldiers had simply set up field hospitals on their side of the border in order to treat injured civilians fleeing the escalating violence which was fast spreading to other areas of the province.

When we returned to the city in the afternoon we found that the much-hated B-Specials had been deployed to back up the RUC, though they had not yet entered the Bogside. At about 5pm a Battalion of the British Army arrived and the battle ended for the time being, in an uneasy cessation of action and without resolution, while all over the Six Counties the fight continued, as it happened, for many years to come.

This was the draft of an article written for *The London Times* on the twentieth anniversary of the deployment of British troops in Ulster.

Dominic's worst fears were realised when Tom Fahy showed him the blown-up stills of the newsreel he had taken. Donal was recognisable, as was Kevin O'Neill in at least two pictures, as being one of those throwing petrol bombs from the roof of the High Flats in Rossville Street.

"Of course, they could not be identified in a normal-sized newspaper photograph," Tom assured him. "However, the RUC might easily demand to see the original footage. Before you ask – I cannot destroy any of this material, and even if I did, other photographers might well provide incriminating evidence."

"Oh God, what will we do now?" Dominic asked despairingly.

"If you can manage to get away, the two of you, it would be a very good idea to go as soon and as far away as possible."

It was with trepidation and many misgivings that Dominic relayed this advice to Donal who, fired up as he was by the events of the past three days, was already impatient for the next confrontation.

"*What*, run away?" he exclaimed, indignantly. "And where do you suggest skulking off to? Don't forget, we don't even exist here officially. How do you suggest we get to Timbuktu or the Australian outback without either passports or money?"

"There is only one other place we can go without a passport, and that is __"

"*England!*" Donal interrupted. "The place where all evil started? Not over my dead body!"

"That's the trouble – it well *might* be over your dead body. They'll be out for your blood, you and Kevin, if the police get those photos. Do you want to spend the rest of your life in prison?"

Surprisingly, it was Geraghty's decision in the end. When he heard about the pictures, he reacted with lightning speed.

His nephew, Kevin O'Neill together with Donal and Dominic Maloney were on the ferry from Belfast to Liverpool the very next evening, with introductions to the foreman of a construction company and enough money for their passage and their first week's accommodation in a boarding house in the Irish quarter of the city.

"Ye're not running away, be any means," Geraghty had assured them. "Sure, there's work to be done over the water as well as here – and I don't mean just earning a living. Ye'll find like-minded people wherever the Irish gather."

***

It was hard, back-breaking work on the building site and Dominic had little time or energy left at the end of each day to keep any kind of diary. However, he eventually found a post office, bought writing paper and stamps and set up a *poste restante* address. He received a prompt reply from Mrs Harrington.

> *My dear Dominic,*
>
> *We were so very relieved to hear from you at last after an anxious few months of wondering how you were faring. This past year must seem like a whole lifetime to you. At least you are safe now, even if the life you are leading at present is not exactly what your earlier education prepared you for!*
>
> *Our newspapers are full of the events in the North, but we had no idea that you and your brother would be so involved. I realise that you cannot give a full account just now for various reasons, but we were interested to*

read of your experience as an observer and are glad that Mr Fahy has asked you to stay in touch. He will be a useful contact when you get a chance to pursue your ambition to be a journalist.

I have passed on your temporary address to Mrs O'Leary and have asked her to inform Cathleen and Mr and Mrs Manning Senior of your whereabouts. I understand that your sisters have been trying to get in touch. They will be very glad to have news of you both at last.

Good luck to you both in trying to trace your mothers. I fear it may be a difficult task: the people who ran those homes for unmarried mothers, especially the Catholic ones and the Magdalene Laundries, covered their tracks very thoroughly when it came to divulging information about adopted babies. Meanwhile, we will do what we can to help. As you say, your adoptive grandmother must know something about your origins.

Please keep in touch now we've found you again and let us know how you get on. My husband and Frances join me in wishing you all the very best.

Yours affectionately,

Moira Harrington

A few days later there was an envelope with a Limerick postmark. Inside was a card with the picture of an ocean-going liner, bearing the legend: BELATED BIRTHDAY WISHES ACROSS THE MILES.

It was addressed within: To dear Dominic and Donal on your 16th Birthday, and signed individually by Maeve O'Leary and Cathleen Shea, with a letter enclosed.

Dear Donal and Dominic,

Cathleen and I were delighted altogether to hear news of you from that kind Mrs Harrington. Praise be to God that your both safe and sound over the water, we have prayed to the Holy Mother every day that you would soon be found alive and well. The two of you are after having a fierce time of it by all accounts. The papers have been full of the Troubles in the north and you being last heard of in Derry weve been very worried indeed. Your sisters, well I should say stepsisters, have been asking for you. I am after writing with your adress but the letters take a long time all that way from America. We wonder, will you please write to us at this address. Mr and Mrs McCausland are very good people though himself is not a believer. Better not to send to Cathleen at the presbytery she says but you can send it here.

Hoping this finds you as it leaves me.

Yours sincerely,

Maeve O'Leary.

PS The card is very late but we had not your adress to send it.

SEVEN

"… Death to ev'ry foe and traitor! Whistle out the marching tune
And hurrah, me boys, for freedom, 'tis the rising of the moon."

The older men tended to prefer the nostalgic songs about the beauty of 'the ould country'; tears would come into their eyes as they sang of their longing for Galway Bay, the Mountains of Mourne and Killarney, places which were merely legendary for most of them. The younger ones, however, were stirred by the rebel songs which told of the centuries-old fight for freedom from English oppression.

"That was well sung, all right, Donal Maloney," said Paddy Keenan one evening in McCarthy's bar.

"It was great, altogether," agreed Eamonn Crowley. "I've not heard the like since I left Cork. But tell me, what's a lad your age doin' here at all? I'd lay a bet that ye're not feckin' old enough to be taking a drink yet."

"People always say that," said Donal.' Tis just that I look young for my age."

"Which is – what- t'irteen?"

"Eighteen last birthday."

"Where d'you come from, Maloney?"

"Limerick City, - though I'm told I was born in London."

"Holy Mother! And you singing the rebel songs! I'm after living there for a while meself when I first came over."

"We aim to be goin' there soon, me and me brother. Where would you suggest for finding work an' all and somewhere to stay – among our own people?"

"Well an' all, tis an enormous city altogether," Crowley said, stretching his brawny arms wide to indicate the size of it. "We were in the North West, - place called Kilburn. There were plenty of Irish there and good navvying jobs to be had, no questions asked, kinda thing." He tapped his nose with a broad forefinger and winked. "When ye're t'inkin' of going there I'll give ye an address or two. Now, be givin' us another song, if ye will. Ye've a grand voice on ye."

THE DERRY RECORD
March 20th 1971

Dear Dominic,

Thank you for your letter. I'm sorry it has taken me so long to reply. It was good to hear that you got away safely and have found work in England. Even if it is not your first choice of a job, it is a living for the time being and will tide you over until you and your brother can establish valid identities. Certainly I shall be able to give you suggestions and introductions into journalism when the time is right.

I can understand your need to trace your mother – or at least some evidence of your date and place of birth. This may prove very difficult if your adoption(s)

were illegal, as false names may have been registered –
or the births might not have been registered at all.

According to the results of my enquiries, there was a
home for unmarried mothers, together with an orphan-
age and a lunatic asylum, run by the Sisters of Mercy on
the site of an earlier Magdalen Laundry in the Kilburn
area in North London. There is a large Irish community
there so maybe you will be able to learn more local-
ly. The place may still exist in some form or other. Do
please let me know how you get on.

The Troubles continue here and will do so for some
time to come, I fear. At least there is no shortage of
work for me, though a change of subject matter would
be very welcome!

Yours sincerely,
Tom Fahy.

PS. I met Mrs Bernadette Geraghty at my uncle's house
recently. She was very pleased to have news of you and
asked me to send her kindest remembrances to you
both. I think she would be glad to hear from you di-
rectly if you have the time. It would be best to address
it c/o Fr. Aidan McDonald, Lismore, St. Luke's Road,
Londonderry.

When the boys got to London, they found that locating
the Convent was not as hard as they expected. Casually

asked questions among their work-mates and in the Irish bars brought forth a wealth of reminiscences and anecdotes. Some of the older men remembered the Laundry. One had walked past it every day, he said; the hot steam pouring from the windows had taken the chill out of many a winter's morning – at least for a few seconds. Another said he had worked on the site when it was demolished. A large block of flats now stood where once the dirty linen of the neighbourhood had been brought in huge baskets. And yes, the work had been done by the women who were no better than they should be: fast girls, prostitutes, fallen women and the like. Behind those high walls they gave birth to their bastards and the nuns put them in the orphanage. If you were one of the lucky little bastards, a childless couple might come and pick you out and adopt you – and pay good money to the sisters. Some children were even sent to America, sight unseen. Old Pat knew one fellow who'd been sent back again, returned empty, so to speak. As for the Lunatic Asylum, wouldn't it curdle your blood to hear the screeches of the mad women? 'Twas as if the banshee herself was after ye when you were out late at night and had too many drinks taken.

The convent was still a home for unmarried mothers, they were told. It was called Magdalene House and was probably the only Catholic one of its kind this side of the Thames, - maybe the only one in England. There were plenty back in Ireland, of course, even stricter than this one used to be.

—ఴ—

"Even if this the right place, where do we go from here?" Donal wondered, as the two of them surveyed the tall gates set in high walls, adorned at the top by shards of broken glass which glistened in the light of the street lamps.

"It will need some careful thought, certainly," said Dominic.

"You spend far too much time thinking, Domino – you always have done. It's *action* that's needed now. We managed to break out before: now we must break *in*."

"Correction: we were *broken* out – rescued, if you like, though I'd not much choice in the matter, if you remember. No, if we're to get information, we need a much more subtle approach. What we need is a name – or *names*."

"**I** have an odd request; am I speaking to the Registrar?" started Dominic in the local Registry Office.

"Fire away," said the clerk behind the counter, in a bored voice. "Registrar's out; I'm in charge."

"I need to know the name of my father. I'm applying for a college course and the form requires this information."

"So why don't you know it?"

"He left home before I was born."

"What about your ma then?"

"She's dead."

"You were registered here, were you?"

"I think this was the place."

"Date of birth?"

"25th of August, 1954."

"Name?"

A telephone rang somewhere behind a wall of filing cabinets, and was answered promptly.

"Your wife for you, Mr Green," a girl's voice called.

"Deal with this then, will you, Sally. I may be some time."

Sally was petite and blonde and regarded Dominic with evident approval. She patted her hair and smoothed her flamboyantly-patterned mini-skirt as she approached the counter.

"Now, where were we, sir?"

Dominic gave her what he hoped was his most engaging smile.

"Could you check the births registered on or around the 25th of August, 1954, please?"

"Certainly, sir," said Sally, fluttering heavily made-up lashes at him.

She disappeared for a short while and returned carrying a ledger.

"There's only a still-birth recorded on that actual date: Baby Trelawney – Female."

"How odd. Who registered it?"

"A Mrs Dorothea A. James."

"And the father?"

"Not known. Mother: Cecily Rose Trelawney of the same address."

"I don't recognise either of the names. What about any male births registered in the days before and after that date?"

Sally ran a finger down the register. Let's see … female… female, female …… Ah, there's a Declan O'Shaughnessy on the 22nd. Mother: Brigid O'Shaughnessy of Magdalene House; father unknown; registered by Sister Mary Noreen Kenny of the Convent of Jesus and Mary, Station Road North, - that'd be that big ugly house that backs onto Fenton Street."

"No, none of those names mean anything to me," Dominic said, truthfully. "I think I may have come to the wrong office.

But, just in case, would you be kind enough to write down Mrs James's address?"

He was reassured, by the occasional sound of the clerk's voice, that the telephone call was still in progress. He watched Sally's little pink, pointed tongue peeping out of her mouth as she wrote the address, and was amused to see that she had written her own telephone number underneath.

"If I can be of further help," she said archly, "Please let me know on *this* number." She underlined it heavily as she spoke.

Armed with more information than he could possibly have hoped for, Dominic left the office and hastened back to the building site to tell Donal.

The door of 11, Charlton Walk, Hampstead, was answered by a stout woman in a striped overall. She was clearly in the process of washing the tiles on the hall floor.

"There ain't no-one of that name lives 'ere now," she said, in answer to Dominic's enquiry. "Mrs Blumenthal don't like me answering the door when she's aht but I was just about to slosh this bucket of water over the path."

"Oh, I'm sorry to have bothered you – but would you have any idea how long ago Mrs James moved from here?"

"Well, I've bin working for Mrs B. ... let's see... it'd be two years come Christmas – and they'd not long moved in then. Try Mrs Stevens, the old lady next door. Lived 'ere for years and years, she 'as. 'Ere, I'll knock for you if you like. You seem a nice young man; I don't think you look as though you're the bailiff's lad, or someone come to steal the silver." She laughed heartily at the very idea.

—⚭—

"Oh yes," said Mrs Stevens, "I remember Professor and Mrs James. We still exchange Christmas cards. They live in Cambridge now. The professor lectures at the university."

"Would you be kind enough to give me their address? Mrs James is some sort of relative. Before she died, my mother asked me to get in touch with her. Do they have a family?"

"No children of their own – but there is a niece, Cecily, who often stayed with them here. Lovely looking young lady, with beautiful red hair – dark red, well, auburn I suppose you'd call it."

"Would her surname have been Trelawney, by any chance?"

"No, she was a James, too. I think the Professor and her father were brothers. Step inside a moment and I'll find the address for you."

Dominic stepped into a hall similar to the one next door. The Victorian patterned floor tiles reminded him of the little painted wooden bricks he and Donal used to play with when they were small children, and a wave of nostalgia for those days of uncomplicated contentment washed through him. He heard Mrs Stevens opening and shutting drawers and muttering to herself as she searched for her list of addresses. At last, she came back with a sheet of paper.

"I'm sorry to have been so long," she said. "My Christmas list wasn't where I thought I'd put it. Anyway, here is the James's address in Cambridge – and Cecily's too, now Mrs Knight; she married a clergyman. Mrs James herself was an R.C."

"Thank you very much for your help, Mrs Stevens. That is more than I could have wished for."

"I'm very glad to have been *able* to help you, Mr ...?"

"Dominic."

"Mr Dominic. I wish you every success in your search. I'm sure your poor mother would have been so pleased to know that you were carrying out her wishes." She held out her hand and Dominic shook it politely, ashamed not only of his callused palms and rough fingertips, but also of the fact that he had lied in order to obtain the information he needed.

D ominic was very unhappy that all the information he had gathered had been shared with Geraghty and O'Neill. After the introduction of internment without trial that year in the six counties, the former had decided to lie low in London himself for a while, in case he was identified as a member of the new 'Provos'. Now he wanted 'a slice of the action' as he put it. The boys would need a driver and an escort when they went to accost 'the Protestant hoor' in her lair. Whosoever mother she turned out to be, she was going to have to pay. The boys needed money, papers and passports, and Geraghty and O'Neill wanted their cut, both for expenses and for 'the cause'. Yes indeed, there was no time like Christmas to give Mrs P. R.T. Knight, wife of the vicar of Hutton-on-the-Wold in Gloucestershire a nasty surprise: a present that she was not going to relish opening at all, at all.

PART 3

ELEVEN

As so often happened, I had a strong sense of Bruno's presence as I put the finishing touches to the Christmas tree. We had never discussed Christmas, as far as I remembered, let alone been together for any part of the festival, but this afternoon he seemed especially close. It was as if he were sitting in the same room, composing or arranging music, while I fiddled with the tree lights and added another glass bauble here, a piece of tinsel there. The smell of freshly baked mince-pies wafted in from the kitchen, mingling with the aromatic scent of applewood burning in the grate. Peter was out, visiting a sick parishioner and going on to a meeting afterwards; the children, now teenagers, were staying at their aunt's in Bath until the following day. Except for shutting up the hens, I was in for the rest of the day.

"So it's just you and me, Bruno, - alone at last," I said over my shoulder. The cat, Hieroglyph, jumped off a chair and stalked across the room, tail in the air and plainly offended. "Oh, and you too of course, Glyph. How could I forget *you*?"

The peace was suddenly shattered by a determined knocking on the front door. It came again, more demanding now, before I had time to open the door. Two young men of about the same age as Edmund stood there. Glyph shot out between them and sat at a safe distance, regarding them warily.

"I'm afraid Ed's away till tomorrow ____" I started to say, but one of them interrupted:

"Cecily Rose Trelawney?"

"Knight, actually," I corrected, intrigued. "But my mother's family name was Trelawney."

"Well, we're not here to make polite conversation," said the same boy, while the other looked distinctly ill at ease. "We're here to give you a nasty surprise, not to wish you a happy Christmas and all that rubbish." He spoke with a roughish accent; Scottish, Irish? The latter, I decided.

"Well, perhaps you had better come in," I said coolly, "and tell me what this is all about." This young man was evidently very angry and I felt confident that I could handle the situation.

"What it's all about is that we've come to spoil your happy, cosy little Christmas party, *Mrs* Knight." He pushed past me into the hall and I felt the first flutter of alarm. The other boy followed, giving me an apologetic look. He seemed to catch his breath as he stepped into the room, looking first at the tree, at the fire and around the room, his gaze lingering on the piano. Finally, he looked directly at me for a moment. The first boy came in behind us, stuffing a mince pie into his mouth and handing another to his companion who looked at me again, his expression part apology, part enquiry.

"Please, go ahead," I invited him, and to the first youth I said: "I see that good manners are not your strong suit. Perhaps you'd better introduce yourself so that I can *offer* you another mince-pie."

"Perhaps *you'd* better sit down on that chair, Mrs Knight – or should we call you *Mother*? I'm Donal and he's Dominic." He pointed first to himself and then to his companion in an exaggerated manner. "We don't know our *real* surnames but we do know that one of us is your son, - the little bastard you gave away in 1954 because you didn't want him, Protestant *whore* that you are."

"Donal, that's enough! Let me do the explaining." Dominic spoke for the first time. He too had an Irish accent but was much more softly spoken.

But Donal was not to be silenced. "Shut up, will ye; I shall handle this." Looking me full in the face, he asked in a declamatory tone: "Prisoner at the bar, were you or were you not resident in the Magdalene Home in Kilburn, London on or around the twenty-fifth of August, 1954?"

"Are you here to blackmail me; is that it?"

"Did you or did you not give birth to a bastard son on or around the aforementioned date?"

"Why are you asking me these questions – and why should I answer them?"

"Because we have reason to believe that one of us is the child born to you that day." It was Dominic who spoke this time. The gentleness in his voice diffused my indignation and I collapsed onto the nearest chair, head in hands to hide my sudden tears.

"My own baby, a girl, died at birth," I said, when I had collected myself a little.

"Oh yes, that's what it says on the register: stillborn. A very convenient lie." The rough voice again – Donal's.

"It is no lie," I protested, sobbing. "It was a difficult birth … and she did not survive."

"Then tell me this: why were we told – by a solicitor no less – that one of us was the bastard of a Protestant woman, born in a Magdalene Institution in London?"

"I'm sorry, I don't know," I said hopelessly. "All I know is that my own baby died."

"How do you know? Did you see it – dead, I mean?"

I was distraught by this time at being forced to recall that dreadful day.

"Don!" said Dominic, "Will you lay off; you can see how upset she is."

"She *would* be," retorted Donal. "She's been exposed as a liar. I wonder, *Mother* Knight, does your holy husband know about your wicked past? And your children; how many more little bastards did you give away?"

I stood up and took two paces towards him, my eyes on a level with his own. "If my child had lived, I would never, EVER, have 'given her away', as you put it. I have been unable to bear children of my own since that time: the children here are my stepchildren. How *dare* you march into my own home and make such accusations? Is it money you want? If you were to kidnap me, my family could not afford the ransom; if you were to blackmail me, the same would apply. So what *do* you want?"

Dominic answered my question simply. "I suppose we want recognition from a parent, really. We have no adoption papers, birth certificates – anything - to prove who we are, since our parents – adoptive parents – died. I suppose we do not exist in the eyes of the law, either in this country or in Ireland where we were brought up."

"I think we had all better sit down and you can tell me the whole story," I said. "I will do what I can to help. All I ask is that we are honest with each other and that we try to speak without anger."

"You seem to be alone in the house," Dominic said. "What will we do if your husband comes home?"

"I shall have to explain why you are here," I said.

———✷———

As I listened to the boys' extraordinary story, recounted most-ly by Dominic, with angry interjections by Donal, I found myself questioning the truth of what I had been led to believe all those years ago. I searched their faces and studied their manner-isms for any signs of likeness to Bruno or to me. They resembled each other only in that they were the same age and similar height, and both were black-haired and good-looking; in temperament, however, they were clearly very different. Dominic, the more ar-ticulate of the two, resembled Bruno in his gentle firmness; Donal had my earlier fieriness and tendency to anger. I hoped fervently that the former might be our son, but very much feared that it would turn out to be the latter. Any suggestion of instant mutual recognition belonged in the realm of fiction.

"I am truly sorry if any action of mine resulted in so much trouble for you both," I said when Dominic had finished speak-ing. "Would it help you to know that I have never stopped loving the father of my baby; that the baby was conceived in one act of love – not of lust?"

"What help is that?" Donal asked scornfully. "Anyway, who was he and what was his name, Mr Blank?"

"When we know the truth of all this, I may tell you more about him."

"I could make you tell us," he said threateningly.

"I've no doubt you could try, Donal," I said, "But first we need confirmation of the facts. My aunt must know what really hap-pened in that dreadful place."

"I could make her talk, too," he said confidently.

"You probably could; but threats and violence are not the only way. I shall do it myself. As soon as Christmas is over, I shall go to Cambridge and demand to know the truth."

"*Before* Christmas," he insisted.

"I have obligations here; please understand that. In other circumstances I would invite you to stay – but I think that would be awkward, don't you?" The daylight was fading and I went round the room switching on table-lamps.

Dominic sighed wistfully as he looked at the tree, the pools of light cast by the lamps and the warm glow of the fire.

"It seems a long time since we had a real Christmas," he said.

"One day we may celebrate it together," I said. "Tell me, how did you get here – and how are you getting back to London?

"By car. Geraghty and his cousin drove us here and said they'd wait at the gate – about now," Dominic said, looking at the clock on the mantelpiece.

I packed up the rest of the mince-pies and handed them to Donal. "Take those to share on your journey," I said. "I can always make some more tomorrow."

"Huh!" he said. "D'you think you can buy us off with a few pies?"

"No," I answered. "I hope to be of more help in the future. Just let me tell you this though: no son of mine would turn out to be as ill-mannered as you are. So that puts *you* in the clear."

I put on a jacket and walked out of the door with them. Dominic bent to stroke Glyph who was waiting on the doorstep. "I have to shut the chickens up for the night," I said, "So I'll say good bye. I think that must be your car at the end of the drive. I'll be in touch as soon as I've been to see my aunt."

I held out my hand to Dominic who took it with a firm hand-shake. It seemed a strangely formal action but my social training had not prepared me for this eventuality. Donal ignored my out-stretched hand and turned away towards the gate.

—⚬⚬⚬—

I was grateful for the two hours or so that remained before Peter was expected home. The multi-layered complexity of the afternoon's revelation needed intellectual examination to balance the considerable emotional reaction. Suddenly, and without warning, the past had caught up with the future.

I made more mince-pies, the simple domestic task serving to stop me from pacing about the house in a tangle of uncertain-ty. Firstly, there was the dilemma of how and when to tell Peter. The most treasured and beautiful episode of my young life had brought about the collision of two worlds, but I could hardly put it like that to him. He would see it as a sordid secret which I should have revealed to him before our marriage. On his reaction would depend the impact of all this on his children and his flock.

Then, there were the boys themselves – and the influence of the man, Geraghty, particularly on Donal, to whom the very word 'Protestant' was anathema. This might turn out to be a put-up job, the blackmail attempt that I had at first suspected … and yet … these boys, whoever they were, had had a raw deal. They had been pitched from a secure, well-to-do home into institutions where boys suffered unspeakable degradation; schools which purported to be religious foundations but seemed to be a cover for perversion and brutality. Evidently Donal had undergone worse than Dominic, which would account for his anger and bit-terness. The irrational thing was that he vented his wrath upon the Protestants, whereas the Catholic, so-called *Christian* Brothers had been his true persecutors.

Once the pies were in the oven, I phoned Aunt D., saying that I had research to do in Cambridge, and asking if I might stay one night, arriving two days after Christmas.

Finally, there was Bruno to consider; Bruno, whom I consid-ered every day that dawned. If there was any substance to what I had heard today, I would break the silence of over thirteen long years and tell him that he had a son.

I took the mince-pies out of the oven, placed them on a rack to cool and went into the sitting-room to make up the fire and draw the curtains. The comfortable, softly-lit room left no trace of the boys' visit; the lights on the tree twinkled festively. Nothing had changed – except the future. I heard the front door open and close, and Peter's step in the hall.

"I'm home, Cecily. Mmm – smells good! Mince-pies? Have you had a nice, peaceful afternoon?"

Peter took it very badly as I expected he would. I told him as succinctly and unemotionally as possible as soon as Edmund had left the house with Agnes and Elizabeth to go to the Boxing Day Meet.

"It pains me that you have deceived me all these years," he said.

"It was not something I could bear to talk about. I suffered the pain and loss of losing a full-term child, but had to put it

behind me and make something of my life long before I met you.
I was not consciously deceiving you; there is a difference."

"Nevertheless, at present I cannot forgive you, Cecily. I must
seek guidance from God and pray for a change of heart. I would
not have entrusted the care of my children to you, had I known
that you had a – tarnished reputation."

"Tell me, Peter, have I otherwise been a satisfactory wife and
mother in the ten years that we have been married?"

"Of course you have; but I still cannot find it in my heart to
forgive your deception. It will take time and much prayer."

"Then I shall go away for a while and leave you to pray. I intend to go to see Aunt D. tomorrow and find out the truth. I shall
have to tell the children that she's ill – as she very probably will
be when I tax her with this."

"The repercussions of one sinful act can be endless, I fear.
The poison may spread down the years."

"Peter, I repeat: it was an act of *love* – and long, long before
I knew you. If there was sin, it was as much that of those who deliberately deceived *me*."

I found the house in Trumpington Road without difficulty and
turned into the driveway. I had visited my uncle and aunt
seldom in the years since I had left their care. Aunt D. greeted me with an awkward peck on the cheek and showed me to
my room. My uncle, she said, had gone for a walk and would
be back for tea. After I had freshened up, I went down to the
drawing-room.

"I will tell you the real reason why I'm here," I said, without preamble. "I want the absolute and unvarnished truth of what happened in the Magdalene Home in 1954."

Her eyes widened in surprise and alarm at my direct and determined approach. She sat down suddenly as if her legs had given way. Still standing, I told her of the boys' visit and the claims that they had made, sparing her no detail of their incarceration in the infamous Industrial schools to which they had been exiled, and emphasising the threats of IRA involvement.

"So you see why it is vital that you tell me the truth," I finished. "Did you falsify the records? Have I been mourning, all these years, a still-born child who never existed – while another was taken away?"

She was shaking noticeably as she answered: "No – the girl *was* still-born."

"The girl?" I shouted. "Was there a boy as well? *Twins?* Oh *God!*"

"Cecily, I did what I thought was best for you. It would have ruined your life to have been saddled with a baby – and you did seem determined to keep it. There was the couple from Limerick wanting to adopt a baby from … a good background. Dr Manning was an erstwhile colleague of your uncle's. It seemed a heaven-sent solution at the time."

I was the one to tremble now as anger took hold. "*Heaven*-sent? Direct intervention from a good *Catholic* God, you mean? And what about the other boy? They were brought up as twins, you know. Which one of them is *my* son?"

"The other boy was born to a ____"

"Brigid O'Shaughnessy?" I asked.

"That may have been the name – it's so long ago now. She was maid in a big house in Hampstead. The son of the house, who was still at school I believe, got her – into trouble. Dr and Mrs

Manning adopted both babies and took them back to Ireland with her as nurse."

"And what became of her? The boys remember a succession of maids and one elderly nanny, but no-one of that name. She must have known which of them was her *own* baby, surely."

"The Mannings were very good people, - very suitable as parents for your child," Aunt D. said piously. "They promised to set her up somewhere well away from Limerick as soon as they had engaged a new nanny ... to save her reputation, you know. They would give her a modest income, they said, until she married."

"And now nobody knows which boy is which, and untold misery has been endured by two helpless innocents," I said bitterly. The irony did not escape me that this very day was Holy Innocents' Day. "As for me, I have earned the hatred of a boy who may very well be my son – a boy of whose existence I was completely ignorant until the other day - and all because of the manipulation of self-righteous religious *bigots*. I suppose a large sum of money was involved?"

"Well, there are always expenses," she said, pursing her lips primly.

"And the law of the land; was that observed?" I answered my own question. "No! Only the law of God, as conveniently interpreted by the Sisters of Perpetual Malediction, or whatever they were called. Consequently, these two boys were not only disinherited from their late adoptive parents' estate, they have no identity and no rights, either in this country or in Ireland."

"You are very angry, Cecily. Would you like me to leave you alone to calm down while I make some tea?"

"No, I would not," I answered. "In fact I don't think I can bear to stay here any longer. Two more questions, though. How much of all this did my parents know?"

"Oh, it was all done with their approval: they agreed that it was for the best ... for you, in the long run, you know."

My voice faltered over the next question. "And my baby girl: was there – is there - a grave? I never asked."

"It is in the Sisters' own burial ground behind the convent. I insisted on a proper interment and paid for a mass and a small stone, myself." Again, the pious tone in her voice, as if she expected thanks or congratulation.

When she went to the kitchen to make the tea, I fetched my case from upstairs and went to the car without saying good bye. As I drove towards the London road, I passed Uncle Guy on his way home. He did not see me.

———

I drove badly, distracted by my thoughts, and so intent on unravelling the tangled threads that I paid little attention to the road. After a few miles I realised the folly of arriving in London in the dark with nowhere to stay, so I turned off into a biggish village and found a telephone box. It was irritating to find it occupied by a girl who continued to feed coins into the slot for several minutes, although she was well aware of my presence outside. When she finally hung up and tottered down the road in her high heeled shoes, I found the box smelt of cheap scent and stale cigarettes, with overtones of urine. I lifted the sticky receiver with a shudder and dialled Wat's number, willing him to be at home. His phone rang and rang, and just as I was about to hang up, he answered.

"Wat, it's Cecily," I said in relief. "I'm on my way to London from Cambridge. Have you a sofa I could sleep on tonight?

"Cecily! Wonderful to *hear* you. Come by all means, darling. You can have a real *bed*. My flatmate's just moved out – in fact, I need a shoulder to cry on, and whose better than yours?"

"I know that feeling, so have your shoulder ready, too." The pips went, demanding another coin in the slot. "See you soon-ish. 'Bye."

⊸⊶

Wat and I had kept in touch over the years and had the kind of comfortable relationship that often exists between a woman and a man who 'bats for the other side'. (A euphemism often used by heterosexual men!) He hugged me warmly and proceeded, literally, to cry on my shoulder, his latest 'flatmate' having walked out on him on Christmas Eve, taking with him any of Wat's possessions that might have a street value. I grieved for this dear, weeping man, with his brilliant mind and incisive wit, that in forty years he had never found the soul-mate who he believed was 'out there somewhere'.

When he had finished pouring out his anguish, he said: "Now dearest girl, what about you? What are you doing in London? Catch me up on the last hundred years while I get us something *delicious* to eat. Actually, it will have to be cold turkey and reheated veggies. I cooked a *lovely* dinner on Christmas Day, just in case Jules came home, - but no show."

Hitherto, I had told Wat nothing of the events of Summer 1954 and my sudden departure from Hampstead 'to do a summer teaching job'. We had exchanged the occasional letter while I was at Richmond and again when I first went to Shropshire; after that we resumed our friendship at Cambridge. He opened a bottle of Chablis. ("For the first course, darling – but let's start

191

on it now. I think we both need it.") I sipped it gratefully and soon began on my own shoulder-weeping account.

"Dear God!" he breathed when I stopped speaking. "And I thought I had problems. To think that you found the love of your life, - and he wouldn't stay with you, while mine is out there in the wilderness, waiting to be found. *Amare et supere vix deo conceditur.*"

"Which means? I'm too lazy to translate it."

"To be in love and to be wise is scarce granted even to a god. You *will* tell him that you have a son, won't you? You must, Cecily."

"Yes, but *which* son? Which of them is ours? I shall have to treat them as brothers until I can find out. Yes, I will tell him. Tomorrow I'd like to visit the Polish priest. Perhaps you'd help me find him, if you're free. He's the only mutual contact we have, Bruno and I."

"Count me in. I can always just sit in the car and wait."

"Then, in the evening I must go to see the boys," I said. "They told me I would find them in O'Flaherty's pub in Kilburn. Can you believe it, in all my thirty-six years, I've never walked into a pub alone? I dread it."

"Then I shall escort you, darling, keeping my sword-arm free to protect your honour."

"With the greatest respect, dear Wat," I said, laughing, "I think you'd be the one needing protection amongst those macho Irish builders."

We left the car outside the flat in Maida Vale and, armed with Wat's A – Z, we went by Tube to Fulham. The housekeeper answered my knock.

"I'm afraid Fr Michal is in Rome," she said proudly, when I asked if I might see him. "He won't be back until next week."

"Oh dear," I said. "I've come a long way to see him. Perhaps you could help. I was hoping to contact Bruno Sabra. I know he uses this as a *pied a terre* when he's in London."

"Oh yes, Mr Sabra. He was here only a month or so ago."

"Would you have a forwarding address for him?"

"Fr Michal usually sees to that if there is mail for him. I could find his address in America for you, - though Mr Sabra – Doctor Sabra, I should say, - said he would be in Hungary for a few weeks after Christmas. Or was it Turkey? I forget which."

"Well, I would be grateful for the American address, if you'd be so kind."

I held my breath while she went to what I supposed would be the priest's study, then wrote Wat's address on a small note pad, under my name, - Mrs C.R. James.

"There, that's the best I can do for you," she said, handing me a piece of paper. "Such a nice man, Dr Sabra. His daughter was with him last time he was here. Lovely-looking girl, very like him to look at – dark, you know. She went for an interview at the Royal College of Music. She'll start there in the autumn, so we'll probably be seeing a lot of her. Have you ever met her?"

"No, I've never had that pleasure," I said, faintly. "Thank you so much for your help."

I left without handing her the leaf I had torn from my note-pad.

"Let's go to an art gallery and look at something *healing*," said Wat as we sat in the coffee shop where he had waited for me. "You look as if you've seen a ghost. Was it bad news?"

I told him about my visit to the presbytery. "So you see, I have Bruno's address, but it was the other information that threw me. I suppose I've never thought of 'the daughter' as being anything more than the four-year-old child she was thirteen years ago. It hurts, Wat, it *hurts*."

TWELVE

I stood outside O'Flaherty's pub at about nine o'clock that evening, steeling myself with several deep breaths before pushing open the swing door. 'God, give me strength to brave this humiliation,' I prayed, - not knowing whether my plea was to a stern Catholic God or the more easy-going Anglican one. Both seemed to have it in for me of late.

I could hear music inside: someone singing a song I did not recognise, accompanied by the beat of a tambourine or drum. Dominic had told me that Donal often sang rebel songs, and that he himself sometimes played his clarinet, though less frequently. With one final steadying breath, I pushed open the door, hoping that I could slip in unnoticed. The singing ceased, the drumming stopped and all heads turned in one synchronised motion. Glasses of stout or cigarettes stopped midway between table and mouth, and in the utter silence at least twenty pairs of eyes inspected me from head to toe and back again.

"Good evening to you, gentlemen," I announced. "Please excuse my interruption, but I would like a word with Donal and Dominic."

Donal, standing on the rostrum was first to break the men's silence, so that the tableau slowly came to life.

"Well, fellas, will you take a look at our *mother*. She's after turning up for the first time in eight-*een y*ears to take us home and tuck us into bed."

Dominic came towards me from the other side of the room and held out his hand. "Thank you for coming," he said, courteously. "What can I get you to drink? Come and sit over here."

"Jesus, Joseph and the Holy *Mother* of God!" said one of the other men. (Geraghty, I wondered?) "Isn't he the gentleman, all right? The trouble is, *Madam*, that this is no place for a lady – or did a little bird tell me that you do not qualify as such?"

"I think it is plain to see, Sir, that I am certainly not a *gentleman*," I said. There was a little awkward laughter before silence fell once more.

"Please, carry on with the music," I invited. "Thank you, Dominic; I'd like half-a pint of Guinness, if I may." Still silence prevailed. Was ever a public bar so quiet?

As Dominic went to the bar, a sudden impulse made me mount the rostrum and open the piano. I seated myself and played a few chords and a run or two to get the feel of the instrument. When I stopped, the silence was so profound that it seemed as if the whole world was holding its breath. I started to sing: *I know where I'm going, 'The Butcher Boy, 'The Bonny Boy' and 'Danny Boy',* without leaving time in between for applause - or lack of it. Then I rose from the chair, turned to face the room and sang *She moved through the Fair'*. Some of the older men were wiping away tears, I noticed, and when I finished the song, after a moment's electric silence, one of them began to clap, and gradually others joined in. I bowed, left the rostrum and walked over to the table where Dominic was sitting. Donal was nowhere to be seen.

The conversation was resumed with a few glances in my direction. This odd departure from normality might well be a topic for discussion and speculation for some time to come. But I had matters to discuss with Dominic.

"That was great," he said. "You have a voice like Mary O'Hara."

"That's a great compliment indeed. Actually, I learnt some of those songs from a record of hers. I'm sorry Donal felt that he couldn't stay. I suppose I embarrassed him."

"He just finds it hard to cope with this whole thing. I feel bad about his rudeness."

"Don't apologise for him; I can understand it. You and he have been through a lot."

I told him then of my aunt's confession to me the previous day, and my intention to help the boys financially to establish themselves with valid identities and the necessary documents.

"My only asset now is my old home in Cornwall," I explained. "I haven't been back since ... all this happened. I intend to raise capital by selling it, though it may take some time. You and Donal will need a large part of it to set you up for the future."

"But one of us is no relation to you!" Dominic pointed out.

"Then that is his good fortune," I said, smiling. "I shall just have to treat you as brothers until I know who's who."

We talked about his ambition to be a journalist and the wish of both of them to go to California to see their sisters. It would remove Donal from the influence of Geraghty and give him some interest in life other than 'Proddie-bashing'.

"This Mr Geraghty – is he here tonight?" I asked. "I shall have to meet him sooner or later."

"He *was* here, but he and O'Neill – his cousin - left with Donal while you were singing at the piano."

Two old men got up to leave. One of them raised his cap to me and said, "Thank you, Missus, for the beautiful singin'. I hope we'll be hearin' you again, so I do."

"Who knows?" I replied. "It was a great pleasure." I flashed him a warm smile. It would pay to have well-wishers around here, I thought.

"It was brave of you to come in here on your own," Dominic said, when I stood up to go. "How did you get here?"

"I left the car along the road a bit and walked."

"It might not be safe for you around here at night. I'll walk with you to your car."

"You are very kind. There's one thing I want to do before I go home tomorrow – and I wonder if you would come with me. I need to see the grave of … my little girl, the baby who died, you know, when you …"

"I will, of course," he answered, gently, this boy who seemed old beyond his years.

"We shall have to ask at the Convent, the old Magdalene Home. I'm not sure where it is, but my friend has an A – Z."

"I know exactly where it is," Dominic said. "Donal seriously thought of breaking *into* it to find out who we were." And for the first time, I heard this solemn boy laugh.

"I just love your unpredictability," said Wat, when I recounted my impulsive behaviour in the pub. "Perhaps you should have been an actress."

"As long as I can act when the occasion demands, I'm happy with that," I laughed, – "and that occasion certainly demanded *some* diversion, to break that ominous silence."

We were sitting over a late supper. Wat had made a delicious Spaghetti Bolognese, and I was relishing every mouthful, in spite of my earlier anguish after the episode in Fulham.

"This is so cosy," said Wat. "I'm sorry you have to go home tomorrow. You fit in so well here."

"If Peter decides to excommunicate me, I shall be back, if that's OK."

Three weeks after that, I *was* back.

———

The nun of about my own age who attended to my request to see the grave was less than welcoming. I had to hint at the irregularity of the unofficial adoption practices of the old orphanage to persuade her to acquiesce. She had been there only four years, she said. Everything was very different now that the Convent no longer administered the home for unmarried mothers, the orphanage and the asylum.

We found it in the far corner of the burial ground, the tiny grave marked by a small headstone. I brushed away the gritty lichen with my gloved hands, to reveal the brief inscription:

BABY TRELAWNEY
AUGUST 25, 1954.

We stood in silence for several moments, then Dominic said, "She didn't even have a *name*. What would you have called her?"

"In my mind, I have always called her Elowen," I said. "It's a Cornish name. One day I will tell you about that connection."

"My twin sister, - or Donal's," he said, thoughtfully. I wiped the tears from my eyes and reached for his hand.

"Thank you for coming, Dominic. It means such a lot to me."

As I drove home in the dismal half-light of that winter's afternoon, I thought of all that had changed in the past ten days: all that had happened in the past two. A few flakes of snow fluttered past the windscreen, and after a few miles I noticed that the fields were pale with settling snow. The lines of one of Robert Frost's poems came to me:

> *For I have promises to keep*
> *And miles to go before I sleep*

New loyalties, new promises: how could I reconcile them with the old ones, - my marriage vows, my duty towards Peter's children, to his congregation? Tomorrow would be New Year's Eve, a turning point in the calendar. It must, inevitably, be a turning point in my life.

I wanted so much to share all this with Bruno. Now there was the added obstacle of Heloise. I felt a stab of jealousy when I thought of her. Had she too stayed at Foxgloves, sung with Bruno at the piano? Worse still, had she found Elowen's well, looked deep into it and drunk of its water? The phonic similarity of the two names occurred to me suddenly and I wondered what it meant. Elowen, my lost child, lay in a cold little grave, while this girl lived and thrived; beautiful, musical and talented, - the confident, all-American teenager, no doubt, enjoying her 'father's' favour and the privilege of his fame as a musician. Another thought struck me: she might have been at the Presbytery with Bruno when he received my annual missive. Each year I sent him a card for St Cecilia's Day, November 22nd. Usually the card was a reproduction of Raphael's St Cecilia and I signed it simply 'C'. Last year I had enclosed a lock of my hair, stuck inside the card in the shape of a 'C'; underneath I had written: *Littore quot conchae......*, - hoping that it would provoke some sort of response.

I took a wrong turning and went five miles out of my way. The snow had turned into a sullen drizzle now, and what light there had been was fading. I should have left London earlier, but had valued the time Dominic and I had spent together after we had left the Convent. We had had a light lunch in a café near the Tube station where we had met, and he had told me more about his and Donal's life in Ireland before the death of their adoptive parents. Poor children, I thought, to have led such a sheltered and well-ordered life in a beautiful house, and then to be catapulted into a world of coarse brutality and perversion. I resolved to make amends, as far as it was in my power to do so.

⸙

"How was your aunt?" Peter's voice was stiff with resentment. "Not at all happy when I left," I replied, taking my cue from him.

Agnes and Elizabeth were sitting at the kitchen table playing cards when I walked in. Glyph was sitting contentedly on a pile of clean towels on the chair by the Aga. The Christmas cake, which looked as if it had been butchered rather than cut, sat precariously at one end of the table. It was a cosy, untidy scene. The girls got up to give me a hug.

"Are we glad to see you home, Ma!" Lizzie said. "Dad's been such a *misery* while you've been away. He made us do all the washing-up and didn't even say thank you."

"Yes, *and* sweep the floor and tidy our rooms," said Agnes. "*And* he came to inspect them afterwards."

I looked pointedly at the sink, where the dishes from at least two meals were waiting to be washed. "So you missed me then," I said with a wink. "Any chance of a cup of tea and a piece of that Christmas cake, before it all disappears? I'll leave it till tomorrow to ask whether you've had time to write your thank-you letters, shall I, seeing that you've been so overworked."

"Oh *Ma*!" they groaned in unison.

Peter stood unsmiling by the door, then turned and walked out, saying over his shoulder: "By the way, there's some post for you on the chest in the hall."

"See what we mean?" said Lizzie. He's just *so* grumpy."

Edmund had gone to a film in town with a friend so I decided to wait up for him, thus putting off the moment when Peter and I would find ourselves alone together. His expression had been ominous all the evening and it was with relief that I heard him shut his study door and go up to bed.

Having restored order in the kitchen both before and after raiding the freezer for a makeshift meal, I sat on the other side of the Aga from Glyph, who smiled at me benignly, to look at the mail which had arrived in my absence. There were a couple of late Christmas cards and three New Year cards addressed to us both, and a thank-you letter from Mrs Gray. At the bottom of the pile was an envelope which set my heart pounding; I knew every flourish of that beautiful, bold handwriting. It had been posted in London on Christmas Eve. I slit it open with shaking hands and took out a card, - a picture of St Cecilia that I had not seen before. Inside it was signed, simply, 'B', with the other half of the Ovid quotation written beneath it: ...... *tot sunt in amore dolores.* Enclosed within the card was a small hand-bill, advertising a concert at St John's, Smith Square on February 22nd – my birthday – by the Orchester und Chor der Matthias-Kirche, conducted by Bruno Sabra. Could this possibly be an invitation, I wondered. After all these years of self-denial, could he be asking me to break the period of abstinence he had imposed upon me?

Hearing a car pull up on the drive, I hastily gathered up the pile of letters and hid them amongst the towels beneath Glyph's cushion.

"Perhaps you feel ready to tell me about your two days away, Cecily," Peter said when we found ourselves alone the following morning. The girls had gone into town on the bus to spend their Christmas money, and Edmund was having a driving lesson with the father of a friend.

I gave a much abridged account of my time away, dwelling mainly on my aunt's admission that though one twin had died, the other had survived and been given away for adoption without my permission, indeed, without my having even been aware of his existence.

"And what do you intend to do about all this?" asked Peter. "Do you feel that you have a duty towards this boy?"

"Yes, Peter, I do; I have a duty to *both* boys because one of them is my son."

"And how do you reconcile that obligation with your duty towards me and *my* children?"

"That depends very much on what conclusion *you* have come to now that you've had time for reflection – and prayer."

"Leaving that aside for a moment, I cannot imagine that you would expect *me* to help support these boys financially – or in any other way. My own daughters' school fees are crippling enough."

I did not point out that these expenses were paid for by his widowed mother.

"Of course not," I said. "No, - I intend to sell Cliff Cottage to raise the money to enable them to go to the United States."

"You have forgotten perhaps that, as your husband, I would be entitled to half the proceeds of such a sale. 'With all my worldly goods ….'et cetera, – being but *part* of your marriage vows."

I had not considered this; it was painful enough to face losing Cliff Cottage to a stranger. In spite of my years of self-imposed exile, I had always envisaged ending my days there.

"Be that as it may," I said, playing for time with the meaningless phrase, "Perhaps *you* would tell me *your* thoughts on this whole situation."

We were interrupted by the sound of a car in the drive, then a knock on the back door. It was a delivery of beer and cider for the bell-ringers that night. It was an age-old tradition for them to come to the Rectory for refreshment after their three-hour peal to ring in the New Year.

Edmund returned from his lesson before we had a chance to resume our discussion.

"Mr Hodge says I still need more driving practice before my Test next week," he announced. "Could you spare me some time this afternoon, Ma?"

"What's up with Dad?" he said to me later as he drove (too fast) along the narrow road through the village. "Was it something I said or did? He's been like a bear with a sore head ever since Christmas"

"Slow down, for heaven's sake! No, it was something *I* said or did. We just haven't had a chance to sort it out yet. Now I want you to stop opposite the War Memorial and do a three-point turn."

I t was not until the following morning that I had an opportunity to look at Bruno's card again. I had removed it from its hiding place early on my first morning home, and placed it in my locked bureau with my other treasures. Now, before the family were up and about, I took it out and scanned it again. The picture, by Sidney Meteyard, 1868 – 1947, was lovely, and typical of its period, showing the Saint seated at the organ. Her hair, though neatly confined in style, was much the same colour as my own. I inspected the writing inside, and the leaflet enclosed, which advertised a concert of Hungarian music, including Kodály's Te Deum and Missa Brevis, for soloists, mixed choir and orchestra.

I decided that this was indeed a request that I should attend, if not a summons, otherwise, why would Bruno have enclosed it? I hugged the card to my heart; there were hurdles to overcome, but nothing in Heaven or Earth was going to prevent me from attending that concert.

———

An uneasy truce between Peter and me lasted until the girls went back to their boarding school and Ed returned to Oxford, where he was in his first year. In the meantime, I had written to Mr Trethewy, my Cornish solicitor, asking him to set in motion the sale of Cliff Cottage. I opened his acknowledgement as Peter and I sat at breakfast on our first morning alone together.

"It seems there is 'an interested party' wanting to buy Cliff Cottage before it has even been put on the market," I said.

"So you have gone ahead with your plan without my permission," Peter said coldly.

"It didn't occur to me that I needed your *permission*, Peter. You knew my intentions regarding the current situation."

"You have made it quite clear where your loyalties lie and I find it increasingly difficult to tolerate this state of affairs. My mother thinks ____"

"Your *mother?*" I shouted. "You've discussed this with your *mother?*"

"Certainly I have. She pointed out that Jane would not have wanted her children to be brought up by someone capable of such calumny and deceit. As you know, she has never been happy about our union."

"Perhaps I should ask you whether you consulted her before or after you consulted the Almighty. It sounds to me as though *she* had the last word."

I shall not recount here the rest of our acrimonious exchange, except to say that it made it very easy for me to leave.

THIRTEEN

I went to the Irish pub again on Friday, January 28th. I remember the date exactly because of what happened on the following Sunday. It was more crowded than it had been on the first occasion a month earlier, so there was no unnerving silence to greet me this time.

"Is it some more songs you've come to sing us then, Missus?" asked the landlord. "Ould Pat is after askin' for ye every night since."

"I may give you a song or two later," I answered, "But I need to speak to the Maloney boys first."

He pointed to where Donal was sitting with the man I had rightly suspected was Geraghty. They did not stand as I approached, and both assumed a hostile expression above folded arms, as if to discourage me from coming closer. I pulled out a chair and sat down at their table.

"No Dominic tonight?" I enquired.

"He'll be after going to Confession," said Geraghty. "Though of all the feckers in this room, he'd be the least likely to have anything to confess."

"You are Mr Geraghty, I believe?" I did not offer my hand, sensing that it would be refused. "I'm glad to meet you at last. I understand that you would know the right people to ask about providing the necessary papers, so that the boys can prove their identities when they turn eighteen in August."

"Where's yer feckin' money then? 'Twill cost you dear all right."

"I will pay you a certain amount now, - say ten percent, - and the balance on completion of the agreement; in front of witnesses, of course."

"What would ye be needing feckin' witnesses for at all?"

"It would protect both our interests," I answered. "You choose one – not Donal – and I'll choose another."

After we had haggled for a while and finally come to an agreement, I walked over to the table where old Pat was sitting and asked him if he would witness my signature to a transaction, in return for one or two songs. He readily agreed and Geraghty brought his own witness over. I handed over the money, and the simple document I had prepared before I came was duly signed by both parties and their witnesses.

All this time Donal had sat scowling into his drink. I invited him to sing with me, but he tossed his head in refusal. This time, I sang lullabies such as *The Castle of Dromore*, and finished with one in Irish, which I had learnt attentively from Mary O'Hara's recording. My audience was amazed, - but it was Donal's attention I sought. He and Geraghty did not applaud with the rest, I noticed.

I took my leave soon afterwards, saying that I would return on Monday to discuss the details of the identity papers.

"Please ask Dominic to be present, too," I said.

"Feckin' women," muttered Geraghty, "Giving their feckin' orders."

"By the way, Mr Geraghty," I said quietly, "The word is 'fucking' in England, - but in both countries it is almost always used entirely out of context."

Geraghty's jaw dropped and for the first time I saw the faintest hint of admiration on Donal's face – and felt ashamed that I had had to stoop so low to impress him.

———

W at had seemed pleased to see me back. "If you stay with me, it will stop me taking in unsuitable lodgers," he said. "By the way, if I can put it so indelicately, dear girl, did you jump or were you pushed?"

"A bit of both, really," I said. "As I got ready to jump, he pushed, - or was it that he pushed so I had to jump? No, I think it was mutual. I said some rather unforgivable things, about his mother in particular and about religion in general; blasphemous too, I was told, - or was it heretical?"

"Blasphemous, angel? Pray expound."

"I mentioned that we are told in the Bible that God made man in his own image, but said I thought it was the other way round: Man has made God in his own image. That goes for all this Catholic v. Protestant stuff as well, don't you think? Where are love, peace and forgiveness? What happened to tolerance and forbearance, beauty and truth? Each faction seems to interpret the concept of God according to its own received preconceptions."

"Well, as a half-Jewish, dissenting Agnostic, I have to say that I just don't know what to believe," he said, whereupon we laughingly abandoned the finer points of Theology and opened the bottle of wine I had brought for him."

"Here's to the future and whatever it may hold," he said, raising his glass and touching it to mine.

———— ⬦ ————

The immediate future, as it befell, held the horrifying event which came to be known, almost from the outset, as Bloody Sunday: the shooting in Derry, by British soldiers, of predominantly Catholic, unarmed civilians on a peaceful Civil Rights march. As I write this now, it has taken nearly forty years for a Prime Minister, himself but a child at the time of the atrocity, to apologise to the people of Derry.

Wat and I had taken the train and spent the day in Brighton, 'for a healing breath of sea air', though it was a far cry from the seaside as I knew and loved it; cold and bleak, too, on a winter Sunday. We heard the news when we got back to the flat, and it was with trepidation that I pushed open the door of the pub on the following night.

To my great relief, Dominic was there and came forward to greet me. He looked drawn and anxious and his voice was grave.

"Donal's gone, - with Geraghty and O'Neill," he told me. "I couldn't stop him. You heard the news, of course?"

"I did," I replied, "And was afraid for him – for both of you."

"They wanted me to go with them, but I told them that I must keep our appointment with you."

"I am very relieved to see you here, Dominic. What can we do for the best? Would it be any use if I went over there?"

"I think it would be dangerous for you, Mrs Knight," he said. "Since I've been in England, I've realised that 'Protestants' are just ordinary people who go to a different church and worship in a different way. In Derry, where the population is mainly Catholic, 'Protestant' is a dirty word. Protestants or Loyalists, as you might say, enjoy rights which Catholics don't have; one of those rights is to dress up and march with banners through Catholic areas. The British soldiers are seen as supporters of those rights, while not respecting the rights of the majority."

"There is so much to understand now I've found myself in a completely different world," I said. "You must educate me further before I go rushing off to defend one of my 'boys'. By the way, please don't call me Mrs Knight. Call me .... I don't know ... something else. I wish it could be 'Mother'."

"I wish it too," he said quietly.

A week later there was a letter from Mr Trethewy, to whom I had notified my temporary address, telling me that contracts were ready to be exchanged on Cliff Cottage and enclosing the necessary documents for me to sign. I had misgivings when I read that the buyer was a London solicitor on behalf of an American client, but he was offering a good price and the money was urgently needed. The remainder of the six-month winter booking (a writer) could run its course, I was assured, and the summer bookings would be honoured. Mr Trethewy said he was sorry to hear that my husband and I were estranged and that he would advance the deposit, less expenses, as soon as possible.

Dominic and I met now, not in the pub, but in the little café where we had had lunch after our visit to the convent. I had to put up with knowing looks from the proprietor, as if I were a cradle-snatching seducer of teenage boys, but otherwise it was a convenient venue, being near the tube station for me and not far from Dominic's digs. He would regularly ring Bernadette Geraghty from the phone-box outside for news of Donal and the others. She would usually say, cryptically, that they were active, but safe. We both worried about the word 'active', which we knew had much more to do with aggression and revenge than peace and reconciliation. After the events of Bloody Sunday they would feel more than justified in seeking to avenge the deaths and injuries of those innocent victims.

The day after I had received the first payment for Cliff Cottage, I went to the box-office of St John's, Smith Square, in person, to buy a ticket for Bruno's Hungarian Concert. I was surprised when the young woman at the desk asked my name. When I told her it was Cecilia Trelawney, she looked puzzled.

"Not Cecilia *James*, then?" she asked.

"That was my maiden name," I said, truthfully.

Her face cleared. "It was the name Cecilia that rang a bell. There is a ticket already arranged for you," she said and, sifting through a small pile of envelopes, she produced one with my name on it. Inside was not only a ticket, but an invitation to a Reception afterwards.

"Nothing to pay," she said, "But there will be a collection for the funds of the Chorus and Orchestra, many of whom are

Hungarian nationals who managed to get out before the events of 1956. But you probably know all about that."

When I got back to the flat, Wat said that there had been an urgent call from Dominic, asking me to meet him at the café as soon as I could. Donal, I thought ... something has happened to him. I was full of foreboding as I travelled to meet Dominic.

My presentiment was right; Donal was in hospital with a serious head injury, having been hit on the temple by a sharp stone thrown by a member of a Loyalist gang while he was working to strengthen a street barrier with a group of Catholic youths.

"I must go to him," Dominic said, desperation in his voice. "Bernadette hinted that Geraghty and O'Neill are being hunted by the RUC. She dare not visit in hospital in case the association with those two puts *him* in danger of arrest."

"No, I will go," I said firmly. "You too could be in danger by association. Can we enlist the help of your friend, Mr Fahy, d'you think?"

FOURTEEN

Although it would have been hard to love Donal, even if I had known for certain that he was my son, it was heart-rending, nevertheless, to see the slight figure in the hospital bed, his head bandaged so that his features were unrecognisable. The fire that had burned so fiercely seemed all but extinguished. Except for a faint pulse in his neck, just visible below the bandaging, and the almost imperceptible rise and fall of his chest, it was as if that wild spirit had already flown, leaving a broken shell in its wake.

"Are you a relative at all?" a nurse had asked when I reached the hospital ward.

"I am his mother," I said, positively. "I've just arrived from England."

"He's in a bad way and still unconscious," she said. "Of course you'll want to see him, but I just wanted to prepare you, Mrs ___"

"Knight," I supplied, thinking it might be best to use the name on my driving licence. "My son's surname is Maloney."

"I should warn you that the police want to speak to him as soon as he regains consciousness," she said.

"Naturally they will," I replied, though with misgivings. "May I see him now?"

215

Tom Fahy had met me at the airport and brought me to the hospital by car. He had arranged for me to stay at his uncle's house. It was well away from the troubled area and quite near the hospital. He would wait for me, he said, and take me there afterwards, before going back to work.

———⁂———

I had not been long in Fr McDonald's house before I decided that, if all Catholic priests were like him, I would convert straight away. So moved was I by his ready kindness, - and by the plight of the boy in the hospital bed – that during the course of the evening I told him the whole sorry story of why I had come to be there at all.

"The catharsis of Confession," I finished by saying. "Now, don't you have to give me a penance? And how do I qualify for Absolution? Or is that denied to me because I was not brought up in the True Faith?"

"I do not recall your having prefaced your account with the words: 'Bless me, Father, for I have sinned'."

"True; but if the world sees me as a sinner, surely, so would a priest. Certainly my husband does."

"That is because he's hurt and confused; lacking in tact, also, by enlisting his mother's support against you. He set fire to his bridges too hastily. Had he been advising one of his congregation in a pastoral capacity, he would have advocated an altogether different course of action."

"Do you think that I was justified in feeling a duty to the two boys?" I asked. "I would value your judgement, as that of both priest and wise counsellor."

"I am not going to *judge* you, Cecily, or your choices and actions. You chose the course which you felt was natural and right. I feel that both you and the boys are more sinned against than sinning – to quote whoever it was that first said that. Dominic told me a great deal about his young life, both good and appallingly bad. The other boy I've not met yet. He sounds to be more in need of 'saving'. There is something incorruptible about Dominic himself."

"It was Shakespeare – *King Lear*, - the sinning bit," I said.

"Was it? I'd forgotten – if I ever knew. God protect me from the woman who knows more than I do." He roared with laughter. "There's catharsis in humour too, you know."

"I value it greatly," I laughed in agreement, "Though life has not been very humorous of late. To get back to the boys: I worry that I will be the last person Donal wants to see when he comes to," I said. "But what else can I do?"

"If it would help, I can come with you. At least if he sees my clerical black he won't think I'm St Peter at the Pearly Gates when he opens his eyes."

"Ah – but what about Purgatory?" I said. "Doesn't that come first?"

Fr McDonald groaned. "Let's not go into that tonight. It'll take more than one evening to indoctrinate *you*, I can see," he said, laughing again.

———

M y days fell into a pattern: sitting at Donal's bedside during the day, reading, writing letters or silently learning songs, and later, discussing everything under the sun with Fr

McDonald, or taking a back seat at his Peace meetings. Dominic would usually phone each evening to ask after Don, and at last, one evening I was able to give him the good news that a nurse had just phoned to say that he had regained consciousness.

The priest accompanied me the following morning, and went ahead of me to introduce himself and tell Donal that I had sat at his bedside every day for the past week. At length he beckoned me over.

"Welcome back, Donal," I said. "I was so afraid we had lost you."

He said nothing, but looked from one to the other of us as if trying to work out how we came to be together at his bedside.

"Cecily came over as soon as she heard that you'd been injured," he explained again. "She is going to stay at my house until you are better and then take you home."

"Where's Domino?" the boy asked faintly.

"He's back in London," I said, "but he rings up every night to see how you are. He said to be sure to give you his love and say he's longing to see you back soon."

Donal nodded; then his eyelids drooped as if he wanted to sleep.

"We'll go and get some coffee and come back later on," I said. "I expect it's all a huge effort for you at the moment."

—⁂—

"Wasn't that easier than you expected?" Fr McDonald asked as we sat on a bench outside the ward, sipping our slot-machine coffee.

"Yes, it was; thank you so much for being there," I said. "There was none of the old aggro, - though that doesn't mean that it won't come back when he's better."

One or two of the staff and visitors greeted the priest as they passed. One old woman stopped and stared openly at me.

"Now then, Rosaleen, who d'you think this lady is then; my wife or my daughter?" he joked.

She laughed nervously. "Oh Father, you will tease me so," she said in a shocked voice, and passed on her way.

Just then we saw two RUC men go into the ward.

"I think we'd best be party to this if it's Donal they're after," said my companion. We rose from the bench and followed quickly, slipping past them as they spoke to a nurse at the desk.

I tapped Donal lightly on the shoulder and he opened his eyes. "When the police come to you, tell them nothing. Pretend to be even more dopy and confused than you already are." The boy looked at the priest for affirmation and he nodded briefly.

"Father, Missus, would you excuse us a moment? We need to talk to this young man."

"He is hardly in a fit state to help you," Fr McDonald said. "This lady is his mother. I'm sure she will answer any questions."

"We have reason to believe that you and two persons known to you were involved in a nail-bomb attack on British Army personnel on Sunday, January 30th." The spokesman addressed Donal directly. His eyelids fluttered, and then closed.

"As you can see," I said, "he is barely conscious. I must insist on continuing this interview on his behalf. For one thing, I can tell you, without any doubt that he was in England on the date in question. Perhaps you would like to tell me the names of the two acquaintances you mentioned."

"We are holding two individuals, known troublemakers, who deny that they were taking part in the Civil Rights march on that day."

"If their names are Geraghty and O'Neill, I can confirm that they and my son were in a public house in Kilburn, London, that day. The landlord and several customers would corroborate that. Here, I have a telephone number." I rummaged in my bag and produced a piece of paper with the number written on it. The other man copied it into a notebook, after which he addressed me for the first time:

"And what is *your* address, Madam?"

"I live in London and have come over to take my son home. At present I am staying with this good friend of mine who, as you probably know is a prominent figure in the Peace Movement – a cause made considerably more difficult by the *appalling* events of the day you mentioned, the shooting *in cold blood* of innocent civilians, attempting to secure equal rights with those given to a usurping minority hundreds of years ago. I tell you, sir, it makes me ashamed to be English and Protestant."

"That was quite a speech, Madam. Tell me, what do you intend to do about it?"

"Oh," I answered, fired up now and warming to my subject. "I know people in high places: my father has recently retired from the Foreign Office, for instance. Perhaps I'd better come and talk to your Superior Officer."

"That will not be necessary, Madam," he said.

I had glanced at Donal whilst delivering this spiel. His eyes had opened momentarily and widened in astonishment before closing again, I noticed.

"I *will* come to the Police Station, however, when I have finished here," I said. "I would not like to think that two men might be thrown into prison if my evidence could prevent it. This internment without trial is another disgrace."

———⊶⊷———

That same night I met Bernadette Geraghty for the first time. She came to the house to ask after Donal and to say that her husband and his cousin, who had been held for questioning by the RUC, had now been released with a caution. Fr McDonald introduced us.

"I think you should let them know that their release was due to Mrs Knight's confirmation of their alibi," he said. "What they do now is up to them, but it is important that Donal should go somewhere right away from their influence as soon as he is better."

Bernadette agreed, while looking at me closely. "So you're Donal's mother," she said. "Couldn't he have done with your guidance long ago, instead of being abandoned to that terrible institution?"

Fr McDonald stepped in quickly. "I think we can trust Bernadette with the truth, Cecily. Just outline the situation for her, will you? I'll leave you two to talk for a while."

It was later that evening that I realised with a wrench that I was not going to be able to attend Bruno's Concert in two days' time. One day had run into another while we had waited for Donal's recovery, and the most important date in my calendar had approached almost unnoticed. I phoned Wat in desperation and asked if he would go in my place and try to explain to Bruno why I could not be there.

"My darling, I am lecturing that night, otherwise I would go like a shot. Can I find someone else for you?"

"No, I think I shall have to ask Dominic." I told him where to find the ticket and the invitation.

I phoned the pub and asked for Dominic again. I had already told him the good news about Donal. To my relief he was still there.

"Dominic, dear, I'm going to ask you to do something very, very important to me …"

FIFTEEN

The immediate problem now was how and when to move Donal to safer ground than the hospital. Tom Fahy came round the next evening to discuss the options that we might consider. One of them was that it might be better to return to England via the Republic of Ireland because of Donal's suspected association, through Geraghty and O'Neill, with the Provisional IRA. He thought it was only a matter of time before they were held on some other charge. There were ways and means of getting over the border checkpoints, - or even circumventing them – he said; an ambulance was one possibility; a funeral car was another and, being less dramatic, might attract less attention.

It was not only these preoccupations that kept me from sleeping at night: the other burning question was whether Dominic would succeed in attending not only the Concert, but the Reception afterwards; and then, whether he would get a chance to speak to Bruno and explain my absence.

Dominic did not phone on the evening of my birthday. I missed his call, but at least it meant that he had attempted to fulfil his mission.

"You're like a cat on hot bricks this evening, Cecily, "Fr McDonald said after supper. "I know you've a great deal on your mind, but you've hardly eaten a morsel and your mind has been quite elsewhere. I'm not used to my pearls of wisdom dropping unheeded by the wayside – to mix my metaphors. Women, in particular, usually hang on my every word."

I had to laugh. "I *am* sorry, Father. Actually, it's my birthday today and I suppose I'm remembering happier times – not that the present company isn't absolutely delightful," I added hastily.

"You silly woman! You should have told me. I may be a man of God but I'm not psychic. I don't suppose you ever thought you'd spend a birthday with an ancient R.C. priest," he chuckled

"No, but the last ten have been spent with a younger, but much stuffier, Anglican one."

"Who by now is wishing that *you* were there instead of his mother, no doubt. Incidentally, did you know that this date is traditionally held to be the birthday of St. Mary Magdalene?"

"I thought that was in July."

"That's her Feast Day – the 22nd."

"Well, I suppose it figures, as the Americans say: I share a birthday with the woman taken in adultery, - the fallen woman, the sinner."

"On the contrary: modern scholarship is beginning to dispute this long-held assumption so beloved of the Church – the penitent sinner, saved from stoning and forgiven by Christ; the sinner turned saint, her name given to the shameful institutions which still exist today, as you well know. This is now thought to be another Mary and not the Magdalene at all. Anyway, whether you are sinner or saint, I have just the thing for a celebration of *your* day. Come with me to the cellar. I think it will be well chilled."

We sat up well into the night, sharing a bottle of champagne in front of the dying fire. And it was well into the night when the shrill summons of the telephone halted our comfortable conversation.

"It's for you Cecily," said the old priest. "Not Dominic, not Wat, - the husband, perhaps?"

"He doesn't know I'm here," I said, under my breath.

"Well, I'll go to bed and leave you to it, shall I? Good night, my dear."

I went to the study and picked up the phone cautiously. "Hello?"

"Cecilia! Can that really be you?" The line was crackly but the deep, rich voice was unmistakable. It was several seconds before I could speak.

"Bruno?" I breathed; "Oh Bruno!"

"My dearest, lovely girl," he said. "The charming young Dominic explained everything to me."

"*Everything*, Bruno?"

"He explained where you were, and why you could not be at the Concert tonight."

"Did he explain who *he* was?"

"He was very correct and diplomatic, but he was so concerned for your safety and that of the other boy that I persuaded him to tell me all he knew. He gave me a mere outline, - but what an incredible story."

"And did he realise ... ?"

"On some deep level, perhaps; but I think I gave nothing away, except that I too was very anxious for you and would do all I could to help."

"Oh Bruno!" I could only sigh and sob in my relief at hearing his voice. Gone was the steely resolve of the last few days.

"I shall change my plans and come to you tomorrow. I cannot leave you to face this alone."

"No, Bruno," I pleaded. "There is nothing on earth I need more than to see you here beside me at this moment, but there are plans for our return as soon as possible, - and I have wonderful help and support. Just promise me that you'll be there when I get back – and never, *ever*, send me into the wilderness without you again."

"We will talk about that when we are together. I shall go to Foxgloves and do some reading and composing while I wait for you. Will you come there to me?"

"As soon as I am able. I cannot tell you what it means to me to hear your beloved voice."

"My sweet Cecilia! Am I too late to wish you a happy birthday?"

"Yes, it's after midnight, so you're a day late. Promise me we shall spend my next birthday together."

"Go safely, my love," he said. "Telephone me whenever you can." The line began to break up but I just heard him say: "God bless you and bring you and the boy safely home."

Fr McDonald did not ask questions the following morning but his eyes were bright with curiosity. Instead, he elicited my confidence with a few well-placed observations.

"You look a different person this morning, Cecily," he said. "The champagne must have suited you; it's left some of its sparkle."

"Has it, Father? It was so kind of you, and it *was* a happy birthday."

"It seems as though it ended in a rapprochement. I wonder who told your husband that you were here."

"The phone call wasn't from my husband."

"A mystery man, then; with a very pleasant voice – an un-English voice, I noticed. Not your father, clearly: it was hardly an Old-Etonian voice."

"Nice try, Father! Actually it was my … someone I have known for a very long time."

"Not the father of your _____"

"Yes."

I told him about the concert which I was hoping to attend, and that I had asked Dominic to go in my place.

"Oh Cecily, this is the man you think of as your true husband, is it not?" The mischievous look had gone from his face which was now full of compassion.

"I would have followed him to the ends of the earth and beyond if only he had let me," I said.

"And yet you put this headstrong young fellow – violent, even, – who might or might not be your son, before your lover."

"Yes, I suppose I did; duty before love, - or is it guilt? I just don't know."

"Just call it love, Cecily. There are so many different kinds in the world. I pray that one day it will prevail over hatred and violence, prejudice and bigotry."

———

I went alone to see Donal that day. He seemed much better, but I was not pleased to see the look of defiance returning. I decided to nip it in the bud.

"Look here, Donal," I said quietly but firmly. "When you are discharged from here, you have two choices: either you go back to Geraghty and rejoin the militants, in which case you will very soon find yourself, and them, in prison; *or* you do exactly as you are told by the people who are prepared to put their lives and reputations on the line to save you. And that number includes me. I have an urgent need to get back to England as soon as possible – alive. If you want to come with me, well and good; if not, you must sink or swim on your own."

"I want to get the fellas who did this to me," he said, touching his head gingerly.

"Oh well, in that case I'll go home right now, shall I?"

"No, I will come," he said, grudgingly.

"Please yourself," I said, feeling real resentment towards him. But for his cussedness, I thought, I could have been in Bruno's beloved presence at this very moment.

D ominic sounded animated on the phone that evening. "I had to keep pinching myself," he said. "The great Bruno Sabra! Did you get his call?"

"I did, Dominic; very late. Thank you so much for going."

"It was such an experience. I never thought I would ever meet someone as famous as that."

"I'm afraid it won't cut as much ice with your friends and workmates as it would have done had it been the Beatles or the Rolling Stones."

"Who are *they*?" he asked, laughing. It was good to hear him so happy. He told me of the difficulty he had had in gaining admission on my ticket. I had anticipated this and had told him to go very early and expect to be treated like a Soviet agent.

"Security was very tight," he told me. "I had to beg and plead like some crazy fan. In the end, someone took Dr Sabra the note I'd written, - with the three Latin words like you told me – and he sent one back saying, 'Please admit Mr Dominic James in place of Mrs Cecilia James.' Why does he call you 'Cecilia'?"

"It's a long story, Dominic. I gather you told Bruno quite a long story too."

"I hope I didn't say too much. There were loads of people wanting to talk to him but he spent ages talking to me at the party afterwards. He wants me to take up the clarinet seriously again, and he introduced me to one of the Hungarian clarinet-tists, István Klafsky, who wants to hear me play."

"That's wonderful for you; I'm so glad."

"It made me want to play in a proper orchestra – especially under a conductor like Bruno Sabra."

"I'm sure you will one day, Dominic. Now you have made his acquaintance, I think he will help you in every possible way."

"He said you had once helped him with an opera he was composing when you were about my age – that you were his Muse."

"That's right, I did, yes. I'll sing you some of the songs one day."

"He thinks a lot of you and is worried about you being over there. I am too."

"Don't worry, Dominic. We shall be home very soon."

SIXTEEN

Four days later, a large, black car passed safely through the checkpoint on the border southwest of Derry. Apart from the black-suited driver, it carried a black-cassocked, white-haired priest, while in the back seat sat a woman in a black suit and black-veiled hat, and a young, cowled Franciscan monk. They were on their way to a funeral in Sligo. Only the priest and his driver would return later in the day; the other two occupants of the car, being close family of the deceased, planned to stay on after the obsequies.

Tom Fahy and a trusted colleague had masterminded the plan, which included arrangements for our onward journey by rail to Dublin, where we were to be met by Dominic's erstwhile benefactress and 'godmother', Mrs Moira Harrington. Tom had called round the previous evening to tell us the order of events. I insisted on settling my account with him for all he had done, including a contribution to my living expenses for his uncle, which he promised to give him after my departure.

The parting from Fr McDonald himself was emotional, especially on my part. Nowadays, many people hug each other unrestrainedly on greeting or parting if they wish, but it was not so then. However, I did embrace the old man as I thanked him for all he had done for us, his hospitality to me in particular.

"My dear, it has been a great pleasure. I hope we shall meet again in less troubled times. I shall pray for you, especially as you try to cope with all the various men-folk in your life. Give my love and blessings to Dominic, won't you."

"I will, Father, - and I'll write to you and tell you how things are going." I promised.

To Donal he said: "If this lady is indeed your mother, you are a very fortunate young man. If she is not, you are just as fortunate, for a complete stranger has been prepared to sacrifice a great deal for you. Honour her and care for her and try to find it in your heart to love her." He laid a hand gently on the boy's head. "God bless you, my son." Donal glanced at me briefly and looked at the ground; I noticed that he had coloured slightly.

We had a compartment to ourselves on the train, and whereas I would have welcomed the opportunity to get to know Donal better, - it was, after all, the first time we had been together without an audience - small talk seemed to be a useless preamble to a more fruitful dialogue. My remarks on the scenery were all but ignored, so I took a book from my bag and started to read. Donal closed his eyes and appeared to be dozing.

"What's it about, your book?" His voice startled me.

"It's a history of Ireland?"

"Why would you want to read that, being English?"

"It seems a good idea to learn about this country. It's so beautiful, the people are so warm and welcoming, and yet it has such a tragic history; and, before you say it, yes the English have a lot to answer for."

"Haven't they altogether; that's why it's time for revenge."

"But it isn't a new problem, Donal. There are layers and layers of history to unravel. Oddly enough, when you spoke, I was reading about your namesake, Donal óg O'Donnell, the Donegal chieftain. In 1258 he returned from Scotland, bringing with him a fighting force of mercenaries to fight the Anglo-Normans. This was hundreds of years before the Catholic-Protestant trouble. To my mind, the present troubles are more racial than religious. But I expect you remember all this from your school History lessons."

"I can't remember much about that. History's boring, anyway." He closed his eyes again as if to discourage further converse, and I did not seek to pursue it further.

—∞—

M rs Moira Harrington had no difficulty in identifying us when we alighted from the train in Dublin. She had been told to look out for a red-haired woman with a dark-haired young man, she said. She greeted us warmly and asked after Dominic; then drove us to her very pleasant house where she welcomed us with tea and cakes.

Later, after an evening meal, over which she must have taken considerable trouble earlier in the day, she and I sat on, talking in the dining-room, while her husband, Gerald, suggested to Donal that they watched television. She offered a solution to a problem that had been occupying my mind for some time: what arrangements to make for Donal in the immediate future and how to keep him from pursuing the burning ambition that had nothing to do with his intellect, namely, his willingness to fight to the death for the dream of an Ireland once more united.

"I can't see any future for him if he returns to the building site," I said. "Only a return to the influences of Geraghty and his cronies."

"Oh, the idealism of youth!" Moira sighed. "Unfortunately, one cannot rewrite History; 'the sins of the fathers' et cetera."

"I think it's the sins of the mothers that Donal has difficulties with, as well."

"Ah! The men of Ireland have always thought those more reprehensible," she said.

"Especially when they are committed by a Protestant?" I asked.

"Oh no! They are far more unforgiving of their own. Think of the Magdalene Laundries in this country. They are not just for girls who have babies out of wedlock: many of their permanent residents – prisoners, really – are daughters or sisters of men who *think* that the girls have 'sinned' sexually, or might do so in the future."

"Strange to think how close the attitudes of Puritanism and Catholicism are, in many ways," I observed. "Yet the men of the North, while setting similar standards for their women-folk, fight and kill each other according to whichever religious persuasion they were born into."

"Or adopted into, in the boys' case," Moira said, smiling. "Which brings me back to Donal. Gerald and I would be very willing to have him stay here while his head is mending, - or even until valid papers can be procured. Dominic could join him here if he would like to. The boys deserve a taste of normal family life again, - if you can call this family normal." Her laugh was warm and infectious. "We might be able to mend Donal's head internally, too. Think about it, my dear. You can hardly absorb them, even temporarily, into your own household, can you?"

"That is such a kind offer," I said, tears springing to my eyes at her concern. "Are you sure that you won't regret this?"

"Not at all. We too bear guilt on behalf of a Government and a Church which have allowed such dreadful institutions as those the boys were forced to endure, to flourish for all these years. But it is not only that: I really took to Dominic. He is an exceptional young man; a brilliant clarinettist, - and having the leather-tipped fingers of a builder will not improve his playing. We have corresponded frequently over the last three years. It would be good to have him here, and company for Donal. Our daughter, Frances would be delighted, too."

"If I may use your phone," I said, "I would like to speak to him right now – or perhaps you would like to invite him yourself?"

Dominic was delighted to know that we were safe, and at the prospect of seeing Donal again. At the end of the call, I asked him to ring Polburran 331 and say that all was well and that I would be home in two days' time.

"There's a pile of letters for you, darling," Wat said, after greeting me warmly when he let me into the flat.

"I can deal with those on the train tomorrow," I said. "I must go and see Dominic tonight."

"You won't have to, pet. He's coming round here later on. We thought you'd be completely exhausted after your travels. I'm lecturing tonight so I'll miss seeing him. God, he's such a dish! What a crying shame he's not 'one of us'."

"Wat!" I protested. "Hands off at once. That would be a complication up with which I could not possibly put."

There were practical matters to attend to before Dominic came round, such as a trip to the Launderette along the road and various phone calls, the most important being that I would be coming *home* the following day.

SEVENTEEN

Once I was settled on the train to Cornwall, I opened my
pile of mail, starting with my mother's letter.

Dear Cecily,

*Your father and I were very shocked and upset to
read your letter when we returned from Jo'burg last
week, - where, by the way, we spent a <u>wonderful</u> few
months.*

*It does seem that you are determined to make a
mess of your life, even now you are well on the way to
forty, and we both feel that it is <u>very unfair</u> to blame us
as well as Aunt D., when we all thought that we were
acting for the best when you got yourself into trouble
all those years ago. It is unfortunate that these youths
have turned up on your doorstep, but now that you
have told Peter about your past mistake, they can have
no hold over you or claim on you.*

*I know that we were not pleased about your mar-
rying him in the first place, when you could have done
so much better for yourself, but you should not have
<u>walked out</u> on him; it is simply compounding your*

wrong-doing, especially as you are living with another <u>*man*</u>*. Who is going to believe that he is 'just a University friend'?*

Both your father and I think that you should write to Aunt D. and apologise for your harsh words, - and for walking out on her as you did after Christmas, for which she is justifiably upset. A letter of apology to us would not come amiss, either. In spite of your having enjoyed a good education and having wanted for nothing, you seem to have thrown away your chances of a stable marriage by your foolhardy behaviour.

If you do not return to your husband you will have to find work and support yourself. Please don't expect us to subsidise you or bail you out <u>in any way whatsoever.</u>

Needless to say, I shall not say a word about all this to the neighbours here. Ben Probert always asks after you. Only yesterday he stopped his tractor in the lane to talk to me. He and his wife have just had a third son. The eldest is eleven now. Mr and Mrs Probert Senior have moved out of the farmhouse into a new bungalow they had built.

We look forward to hearing from you when you have acknowledged the error of your ways and returned to Hutton.

Your affectionate
Mother.

I was tempted to tear the letter into small pieces and throw it from the train window, but I did not want to litter the countryside, and for some reason have kept it all these years.

My dear Cecily,

It is now some weeks since you went away and I have had time to reconsider our future together. After a useful discussion with the Archdeacon, I realise that I may have been rather hasty in my judgement of you, and in view of your past loyalty, I am willing to give you, - and our marriage – another chance.

Mother has been a tower of strength during your absence, stepping into your shoes in the matter of parish work and looking after me very well. Her heart problems, however, give me cause for concern and we both think that it would be as well for her to sell the house in Worthing and move in here. It is only a matter of time, I feel, until the Church Commissioners sell this house to some rich businessman and build a modern vicarage. When that happens, we can perhaps find Mother a suitable bungalow close by.

I look forward very much to your return. People are beginning to ask why you are away so long. The children, too, missed you at half -term, though they told me you had written to say that you had to deal with a crisis in your family. Well, I sincerely hope that 'the crisis' has been dealt with and that you will come back where you belong.

With my love and blessings,

Peter.

Darling Ma,

Where are you??? It was simplylutely garstly without you at half-term. Granny Knight was there so life was no fun at all – no laughs, no yummy cakes, no outings, *no shopping, TV censored etc etc. The only thing there was too much of was bossing and CHURCH!! Actually for once I was quite glad when it was time to go back to school, can-u-believe it – me??!! All my friends said they had a FAB time and I had to admit that on a 1 – 10 scale of absolute awfulness Ag's and my half-term scored 9.99999 recurring. Wait for it ... there is worse to come...... I overheard Granny and Dad talking and they were planning for her to come and <u>live</u> with us soon – horror of horrors! Can you please PLEASE stop that from happening? Another thing that <u>really</u> upset Ag and me was that G. wouldn't let Glyph sit on <u>his</u> chair near the aga. How mean is <u>that</u>???? She shuts him out in the cold and says go and catch a mouse, that's what you <u>exist</u> for. Anyway we sneaked downstairs and let him in and he slept in my bed both nights.*

Got to go and get ready for hockey now, ugh!!

Please write soon and <u>promise</u> to be back home by the hols.

Lotzandlotzovluvandhugz,
Lizzie. XXXXXX

Dear Lizzie: she had been only two when I came on the scene, so had no memories at all of her own mother. At twelve she was young for her age, fun-loving, affectionate and spirited. I had talked to her and prepared her for 'becoming a woman', and had asked Agnes to look out for her if it happened at school, but there was no sign of it so far. Agnes herself was quieter, studious and very anxious to earn her father's praise in whatever she did. I realised that both girls would be devastated if I did not return. However, as I sat on the train speeding towards Bruno on that blustery March day, I refused to think about anything beyond the next few days and packed away a host of problems and concerns to deal with later. The time would come all too soon, I felt sure, when they would confront me again.

EIGHTEEN

And so, after eighteen years of exile, - half my life thus far – I was travelling towards my homeland again, speeding past all the familiar landmarks: towns and villages, fields and hills, sea and moorland and at last the great bridge over the Tamar; primroses, daffodils and rhododendrons in wooded valleys, and, further on, the lunar landscape of the china clay heaps. Sea, mining country, stations, sea again ... and at last the end of the line approached: that place of long-remembered arrivals and departures, of greetings and partings. Being alone in the compartment, I checked my appearance, applying fresh lipstick and a touch of mascara. The clear grey-green eyes that looked back at me from the glass told nothing of the nervous flutters in my stomach. Bruno had told me that he had arranged for Mr. Burrows to meet me at the station and take me to Foxgloves. Only a few minutes' journey separated me from my beloved man. I took deep breaths to steady my pounding heart, and lifted my suitcase down from the rack.

As the train drew in, the fleeting glimpse of a silver-haired man waiting on the platform reminded me for a moment of Grandpa Joe. Recalling the intense joy of those childhood home-comings, I made my way towards the exit, borne along on a wave of nostalgia for those lost days of my childhood.

"Cecilia!" The unmistakable voice stopped me in my tracks. I dropped my suitcase and turned.

"Bruno?" The silver-haired man stood before me and took me in his arms and we stood heart to heart, clasped together, oblivious of time and place. Eventually, he held me away from him and we stood regarding each other wordlessly, shaking our heads in disbelief that this moment had actually arrived: that it was a homecoming in every sense; an acknowledgement of the affinity of spirit which had bound us from the beginning, which would bind us beyond the end.

We spoke little in the taxi; simply sat quietly together in the back seat, holding hands and looking at each other from time to time in the fading light to reassure ourselves that we were not dreaming.

The warm, golden lights of Foxgloves shone out to welcome us and, as the rear lamps of the car receded up the long lane, Bruno said:

"Perhaps I should carry you over the threshold, my own true bride."

"Just lead me in by the hand," I said. "That is symbolic enough. It would be tragic if you strained your back with such a romantic gesture. I am no longer the slender weeping willow I was when I last came here: more the mature birch." I laughed, but shakily, as he took my hand and led me into the warm kitchen, closed the door behind us and put his arms about me again.

"No. You are the noble beech in all the copper glory of autumn," he insisted. And he spun me round and unplaited my French-braided hair, lifting and parting the heavy weight of it to touch his lips to the nape of my neck. When I turned to face him again I saw that his eyes were bright with tears. Wonderingly,

I took his face in my hands and kissed each eye in turn, tasting the saltiness and drinking in the sight and the scent of him, the sound of his breath, the touch and the feel of him; the massive, magical presence of this man who had commanded my love, my respect and, yes, even my *obedience*, for more than half of my life. But never again, I swore to myself, would that obedience bow to my being banished from the court of our love to exile in the wilderness of separation.

"What am I thinking of? You must be exhausted and thirsty after your long journey," Bruno said. "A cup of real Cornish tea, would that be good?"

"Yes, it would be *very* good," I said. "They grow such excellent tea hereabouts." We laughed in the old, easy way.

As he put the kettle on to boil – an electric kettle this time – I looked around the old kitchen and saw that little else had changed.

"All this is mine now," Bruno said. "My aunt died about ten years ago and left it to me in her will, God bless her. It is still my secret hideaway."

"What about your ... family? Do they not visit here?"

"Never! Would I let them tread the place that your spirit has inhabited for all these years? And now you are here and it is yours also. It has upon it the imprint of our loving."

"Oh, my dear Bruno," was all I could say.

After I had drunk my tea, Bruno carried my case upstairs and showed me to a pretty bedroom opposite his own. It was feminine without being frilly and fussy.

"The best Truro has to offer," he said, as I took in the soft, peachy tones of the walls and carpet and the patterned curtains and bed-covering in a russet William Morris design; the small jug of wild daffodils on an old chest-of-drawers of stripped, waxed pine. "A most helpful lady in the store gave me her advice. When I described the hair of my very special guest, she knew exactly which colour scheme would best suit."

"But surely you cannot have had all this done in the few days since you came here this time," I said.

"It has been waiting for you for some time. I knew you would come here sooner or later," he said, pulling me towards him and kissing my neck.

He led me into the newly fitted bathroom where I admired the ivory suite and the glass-cubicled shower.

"I think you had to go further than Truro for all this," I observed.

"It is American in design, I admit. I acquired it with the help of the manager of an American-owned hotel in London. There were problems with matching pipe-work and fittings, but a wonderful London plumber installed it all in return for a fortnight here with his family."

Bruno told me that he had arranged for 'something simple and delicious' to be sent down from The Trevelyan Arms at Polburran for our supper.

"I can spare you for an hour if you would like to relax in the bath. You must be so tired. I shall not invade your privacy, my love. Just slip on the bathrobe and come, refreshed, to eat with me when you are ready. There will be champagne waiting when you come down."

How well I remember those first hours of the time I stayed at Foxgloves. I have to tell it – even if I expunge it later for decency's sake!

I emerged from the bathroom in a state of languorous lassitude and a cloud of fragrance, clad in a bathrobe of thick, soft, white American towelling. Strains of piano music had drifted up to me as I lay in the scented water: a Mozart sonata, a Chopin nocturne, a Brahms intermezzo. Now, as I entered the long music-room, Bruno leapt up from the piano stool and, sitting down at a beautifully painted harpsichord, played the Air from Handel's Water music, - a musical pun that was not lost on me.

He leapt up again and led me to a small table in front of the fire at the far end of the room. Taking a bottle of Veuve Clicquot from a silver ice-bucket, he popped the cork and filled two old-fashioned, shallow champagne glasses. Handing me one and raising his own, he said simply:

"Welcome home, dearest Cecilia."

The tiny, cold bubbles danced upwards into our faces as, eyes locked, we drank in silent celebration of our longed-for reunion.

Later, as we sat facing each other across the candle-lit table eating our 'simple and delicious' supper, Bruno said:

"There will be time enough tomorrow to walk and talk and sing and play; tonight let us simply *be* and love."

"And sleep, maybe?" I suggested.

"Indeed. I need much of that nowadays." He raised both hands to his hair. "See, I am an old man of sixty. How shall I cope with the beautiful young woman you have become?"

"Just hold me in your arms," I said. "I shall be no trouble at all to you tonight."

Tr ue to my word, I must have fallen asleep as soon as he climbed into the soft, downy bed beside me, only briefly aware of his encircling arms. It was much, much later, in the deep dark before dawn that I awoke to hear the sound of the waves dashing against the rocks below. We must have moved apart in our sleep. Blindly I reached out as if to catch a departing dream of him. To my relief, my questing fingers encountered the hair, the eyes and lips of my beloved; moved down his arms, hands, hips and over the firm, flat belly. And then .... Oh! And then ... suddenly, there was life and fire and passion; there were earthquakes and tidal waves; meteoric collisions and elemental storms. The moon and stars fell out of the sky and the whole world turned upside down. (How otherwise can one describe such a coming-together but in extravagant imagery?)

When at last the seas subsided and the wild music died away, we lay like shipwrecked sailors washed up on the shore in the first light of dawn; lay looking at each other in awe and wonderment.

"You see what happens when you postpone something for eighteen years?" I said accusingly, but tenderly, kissing his eyes, his nose, his mouth.

"We perhaps should not leave it so long before the next time," he murmured, spreading my hair over my breasts. "I see a shipwrecked mermaid; how can that be?"

"She came to the aid of Poseidon," I replied. "He could not control the force of the sea, god though he is."

"And he discovered that she was not a *mermaid* after all. Oh, Oh, Oh, my Cecilia!" There followed several minutes of tender intimacy every bit as wonderful as our earlier passion.

When Bruno drifted off to sleep again, and after I had feasted my eyes on him for some moments longer, I rose, showered quickly, pulled on Levis and a warm sweater and crept downstairs. By the back door I found a raincoat and gum-boots and, donning these, I ran across the wet lawn and along the secret path. I swear to this day that Nimrod was at my heels as I squeezed between the stone posts; that he stood beside me as I scooped the water out of Elowen's Well and brought it to my lips; that he heard my words of thanksgiving to the God who had brought me safely home.

"I knew where you would be – once I had put behind me the panic that you had vanished back into the sea," Bruno said, as I came back through the door carrying a small bunch of primroses. "I would have followed but someone stole my boots and coat."

"It was a small pilgrimage I needed to make," I said, "A devotion to the spirit of the Well of St Elowen; a morning thanksgiving."

He stood there in the kitchen with nothing on except a pair of unmatched socks. I put down the flowers, took off the wet coat and pulled him to me and hugged him, breathing in the scent of him to store in my sensory memory for the barren times that I knew must lie ahead, though I refused to dwell on them then. Soon he drew away from me.

"Today we must talk, Cecilia; *you* must talk and tell me all that has happened. There must be no more of *this* until all is told." He indicated the effect that our embrace had had on him.

"Then go and put some clothes on, for goodness sake," I whispered hoarsely, "Or I shall lose the power of speech. I'm not used to such visions."

I made breakfast, suddenly very hungry in my state of euphoric wellbeing. Bruno came down, shaved, showered and dressed this time, to scrambled eggs on buttered toast, fresh orange juice and coffee. I reminded him that breakfast was the first meal we had shared all those years ago.

"As if I could forget that day," he said. "I still cannot believe that you are here. It seems at the same time natural and normal and yet like a wonderful dream."

"It was you who made the dream come true. Tell me, my love, what made you relent after all this time and break the long fast?"

"The card with the lock of hair," he said. "That was it, of course."

"I hoped it would break your resolve," I said.

"It nearly broke my heart. I thought to myself: one day that beautiful hair will fade to grey and my lovely girl will be old. And when *she* is old, *I* shall be dead. If she sends this token after all this time, she loves me still and needs me. I must see her and hold her and love her before it is too late."

After we had cleared away and washed the dishes, we made fresh coffee and sat down again at the kitchen table facing each other.

"Now tell me everything of the past years," Bruno said, "Starting with the day we said goodbye in Cambridge."

"Everything?" I laughed. "That would take up all our precious time. No, I'll start with the most recent events and work backwards." I looked up at the old station clock on the wall. "And every hour, on the hour, we'll stop for a five-minute cuddle. Is that acceptable to you?"

"I'll show you *how* acceptable in half an hour," he said with his heart-stopping smile. "But for *three* minutes only, not five, or we might get carried away again."

NINETEEN

"And suddenly it seems that we have a son," Bruno said, wonderingly. "The young man, Dominic, - I would be proud to be his father from the little I saw of him."

"He is exceptional; and there is much of your own special quality in him, Bruno. But Donal: there is wildness and a passion in him which I recognise in myself. He would like me even less if he knew for sure that I was his mother; and I dare not tell him – or Dominic, therefore – about *you*. He could make all kinds of mischief for you – for us."

"My darling, you are no longer alone in this responsibility. At this moment, we have two sons and will provide for them both. I am content for now to stay in the background."

"I had to sell Cliff Cottage to raise money to get them to America. Completion should be any day now."

I expected Bruno to look shocked and dismayed at this revelation but he gave an enigmatic smile.

"Fear not, my love; Cliff Cottage has not gone … out of the family."

"What d'you mean, not gone … ?"

"To whom did Trethewys say it had been sold?" he asked.

"To an American buyer, dealing through a London solicitor."

"Precisely. To an American buyer – or at least one who has an American passport - who happens also to be your lover."

"Bruno! *Bruno!* But how did you _____?"

"How did I know that it was for sale? I long ago registered an interest and asked for first refusal if it ever came on the market."

"Oh, you darling, *darling* man!" I rushed around the table to hug him. "My cup over flows," I said. "You have piled happiness upon joy upon ecstasy upon _____"

"Love," he supplied. "That is the theme that runs constantly through our own particular symphony. Now take, please, your lovely bosom away from my face and sit down and continue." He looked at the clock. "There is still twelve minutes to go before it is cuddling time."

Over the course of that day the rest of the story unfolded. I finished by showing Bruno the three letters I had read on the train. He smiled wryly when he read Lizzie's.

"And because of *this* one you will leave me and return to your home." It was an observation rather than a question.

"This is my home, Bruno – or wherever *you* are. But yes, I shall have to be the one to leave this time – at least for a while."

"I cannot bear to lose you again, Cecilia."

"Oh Bruno, the irony of it all! This should be the 'happy ever after' scene, the couple walking off together into the sunset. Instead, there are loose ends to tie up or, in my case, massive obstacles to overcome. For one thing, we are both married to other people."

"And you will go back to the husband and sleep in his bed and do the things we did ____"

"NEVER!" I interrupted, loudly. "It has *never* been like that. I have viewed it as a duty, really; he has been a very undemanding husband in that respect. There is absolutely no comparison."

"Forgive me, my dearest. It was just that last night you were so wonderful, so passionate ____"

"__ that you thought I might behave as – wantonly – with anyone else? There has only ever been you; you lit the flame and it burns only for you. You *must* know that. Now, can I sing to you The Songs of Love – and try out your beautiful new harpsichord?"

That night our lovemaking was gentle and leisurely, the wild hunger of the previous night having given way to an infinite tenderness, a silken blend of precious belonging.

———

"What became of the lovely green car?" Bruno asked at breakfast the next morning.

"It didn't, after all, attract the sort of husband-material my mother had in mind," I said, laughing.

"No, actually, Peter – my husband - pointed out that it was not a practical family car, so we sold it – and his – and bought an estate car."

"You will need one here eventually, Cecilia, but for now perhaps we should hire one and explore a little."

"Have you never driven, Bruno?"

"Never. I would have no idea how to manage all those controls."

I shook my head in disbelief. "But here is a man who controls the great orchestras of the world; massive choirs, pianos, harpsichords and huge, six-manual pipe organs with enormous pedalboards, saying that he could not manage a simple car!"

"Ah, but a wrong note here or a missed beat there is not as dangerous as a wrong move in a car might be."

"Well, perhaps you are safer in the passenger seat, my wonderful man. I'll be your driver and show you my beloved Cornwall."

We hired a car that very day and, in a spell of fine spring weather, toured the surrounding area and ventured farther afield, driving along narrow roads deep between banks of primroses and celandines, to visit old haunts of mine, little beaches, rocky coves and old churches – anywhere our fancy took us. When we were amongst people, I piled my hair under a hat or scarf and we both wore tinted glasses to avoid being recognised. We wandered hand in hand, walked briskly or sat together over a drink or lunch in a pub, delighting in each other's company.

On one such outing we were walking past a Gypsy encampment when we saw a Nimrod-in- miniature being kicked out of a caravan by the heavy boot of a large, swarthy man. The young dog ran, cringing, to hide in bushes some way away. It was Bruno who remonstrated with the man. Less than ten minutes later, a sum of money having changed hands, we were the proud owners of Nimrod 11. The man, glad to be rid of 'the thieving *jookel*', called a woman from the van and told her to read my palm as a bonus. She took my left hand in hers, ran rough, brown fingers over the palm and studied it for several seconds.

"The man you love is not your husband," she said at length, "But you will be faithful to him all your life. You have the triangle *and* the mystic cross; trust your premonitions and follow your heart. I see several children, only one your own. Beware of a woman who ill-wishes you." She dropped my hand abruptly.

"My wife's a true Romany," the man said proudly. "Lavendi is never wrong."

"Then kindly tell your husband to treat animals always with respect," Bruno said sternly to the woman. He put his hands together and bowed to her. "Good day to you both."

"Our family is increasing," he said as we led the latest member away along the path on a length of old rope. "We must find a shop on our way home and provide for him according to his new status."

"And I thought *I* was the impulsive one, Bruno. But thank you so much; I am delighted. He's so like Nimrod and will be especially loved."

———

I left it as late as possible before leaving. The school holidays loomed and I knew that the girls would be devastated if they found that their grandmother was still in residence, taking my place. I sent a brief letter a week ahead to give notice of my return, hoping that my mother-in-law would be returned to Worthing beforehand. (There was no mystery in my mind as to the identity of the malevolent woman of the Gypsy's warning!)

Bruno decided that he would go back to London rather than stay on at Foxgloves without me. He had engagements in New York during May, and in Vienna and London, including two Proms, in the late summer. He would spend the month of June at Foxgloves, he said, if I would join him there. I promised to do my utmost.

Nimrod 11 had settled in well and was no longer the cowering creature we had brought home. The vet to whom we had taken him to be checked over judged him to be about six months old. He would grow to twice his present size, he warned; there was a lot of wolfhound in him. I thought wryly of the reception he would get at home, although I knew that the girls and Edmund would be delighted.

In view of the dog's presence in our lives, Bruno had insisted that I should have a car of my own so that I should be spared the inconvenience of public transport, as well as enjoying more independence at home. The day after Nimrod's arrival we had returned the hired car and bought what Bruno termed a Nimrod-wagon, a second-hand Ford Cortina Estate, sea-green in colour.

Our last day together was poignant, however hard we both tried to make it one of happy memories. The weather was cold and dull, so after a short walk, we spent most of it indoors, making music or talking about the future, - our future and that of Donal and Dominic. That night we clung together as if sheltering from waves which would tear us apart and cast us adrift, never to be reunited. We slept a little, made love sadly and slept again, until dawn, relentless as ever, sent arrows of light through the half-curtained windows, to pierce our eyes and announce that the day of parting had arrived.

TWENTY

Cecily darling,

Herewith letters which arrived since you left Cornwall, including one which no doubt you'll tear open before the rest! As I can't very well phone you now, I thought I'd add a few lines.

I do hope everything is going as well as can be expected. It must be very difficult for you, especially after your idyllic few days with B. He phoned me yesterday and suggested we meet so that he could deliver his letter in person to make sure that you received it before Easter. He is certainly a personage: that vigorous hair, those eyes – so <u>intense,</u> so <u>dark</u>! (No, no, he's not my type, but I <u>was</u> impressed!) And how he loves <u>you</u>! He thanked me sincerely for 'being such a good friend' when life was difficult for you.

I have a little bit of news of my own. I met a fellow academic – a Greek - at a symposium last week. We have corresponded on an archaeological matter for some time. When we met for the first time, I think there was a little <u>frisson </u>between us. This time I'm not going to rush anything – just take it slowly and see what develops. Wish me luck!

I do miss you, dearest girl. You are welcome here any time, as you well know.

> With much love,
> Your affectionate
> Wat

March 29, 1972

Cecilia, my own dear love,

It was good to hear that you and Nimrod had arrived safely but oh, how I miss you! Having lived without you for all those years, now I am suffering the loss of you as if a limb has been torn off, a light has gone out. I know that that light still shines somewhere, but upon a scene far away, - and with it has gone all my inspiration. ... *tot sunt in amores dolores.*

I need to do some work in the British Library next week and go to the Fitzwilliam in Cambridge after that to study manuscripts. In that city I shall see you everywhere: walking, cycling or in the green sports car, and yet you will always be out of reach, always disappearing round the next corner .....

Already I long for June and, in my mind, look for the green car coming down the lane to Foxgloves, carrying my dear, beautiful Cecilia and the big dog, Nimrod. And when darkness falls, to see the lovely mermaid hair spread over the pillow while I 'show her all my love, all my heart's adoration.' Do you remember that 'The Lark in the Clear Air' was the first song you ever sang to me?

Your voice has never lost its purity and clarity since that day, my dear girl.

I am in pain: a silly old man in the agony of first love, though I know you will not mock me, my dearest. I shall call your good friend, Wat, and suggest that we meet somewhere for a drink; then I can hand him this letter so that it will perhaps reach you on Saturday. Also, I can talk about you – and that will comfort me just a little.

I do not leave for the U.S. until towards the end of April so there will be the opportunity for many more letters to be exchanged – even a meeting ….if that could be arranged?

All the love in my heart to you, my darling,
Bruno.

24ᵗʰ March, '72

Dear Cecily,

Thank you very much for your kind letter and the cheque which arrived safely yesterday. It is more than enough to pay for the boys' board and lodging and some new clothes and shoes, which we have already bought. Frances enjoyed accompanying them on a shopping spree and advising them on the latest trends. They look bang up-to-date now and are enjoying Dublin as free men this time, instead of <u>prisoners!</u>

Everything is working out splendidly here. The boys have settled in very easily and, between Frances who is training to be a teacher, and Gerald's uncle who is a retired teacher, they are topping up on their education so that at least they will leave this country armed with a Leaving Certificate.

After Easter we are all five of us going to Limerick to meet the McCauslands and bring some pressure to bear on the solicitor and arrange to meet the grandmother who was prepared to consign the boys to such a wicked fate. Matters have been moving in the right direction for some time as far as their official papers are concerned but we feel that the boys' actual presence will facilitate the process. Donal is convinced that public execution for the people concerned is the only solution but I think we have persuaded him that something much less dramatic would be more efficacious!

Dominic sends his love and says he will write after the Limerick visit.

With kindest regards,
Yours very sincerely,
Moira (Harrington)

From: Rev. Fr. Aidan McDonald, Lismore, St. Luke's Road, Derry

My dear Cecily,

April 10th 72

I was pleased to receive your letter yesterday. Thank you so much for finding the time to write to me. Since reading the kind words in your letter from Dublin, for which many thanks, I had been wondering how you were managing your complicated life.

So you and your true love had some precious time together. Did I get the impression that you were asking my absolution for this? My dear, if you were one of my flock, I should be obliged to say 'tut-tut; go and sin no more'. But you are instead a valued friend and I am glad for you that you had that all-too-brief spell of happiness in the place you love.

It is good to know that the two boys are settled in their 'half-way' house in Dublin. What good, kind people the Harringtons are. It must have set your mind at rest and shared the burden of juggling two families! I shall be interested to hear how they all got on in Limerick.

I do wonder how you will fare when M-in-L moves in next week. (Look no further for your penance!!) You say she's allergic to dogs; perhaps it won't be such a long stay after all! But seriously, I wish you all the very best. Please keep me up to date on it all. I remember you in my prayers.

With my love and every blessing,
Aidan McDonald

Dear Mrs K.,

April 12th, 72

We have just returned from Limerick city and I can tell you that we had a pretty eventful few days there. One great surprise was that nothing had changed — except for the different coloured paint on our old house and new curtains in the windows. But then I realised that it is only just over four years since we left and that it is <u>our</u> lives that have changed so much in that time.

We had a kind of conference at Mr and Mrs McCausland's house. Mrs O'Leary, who used to be our house-keeper was present, also Cathleen who was our maid. It was really great to see them again. It seems that, thanks to them, plans had already been made to get us out of those horrible schools, when we were 'rescued' by Geraghty and O'Neill posing as Christian Brothers. I keep wondering how different things would have been if their plans had worked first. I can't help thinking that we surely wouldn't have gone to England and therefore we would not have found <u>you</u>. You would not have known about us either and that has made a big difference in <u>your</u> life. This must be a very interesting study – a single event in one person's life causing an endless chain of events affecting countless people across the world. There is a name for it, isn't there – somebody's law?

Anyway, to the dramatic part of our visit: Donal and I went to Mass at our old church on Sunday with Mr and Mrs H. and Frances. We went in quite late and sat near the back. When we went up to make our Communion, Fr O'Keefe turned quite pale when he saw us and stumbled over his words. Then Grandmother Leahy caught sight of us as she was coming out of church at the end and had a seizure or a heart attack or something. Whatever it was, when someone waved some smelling salts under her nose she did not come round so they had to call the ambulance!! Fr O'Keefe himself was no-where to be seen!

On the Monday we were to have seen Mr O'Dowd the solicitor. The appointment was made by Mr McCausland in the name of Maloney, which he wouldn't recognise. Strange to relate, however, Mr O'Dowd was 'out of the office on urgent family business'.

The upshot of it all is that our passports are in the process of being prepared – in our former name of Manning. This was thought to be the best way to pro-ceed in view of the fact that we only have one mother between us! I hope you don't mind. We were told: 'Don't ask too many questions; pressure has been brought to bear'. At any rate, it will all be more legal than what Geraghty had in mind. I'm really sorry that your money was wasted on that plan.

Mr and Mrs H. took some photographs in Limerick. When they are developed I will send some so that you can see our old home and Cathleen and Mrs O'Leary. I would like a photo of you before we go to America, please. I hope we can meet again before then. I miss our talks on the phone.

I don't know where you are at present so will send this to you at Professor Tyler's address.

Love

from

Dominic.

PS I am typing this on Frances's type-writer. She says it would be useful to learn properly if I want to be a journalist.

April 12 '72

Dear Cecily,

Dominic will have told you about our visit to Limerick, but I thought I would enclose a few lines to thank you for your letter. I am glad you and your girls are enjoying a few outings during their Easter holidays. I'm sure they are pleased to have you back – and must be delighted with the new dog!

I think our recent jaunt was an eye-opener to Donal. He has realised that not all non-Catholics are enemies of the state and that there are <u>degrees</u> of Protestantism! One not of the Catholic faith is Eugene McCausland who has done so much to lobby for the rights of orphans, and children born out of wedlock. As you know, it was through him that contact was made with my organisation (The God-Parents) and was how I came to visit Dominic in the first place.

I think it is only a matter of time before a certain solicitor in Limerick is thoroughly discredited. If he is struck off, it will be no more than he deserves. As for the wicked grandmother, history does not relate whether she recovered after her spectacular – and rather undignified – collapse. Perhaps Mrs O'Leary will inform us in due course.

The troubles in the North continue and are not likely to improve in the foreseeable future, so I think the boys' departure to the United States should not be delayed as soon as their passports arrive. We are in regular touch with the Manning grandparents. We always have the fear that Donal will be tempted to go back to Derry and rejoin the Provisional IRA. I'll keep you posted of any developments.

Yours very sincerely,

Moira.

TWENTY ONE

"Now the girls have gone back we must clear the guest room to make space for Mother's things," Peter said. "We haven't much time before she arrives. She will need your little study too so that she can have a separate sitting room. We shall have to find space downstairs for your bureau and cupboard."

"Hmm. I didn't realise she was coming quite so soon," I said smoothly, trying to picture the ice on top of a volcano.

"Well, I didn't say much when Agnes and Elizabeth were here. They didn't seem to enjoy their half-term holiday last term when you were … er …absent"

"I wonder why that was. You might have told me, however. I thought you and I would have had a little time to sort things out before she moved in here."

"What is there to sort out? You came to your senses and returned; I overlooked your long absence and asked no questions. Can you not just settle down again and forget the past?"

"No, I can't, actually."

"Pull yourself together, Cecily," he said briskly. "There's work to be done. I realise that you probably feel very guilty, but it's over and done with now." (*Had the Rural Dean or the Bishop advised him to adopt this tough line with his recalcitrant wife?*) "And another thing – to return to the subject of Mother: she is not going to be at all happy about that dog."

"Nimrod, you mean?"

"It will bring on her Asthma," he warned, "Which is bad for her heart. I think it should be kept in a kennel outside." (*Perhaps* she *should be kept in the kennel, I thought mutinously.*)

"A kennel?" I echoed in a level voice. "We ... I... rescued him from a cruel and neglectful owner. I really don't feel that he should be banished from the house. If your mother is to have my study as a sitting-room, she won't have to have him anywhere near her." The volcano was boiling away furiously; the ice on top was melting and there might have been an almighty eruption had there not been a knock on the back door.

"' Morning Rector," said a cheery voice. "I've come to look at that decorating you wanted doing."

T his was the day that Bruno was leaving for New York. The previous evening I had seized the opportunity to phone him when Peter was at a meeting. It had been a short, awkward exchange: I was unhappy and jumpy and he was clearly not alone. Now I thought of him on his way to the airport and wondered how I could wait for his return; how I could keep my promise to spend the month of June at Foxgloves with him.

While Peter was showing Bill Dodds the two rooms to be decorated, I snatched up a parcel I had done up for Lizzie – a few 'treasures' she had forgotten to pack when she returned to school, without which I knew she would be miserable – and, attaching Nimrod's smart, red lead to his wide, leather collar, I walked with him up the hill to the Post Office.

"I expect it seems quiet without the girls," said the postmistress. "They must have been happy to have you home again. How come you were away so long? Was it Mrs Knight Senior who kept you away?" I was spared having to answer as she prattled on in her usual manner. "I hear she's coming to live with you *for good*. I must say that I wish you luck, Mrs Knight. I don't mind telling you that she upset a lot of people while she was here. Mrs Barnes told me she'd never darken the door of the church again; turned Methody, she has ......" She proceeded to list several others who had taken umbrage for various reasons.

Having dispatched the parcel, I walked for miles, Nimrod at my heels, lagging behind to sniff at rabbit holes or running on over the next hill. Bruno would be air-borne by now. I banished the pictures which came to my mind of a mid-air emergency, engine failure, a hi-jacking or a bomb, unable to imagine how I could possibly live without knowing that he was alive and well somewhere in the world. Instead, I resolved to do something positive to prepare for Mother-in-Law's arrival. I would have time – just – to buy some material and make new curtains and cushion-covers for the two rooms she would occupy _ *my* private space.

The day before the dreaded arrival, I received an unexpected letter. The type-written envelope, addressed to Mrs Cecily Knight was postmarked Bath, Somerset. Something told me that I should be careful about opening it in front of Peter who was busy looking through his own mail. I slipped the envelope into my pocket and opened two others. When I opened it later I found a handbill advertising a C.P. Snow play at the Theatre Royal, behind which was a letter from the children's maternal aunt, their late mother's sister. Written across the top was the message: TRY TO BE ALONE WHEN YOU READ THIS.

Dear Cecily,

You will be surprised to hear from me, I'm sure. We have never met and I apologise for the fact that I have repeatedly turned down your invitations. Perhaps this letter will go some way to explaining my reluctance hitherto. Edmund, Agnes and Elizabeth have always been loud in your praises and I realise that you have been a good mother to them in Janey's place.

My sister was very dear to me and so are her children, and I suppose, unfairly, I resented the fact that you had usurped her place, thus denying myself the opportunity to meet you. Last week I received a birthday thank-you letter from Lizzie, as you may know. She told me, by the way, that she had a super-brill day and that you had made her the most fab cake she had ever seen! What concerned me, though, was that she seemed to think that Granny K. was moving into the Rectory imminently; also that she had stayed there for some time while you were away in February/March.

It may be that you already know the circumstances of Janey's tragic death. The children have understood that she died of a progressive or incurable disease, but I believe that her suicide was attributable to the prolonged presence of Mrs K. Snr which prevented her getting over her puerperal fever. Our own mother was unfortunately gravely ill at the time and I was juggling caring for her with bringing up a young family while my husband was away in the Army. (My mother never got over Janey's death and now has Dementia)

I suppose the purpose of this letter is to warn you – if you haven't already found out – of how difficult life may be for you, and to offer you my heartfelt sympathy and, more practically, my support in any way I can be of help. Please feel free to phone or visit or to meet half-way. It is only thirty or forty miles to Bath from you, I think.

With my very best wishes,
Yours sincerely,
Isobel Sargent.

Suicide! I re-read the letter to make sure that my eyes had not deceived me. Clearly *Peter* had, however. I too had been led to believe that Janey had died of some unspecified cause associated with Post-natal Depression after Lizzie's birth. It was never spoken of again and I had not asked questions. I knew only that the family had moved to Gloucestershire from Kent shortly after Jane's death. So much for Peter's reaction to my own 'deception'!

Mrs K.'s belongings arrived in a small van that afternoon and we arranged them in the two rooms. The walls of both had been painted pale blue, an unfortunate choice, considering that the windows of both faced north. It occurred to me that the woman had a northerly aspect herself, but I had tried to lighten the effect with curtains of blue and white material with a touch of yellow, in a William Morris design, which I had bought in Cheltenham. I had sat up late for two nights to finish them.

The furniture looked heavy and lumpish in what had been my brightly painted room, my private space for so many years. I thought longingly of my pretty, welcoming bedroom at Foxgloves and the happiness I had known there. I placed a bowl of early yellow roses on the wide window sill and closed the door.

"Those curtains will have to go, for a start," said my mother-in-law as she surveyed her new sitting room. "My maroon Dralon ones are in that ottoman with the matching cushions."

"Cecily made the curtains especially for you, Mother," Peter said, a touch of pride in his voice.

"Quite impractical, as one would expect. Sash windows are always draughty; those are far too flimsy."

"Actually, you'll see that they're lined *and* interlined," I said in a carefully modulated voice, fists clenched so tightly at my sides that my nails bit into my palms. (*It would be well not to throttle her just yet; better leave it until I am really at my wits' end.*)

"Come down when you're ready," I said, hospitably. "I'll make some tea. I think it's warm enough to have it on the lawn."

"In *May*? I think *not*! Serve mine in the drawing room if you please." (*Serve, indeed! Milk and sugar Ma'am? Or a touch of arsenic, maybe?*)

When she came downstairs she was carrying the bowl of roses at arms' length, her thin purplish nose wrinkling as if she bore a plate of week-old fish she had found under her bed.

"Cecily, you know I'm allergic to flowers. Please don't put them in my room again."

I took the bowl from her but she followed me into the kitchen. Glyph, who had been sitting contentedly on his pile of old towels, stood up and arched his back. He jumped down, hissing, and stalked out of the room. Nimrod stood up from his sitting position and looked at her uncertainly.

"Oh my goodness, gracious! What is that *animal?*" she screeched.

"That is Nimrod, my dog," I explained. (*Bite her, Nimrod! Kill! Tear her in pieces, there's a good boy.*)

"A *dog?* Shoo it out, Cecily; get rid of the flea-ridden creature at once! You know I can't abide animals in the house." She shuddered. "They bring on my Asthma – and anyway they're very unhygienic."

I realised that perhaps I should not have sent a telepathic message to Nimrod. He uttered a deep growl and came to stand at my side, watching her warily.

"You go into the sitting room and I'll bring the tea-tray in," I said, soothingly. "Don't worry, he'll stay in here." (*How Bruno and I will laugh over this scene – next month!*)

"So you think you can get into my good books as easily as this, Cecily," Mother-in-Law said, two days later. I had brought breakfast to her room on a tray, taking trouble to arrange it just as she would like: small triangles of (white, sliced) toast in a silver rack, dainty pats of butter in a tiny saucer, shredless marmalade in a pretty pot decorated with oranges and lemons, a pot of tea and a little jug of milk. These were all laid on a linen tray-cloth which I knew she had embroidered herself. The only thing she could find fault with might be the table napkin, which I had made myself from a Laura Ashley material in burnt orange and cream, to match the kitchen curtains and tablecloth. She had made her disapproval of my choice clear to the girls, they had told me.

"As this is to be my home as well as yours," she went on, "I think we should establish some ground rules." (*Ground rules? The only* ground *rule is for you to dig a large hole therein, very, very deep, and jump into it.*)

"Would you like a little air in here, Mrs Knight?" I asked, going to the window. "It's a gorgeous day out there." The room was fusty with stale air and it smelt of old furniture and clothes that had been worn for too long. Outside, the copper beech cast the dappled shade of its glossy new leaves on the lawn and, beyond and above it, little puffs of white cloud danced in a blue, blue sky. It was not a day for staying indoors.

"No, leave the window," she said sharply. "As I was saying: ground rules." She poured tea into the cup and added milk. "I must insist that no animals are allowed in the kitchen. Their hairs and fleas get into everything; and of course *all* animals have worms." (*The worms could do a good job on you when you're six feet under.*) She raised the cup to her lips and grimaced. "You didn't warm the pot, did you?"

"I did warm both the pot and the cup but I'll pop down and make you a fresh pot, shall I?"

(*Perhaps a large slug of hydrochloric acid would warm the cockles of your evil heart.*)

"No, I'll make do with this," she sighed. "Now, as I have you on your own, I can tell you how very shocked I was when Peter told me about your past misdoings – and their recent repercussions. If this *scandal* came to light, it would doubtless compromise my son's prospects of advancement in the Church. Ever since he was a little boy he wanted to become a bishop. Your job now is to help him realise that ambition. Going away as you did for weeks on end is hardly going to help, is it? A wife's duty to her husband is love and *obedience*, - and you seem to have been found wanting in both those virtues."

"I'll bear in mind everything you have said, Mrs Knight," I said, so sincerely that I impressed even myself. (*Oh yes, I'll bear it in mind for years and years, you haggard old harridan, you wizened old witch.*)

I ask myself now as I write this whether, by going into such fine detail about these exchanges, I am seeking to justify my subsequent actions to my readers, to myself. That may indeed be so, and, if so, so be it! I did not actually have murder in mind, I assure you, but it was becoming harder and harder to prevent the volcano from erupting. Had it done so, it would have proved such a spectacular and cataclysmic event that its fall-out might have consumed my dear ones as well as my arch-enemy. Before it reached that stage I had to preserve the ice-cap and make plans.

—oeeo—

That same morning, I drove into Gloucester, made two calls from a public telephone, called at my bank and bought a wicker cat-basket from a pet-shop.

As it turned out, on my return I found that a show-down could not be avoided. I had left Nimrod in the cool back lobby rather than take him in the car on a sunny day. Mrs Knight had passed through the kitchen to put some clothes in the washing-machine and had encountered him in there.

"Peter was out and you were nowhere to be seen," she said in an aggrieved tone. "It was thoughtless of you to go out without telling me. It growled at me and wouldn't let me pass. Supposing it had bitten me!"

"He didn't though, did he? You're all right, aren't you?"

"No, I'm certainly not. It brought on an Asthma attack and there was nobody here."

"Well, I'm glad to see that you've recovered," I said, distracted suddenly by the sight of a large University of London envelope on the kitchen table. Beside it lay a paper-knife which somebody had used to slit it open.

"Excuse me," I said, "I believe that envelope is addressed to me."

"*I* happen to be Mrs C. Knight," she said grandly. "*Your* correct mode of address is Mrs *P.R.T.* or Mrs *Peter* Knight."

"I am also a person in my own right," I said. "Were you expecting anything from the University of London?" I wondered how much she had seen of the envelope's contents.

"As I say, it was addressed to *me*," she said stubbornly.

"How *dare* you open my post?" I exclaimed. "And you have the temerity to talk about *ground* rules!"

"I thought it wouldn't be long before you showed yourself in your true colours. A leopard never changes its spots," she misquoted smugly. "I'll go back upstairs now. Call me when lunch is ready."

There were three letters, mercifully unopened: an airmail from Bruno and letters from Dominic and Lizzie, with a covering note from Wat. Hearing Peter return, I took them quickly to my bureau and locked them away to read later.

TWENTY THREE

"It was then that I decided to leave sooner rather than later," I said to Isobel Sargent – the children's Aunt Izzy. We sat out in the terraced garden of her house in Bath, drinking gin and tonic. It was one of those rare May evenings when it was warm enough to sit outside after six o'clock. Nimrod lay dozing by my side while Glyph, lightly sedated, preferred the safety of his well-padded basket to the freedom of the small, enclosed garden. I felt remarkably relaxed after my escape.

"It's so good of you to come to the rescue," I said. "My main concern is for the girls. They are at such a tender age now and may never forgive me for walking out on them, but I know how they love staying with you here and I had this idea that they - and you - might spend the summer holidays in Cornwall."

"I'd be delighted to see more of them, of course, and they'd be overjoyed to come and see you and the animals – especially Glyph; they're going to miss him."

"At least they'll know that he'll be loved and cosseted. He'd get no such comfort from Granny Knight."

"Who will look after the chickens?" asked Isobel. "You didn't bring them too, did you?"

"No, I drew the line there, much as I shall miss them. I worked out my anger by mucking out the chicken-house while planning my exit. Peter will have to see to them."

"The village is going to miss you – and the church, too."

"I went to W.I. last night and people commiserated with me as if I'd lost an old friend rather than gaining a new foe. I told a group of them that my aunt in Cambridge might be ill for a very, very long while – *very* soon."

We laughed comfortably like old friends. It was strange to reflect that it was our common dislike and mistrust of Mrs Knight Senior, rather than love of her grandchildren, that had brought us together after all these years.

"What will you say to Edmund and the girls?" Isobel asked. "How will you actually break the news?"

"I will write to them individually I think, as soon as I arrive at Foxgloves, - and to the girls' housemistress as well. I had a 'private' letter from Lizzie yesterday to tell me that her periods had started, so I would have sent her a special letter anyway. If I can hold out the hope of them spending August in the cottage at Porthwenna with you, it may soften the blow. There has been a cancellation for four weeks from the 5th, so I've asked the agent not to re-let it till he hears from me."

"In that case I'll say yes then," Isobel said. "Greg will have gone back to Cyprus by then after his leave. "It'll be great fun, - and one or two of my lot might join us if there's room."

"There are three bedrooms, two twin and one single, but they can always bring sleeping bags or use the sofa. If you suggest that to Peter without saying where the cottage is, I'm sure he'd be glad to let them come."

"We'll work something out. You've got enough to worry about for the time being, so leave it to me."

———

W e three set off next morning, human, canine and feline, on the second leg of our exodus, which I labelled Operation Knightmare's End', (though the pun didn't work until I wrote it down the following day!) A second phone call to Wat the previous evening had confirmed that Mrs Burrows, Bruno's caretaker, was expecting our arrival.

The key was already in my possession, Bruno having insisted that I had one of my own. It had been kept with the contents of my bureau: the secrets, treasures and personal documents which now travelled with me in a box. My clothes and other, smaller belongings were packed into bin-liners rather than suitcases. My excuse for such a carload would have been a visit to the vet with Glyph, dropping off generous contributions to the church jumble sale en route, and taking the sewing machine to be repaired My departure, however, had gone unnoticed; Peter was in his study and Mrs Knight had gone up for her afternoon nap. No doubt, when tea failed to appear on time, one or both of them would find the large piece of card propped against the teapot on the kitchen table, bearing the message:

SITUATION INCREASINGLY INTOLERABLE. ADIEU FROM
CECILY, HIEROGLYPH AND NIMROD.

As an afterthought, I had dropped my wedding ring into one of the teacups on the tray I had laid ready for their tea.

It seemed a long journey, regular stops having to be made for Nimrod to stretch his long legs and have a drink. Glyph would neither drink nor leave his basket; all I could do to comfort him was to talk to him soothingly as he sat beside me on the front seat where he could see me.

Both animals seemed to sense that the journey was nearly over when there were only ten miles or so to go. I too felt lighter and less anxious with every mile that passed, and at last we were driving down the bumpy track towards ... *home.*

Even though Bruno was not present – at least in a physical sense, - the house welcomed us. As soon as we stepped inside it seemed to embrace and enfold us as if we had entered a safe haven, a shelter from stormy seas.

A tea-tray was laid on the kitchen table with a welcoming note from the good Mrs Burrows who had looked after Foxgloves and its owners from time immemorial. It told me that there was enough food in the fridge to tide me over till the following day, including cream to go with the freshly-baked scones and strawberry jam she had left on the table. I was particularly touched by the thoughtful addition of a tin each of dog and cat food. Wat must have told her that I was not alone! I dialled the phone number she had added to her note, 'in case you need anything before tomorrow', to report our safe arrival and to thank her for her kindness.

When the animals were fed, watered and settled, I unpacked the car and carried the bags up to the bedroom, pausing in the doorway to breathe in the scent of fresh linen mingled with that of a small vase of garden flowers on the dressing-table. I put down the bags and crossed to the open casement window. 'Behold, the sea itself!' Walt Whitman's words in the opening bars of Vaughan Williams 'A Sea Symphony' came to me as I took in the splendour of the scene beyond and below, at once familiar and entirely strange in its shifting patterns of light and colour and texture.

I turned away from the window, slipped off my shoes and lay on the bed for a few minutes in this room, redolent of past joys and the promise of what was yet to be. Bruno's unseen presence was everywhere. Whatever the future held, this was my home; *He* was my home and I his.

I woke early to the promise of a beautiful day. A golden sun was doing battle with a silver mist with breathtaking effect. Jewels of dew were strewn across the grass as Nimrod and I made our way across the lawn and down the path. The foxgloves, guardians of the Well, were almost in bloom, ready to unfold their bells for Bruno's return. I washed my face and drank from my hands in my customary ceremonial ritual: Pagan or Christian, I know not which; it was simply a thanksgiving to the God of Creation; a prayer for the protection of my dear ones, wherever they might be, and for the soul of the little lost child after whom I had named the Well.

Mrs Burrows called round when I was washing up after breakfast. She seemed unfazed by the cautious greeting from Nimrod.

"I remember him from years ago," she said. "Mr Bruno was looking after him one day when I called in."

"Oh, that would be Nimrod the First," I said. "That would have been about twenty years ago. Unfortunately, dogs don't last as long as that."

Hearing us laugh together, Nimrod relaxed and wagged his tail. Mrs B. was a friend, not another Mrs Knight! Glyph, also, had decided to approve of our caller and smiled across at her from the chair he had already selected as his special place.

"Last time you were here," Mrs B. said, "Mr Bruno said you could manage without me so I went to stay with my sister in Liskeard. I was wondering if you would need me now you're here and whether you still need Burrows to come and do the garden."

"I would love it if you'd come in twice a week or so," I said, sensing that she would welcome it.

"You keep this house so beautifully and it would be a luxury for me to have help to keep it as clean and tidy as it is now. The same goes for the garden."

She looked pleased. We discussed convenient days and re-muneration, and Nimrod and I saw her off, watching her out of sight as she wobbled up the lane on her old-fashioned bicycle.

I spent the rest of the morning on the terrace outside the music-room writing letters. In the afternoon I drove to the Post Office to buy stamps for envelopes to Edmund, Agnes and Lizzie, to whom I had written separate letters; to Bruno, c/o Fr Michal because that seemed the safest way of contacting him; to Dominic, Fr MacDonald and to Isobel Sargent.

I had not ventured to Porthwenna with Bruno on my previ-ous visit but now I drove east along the top road and turned down into the cove, stopping outside Cliff Cottage while the memories crowded in. I visualised the girls arriving with their Aunt Izzie, in less than three months' time, and seeing it for the first time; the excitement of exploring the cottage and its nooks and crannies, choosing which beds they would have, discover-ing the little door at the top of the stairs which led to the small roof-terrace. My reverie was interrupted by a discreet toot from behind me: a large blue van wanted to pass, so I moved on and pulled in a little further down the road. Mrs Pascoe's old cottage had been prettied up for summer letting. Now in her nineties, she had long since moved into a home for dementia sufferers. Each year I received a Christmas card sent on her behalf from her daughter-in-law. I resolved to go and visit her and see if it revived some memories for her.

There was no sign of life at The Ship Inn, which was firmly shut after the lunch-time opening, but further on, two young women, with pram and push-chair, sat sunning themselves and chatting on a bench outside the fishing sheds. They would have been mere infants when I left Porthwenna, I thought, feeling very middle-aged; now they had children of their own! I drove on past the Post Office and two new shops selling children's fishing nets, locally-made giftware and ice-cream. A fish-and-chip shop had opened where the chandlers used to be, with the notice 'FRYING TONITE' in the window, which was adorned with stick-on dolphins in electric blue. The 'Wages of Sin' notice on the Chapel wall had been painted over - long ago by the look of it. A man in T-shirt and jeans was repairing the notice-board outside the porch. I could hear the tap-tap of his hammer through the open window of the car as I rounded the steep corkscrew bend up the hill. At the top I turned right and parked outside the church. There were fancy new gates into the house where I had once spent so many contented hours. Now they bore the legend 'THE OLD RECTORY', which meant that the unremarkable, modern house I had passed a few yards back was probably the new vicarage. The Grays had moved some years ago and now lived in Dorset.

The lych-gate and the bier were just as I remembered them, though two empty beer-bottles stood on the slate-top. I removed them and walked back to dispose of them in the litter-bin, retracing my steps along the path until I found the grave-stone which I had come to see:

IN LOVING MEMORY OF
JOSIAH WILLIAM TRELAWNEY
DEPARTED THIS LIFE JAN. 15TH 1954, AGED 79
AND IVY ROSE, HIS WIFE,
WHO DIED ON MARCH 4TH 1940, AGED 61 YEARS

"GONE BUT NOT FORGOTTEN."

I could not reconcile the thought of the mouldering remains lying below with the vibrant memory of my grandfather's physical form, nor of the vivid presence I felt beside me now, the gnarled hand on my shoulder, the deep, warm voice in my ear, saying; 'Welcome home, Cecily Rose, my little mermaid. Bring that fancy-man of yours next time you come – and that new dog, too. Oh, and while you're here, take away those 'orrible wax flowers. A few foxgloves in a jam-jar will do nicely – your grandmother's favourite, they were, d'you remember?'

PART 4

ONE

(Maddie writing in November 2011)

Cecily's memoir ended there, with her visit to her grandparents' grave. One day, when she was writing that last paragraph, she said to me:

"You know, darling, I'm never going to finish this. I've gone into far too much detail about the first half of my life. I'm so tired today; I think I'll give it a rest for a while. At least I've got as far as the 'happy-ever-after' bit, with the best still to come. Perhaps you'll have to finish it for me."

But you cannot write someone's *auto*biography, can you? Or their memoir. I think I must just try to finish her story as simply as I can; round off our year-long collaboration on this archive, try to tie up the loose ends, take the tapestry off the loom and present it as a substantial, but somewhat hastily finished work. There is always the possibility of adding to it at a later date.

She died a few evenings later, before I had a chance to summon the family. I was watching the August rioting and looting in London and other major UK cities on TV, and thinking how differently the US police would have dealt with it all; also comparing the scenes and eye-witness accounts with Dominic's article about the August 12 riots in Derry in 1969, and the pictures and videos on the web-sites I had visited. Absorbed and shocked though I was, some sixth sense told me to go upstairs and check if there was anything Cecilia needed. She smiled as I came into her bedroom and held out her hand.

"Sit with me a moment, darling."

I sat down carefully on the side of the bed and took her frail hand in mine. The heavy gold wedding band swung round, too loose on the fourth finger of her still graceful hand. I pushed it back gently to stop it from slipping over the knuckle, but she shook her head.

"Take it off, darling girl, Bruno's ring; it's yours now. There, wear it on your right hand. I shan't need it where I'm going. *He* will be there, though; he will be there." She closed her eyes with a little sigh, and those were the last words I heard her say. She died in her sleep later that night. She had had at least two heart-attacks in the past two years, and knew that the next would be her last.

The family and I have had three months to try to come to terms with our loss, although we still haven't gotten used to her not being around anymore … and it's excruciating. To other readers, I must apologise for this sudden revelation; I could not think where else in the manuscript to impart the news of her passing. It will have come as a shock, I feel sure. When I was younger I used to think that, when a book was written in the first person, it would be safe to assume that the main character would not perish – at least not during the course of her or his narration.

But let me take you back forty years to June 1972 now and bring her back to life as she was then: still young, beautiful and radiantly happy in the anticipation of Bruno's imminent arrival at Foxgloves. He had called Mrs B. to say he was flying into Heathrow on Friday 2nd and coming straight down to Cornwall. It was evident that he had not received Cecilia's letter, so Mrs B. said nothing – as requested by Cecilia herself – and promised that the house would be ready for his arrival and that she would ask Burrows to meet his train at the usual time.

Imagine Cecilia's excitement, and Bruno's joy when, their roles reversed this time, *she* was at the railroad station to meet *him*! She hung back behind a pillar as the train drew in and watched the passengers alighting. At last came the one she was waiting for: a man spare of figure and of no great height, yet more distinguished by far than the rest of the small crowd, turning round to shut the carriage door, then making his way towards the exit, carrying suitcase in one hand and briefcase in the other. She stepped out then from her hiding place and watched his eyes widen and his whole face light up as she ran towards him.

"Oh, Cecilia, *Cecilia!* Am I dreaming? Can it really be you?" The cases were abandoned, arms were outstretched and they stood locked together, kissing, gazing, laughing, crying and kissing again.

The ticket-collector looked at his watch. Surely this was the same couple of love-birds who had made him late for his tea that day in March. Yes, he distinctly remembered the woman's incredible hair. He'd been in Primary School in Porthwenna with a girl who had hair exactly that colour.

Maybe it was the constant cycle of arrivals and departures in those ensuing years that kept their relationship fresh;

preventing it from settling into the humdrum predictability so many couples experience. The nearest they ever came to an argument, she said, was during a discussion about how best to write down in rhythmic notation the (irritating) conversation between two woodpigeons, agreeing eventually to differ as to whether it should be in 4-4 or 5-4 time! Every moment with Bruno was unique and precious, she told me on many occasions, and always enhanced by the music they shared: listening, playing, singing, composing. She became an accomplished harpsichordist in her own right and, during one of his longer absences, she learned to play clarinet so that she could surprise and delight him on his return. Although her voice was of a high soprano range, her favourite sounds on the clarinet were the rich, mellow notes of the chalumeau, the 'chest voice' of the lowest register. This had a particular effect on Bruno, she told me without embarrassment, driving him wild in such a way that they would often end up on the thick-piled rug at the far end of the music-room 'playing a different kind of duet', as she put it.

Sometimes Cecilia would accompany Bruno on his travels, attending concerts all over the world. He was thrilled to have her companionship on his tours and she, undemanding of his attention at such times, would amuse herself by exploring whichever great city they were staying in, visiting churches, museums and galleries to her heart's content while he was busy with rehearsals or research. Because of the publicity they might attract, however, she did not travel with him until they were married, and this did not happen till 1980, eight years after they began to live together.

This became possible when Peter Knight thought better of his refusal to divorce her when he found a plain-looking and altogether more suitable helpmeet to support him in his aspirations towards an episcopal enthronement. His own bishop at the time approved of this woman, Cecilia heard, because she used all the right buzz-words, such as 'meaningful' and 'outreach', and advocated and promoted the abolition of 'archaic' language and 'outdated' music in church. "Even if I hadn't left him to be with Bruno," she told me, "I would have been no use to him in his ecclesiastical climb. I was already mutinous about the new services, the mutilation of the liturgy, the abandoning of the King James Bible and the trite modern hymns about concrete and steel – *townies'* stuff. If worship is not about mystery and spirituality, one might as well become an atheist. Just think what the religions of the world – not only Christianity – have inspired in the way of great paintings, music, architecture and literature. Certainly let us retain the simple, but never confuse the truly great with the trivial, the trendy and the transient."

A nyway, rewind to their wedding day in June 1980. Of course, it was long before my time, - before I was born, even. Let me describe a photograph that stands in Cecilia's (now my) bedroom. She and Bruno stand facing each other, hands clasped at arms' length, smiling into each other's eyes. In the center of the picture the ancient priest, Fr McDonald, stands with one hand on Cecilia's shoulder, the other on Bruno's and his stole joining both. She is wearing a flowing maxi-dress of mustard-colored silk, her loose hair tumbling round her shoulders and setting off her cute profile. (She would disapprove of that word but I think it describes her slightly up-curved nose. Bruno, (his nose curving the *other* way due to his Jewish ancestry, maybe) wears black trousers and a smart, striped shirt in mustard, black and silver, with no necktie. The group is standing to one side of Elowen's well, and in the foreground, the intense deep rose color of a clump of tall foxgloves makes a striking contrast with the gold of Cecilia's dress. But for all the color, it is the love which lights the whole scene, adding a radiance which somehow the photographer, Tom Fahy, managed to capture; the love that so many seek but seldom find. It lights up the old priest's expression, too, as he blesses them in this unofficial and private ceremony which followed the necessary civil proceedings at the local Registry Office.

TWO

Although this is Cecilia's story, I think it's time I told you where I, Maddie, fit into the picture. Better still, she can tell you in her own words. Her memoir was written in mostly chronological order but I found in her writing desk a pad of jottings about various events in diary form, the most substantial being the account of my arrival at Foxgloves. Bear in mind that her beloved Bruno had passed away two years earlier and, except for very occasional visits of close friends and family, and delivery men, the gardening boy and the like, she had been a virtual recluse ever since. Here is her account, just as she wrote it:

JULY 21ST 2001

The most amazing thing has happened: I have a granddaughter, a living link with my darling Bruno! There are few visitors these days and I am always glad to see them leave. They bring me food and wine and flowers and think I should be getting over my grief and 'moving on'. This visitor, however, was different and I can hardly wait for her to come back again.

Two afternoons ago there was a light knock at the back door which I ignored as usual. It came again, more determined this time.

"Who is it?" I asked, in a discouraging tone.

"My name is Maddie; Madeleine Grace Manning." The voice was young with an American accent. I unlocked the door and opened it, reeling backwards in shock when I saw ... *myself,* as I was when Bruno opened that very same door to me for the first time.

The girl looked alarmed. "I'm sorry for startling you. Are you okay? You look like you just saw a ghost."

"You'd better come in and persuade me that I haven't, then," I said, standing aside for her to enter. "Can I make you tea, coffee? It'll be instant, I'm afraid."

"A latte would be just fine." She sat down at the kitchen table and with both hands lifted her long, red hair and shook it back over her shoulders.

"Who are you?" I asked, busying myself with the kettle. "And what do you want?"

"I think I'm your granddaughter. I would've called you first but my cell phone ran out of battery?" Her sentences tipped up at the end as if punctuated with a question mark.

I put her coffee in front of her and poured a strong one for myself.

"Thanks, Cecily; cute beaker."

"I think we'd better make it 'Mrs Sabra' until we have established our relationship, if any." I spoke more sternly than I intended.

"Okay, okay. I reckoned you may be, like, kinda crabby, your husband passing away an' all." And suddenly the girl put her head down on her arms and wept. My indignation dissolved instantly; I went to stand behind her and stroked the hair so like my own had been, thinking of the hot tears that had fallen onto the same spot of this very table, one evening nearly half a century ago.

"Don't cry, my dear. Of course we *must* be related. I'll show you a photo of how I looked when I was about your age. That was what gave me such a shock when I opened the door."

I led the way upstairs, suggesting that she might like to make use of the bathroom while I looked in my bedroom for the photograph I had in mind. As I shuffled through the contents of the drawer, I realised that one question alone stood between me and finally knowing which of the two Manning 'boys' was Maddie's father and, therefore, Bruno's and my son. Did I really want to know after all this time?

"Oh wow, I'll say there's a likeness!" she exclaimed, looking through the handful of snapshots I had selected. "And get that circle-skirt – and those pedal-pushers! That could be me in fifties gear." She looked at my hair with raised eyebrows.

"Yes, the colour's gone, I'm afraid," I said. "You're looking at me fifty years ago and yourself fifty years hence." I sat down on the bed and patted the patchwork coverlet. "Now sit beside me and tell me all." Still I did not ask *the* question, and had the feeling of being suspended above a chasm; of walking a tightrope between not-knowing and knowing.

"Where d'you want me to start?" she asked.

I took a deep breath. "Where you've come from and what led you here; that would be a good place to begin."

"Uh huh; okay, I come from San Francisco – the Bay area? - on the coast of California, and Mom and I are over here – well, Dublin, Ireland(?) – to see my other grandmother, who's sick."

The question had been answered without being asked. So 'Mom' was Frances, née Harrington, who had married Donal

Manning years ago; and he was our son, as I had suspected all along. I tried to keep my face expressionless.

"Go on," I prompted.

"It wasn't till I got to Dublin that I found out that I had, like, another grandmother. My dad always said his mom was dead? And Mom was always kinda quiet on the subject."

"And what happened in Dublin?"

"Mo-Mo, - that's what we call her _____."

"We?"

"Yeah, my older brother and sister called her that when they were little, so I, like, copied them? Anyway, Mo-Mo hadn't seen me since I was a kid, only in photographs, and when Mom and I arrived, she said, 'Oh my *God*, you're the image of Cecily! That must mean….' But Mom stopped her and said 'Not now, Mam, *please*, we'll discuss it later.' I wasn't about to leave it at that and when I got Mo-Mo on her own I asked her to please tell me who Cecily was."

I noticed the tears returning to her eyes and shining like little pearls between the long, dark lashes. I patted her hand briskly. "Let's go and walk in the garden and you can tell me more."

I needed a few moments to come to terms with…what, disappointment, anticlimax? Whatever it was, I felt neither surprise nor joy. I excused myself to go to the loo and when I returned she was standing by the window, the light falling on the rich chrysanthemum colour of her hair.

"Hey," she said "This place is, like, *so-o* close to the ocean. Aren't you real scared the cliff'll crumble?"

"I don't think that will happen for a few thousand years," I smiled.

T he garden was fragrant with the scent of new-mown grass, mixed with a slight saltiness borne on the gentle breeze.

"Gee, I'd sure love to live here," Maddie said, sighing. "You could really chill in a place like this. It's, like, so peaceful and far away from troubles."

"Do you have so many troubles in your life, Maddie?" I asked, sensing that there was a good deal more to be disclosed.

"You better believe I do," she answered.

"So tell me about them," I encouraged. "There's an old adage – you may have heard it spoken – 'A trouble shared is a trouble halved'."

"Okay; here goes. You see, I've always had this feeling that my dad didn't like me? He's always been kinda cold around me? And night before last I found out why. My mom came right out and told Mo-Mo and me that he wasn't my *real* father."

I caught my breath and almost choked, coughing and pretending to sneeze to mask the sudden tears that sprang to my own eyes.

"Excuse me," I said into my handkerchief. "It must be the grass-seed. Did she tell you who your real father was?"

"Sure, she did. She told Mo-Mo and me that onetime when my dad – Donal – was real sore at her, he beat her up and walked out on her, as he often did for weeks on end. Any rate, my Uncle Domino, who'd been in Seattle for years, stopped by one day and saw her, like, all bruised. He was her first love, she told me– and he kinda comforted her and they, like ... did it together, you know? Then she got pregnant and ___"

"You were the result." I finished for her, as she dissolved into fresh tears. I took her in my arms then. "And such a wonderful result!" I added, exultant. "Welcome to the family, my dear granddaughter!"

"But do you think it was okay for Mom to cheat on my dad – and with his step-brother; you being old and of a more, like, prim generation?"

"One day I will tell you my own story which is far from 'prim', I have to say. And no, I wouldn't blame your mother for what she did. *No* man who beats up a woman deserves her love and loyalty, or that of his children, either. Your 'father' went through a great deal in one period of his life, but so did Dominic too. Subsequently, he was given every chance, not least by me, but I fear that he may never realise the sacrifices that so many made for him. Forgive me if I speak harshly of him."

She was silent and thoughtful for a few moments. "Okay," she said eventually. "I think I can get my head around it now. It was, like, a shock, you know?"

"I *do* know, Maddie, and we will talk more about this later. Now I want to show you somewhere very special. Come with me."

That scene took place ten years ago now, on the eve of my eighteenth birthday. She was especially interested to know that I'd been born on that date.

"July 22nd, St Mary Magdalene's day," she said. "How odd! My own birthday is the same day as hers is reputed to be: February 22nd. What is it about the number 22? St Cecilia's is on that day of the month too. And that explains your name too, of course: Madeleine. What about Grace?"

"That's after Grace Cathedral back home in San Francisco," I answered.

She insisted that I stay over and that we celebrate it together, though I ought really to be with my mother and Mo-Mo, she said. I explained that I had stormed out after hearing the disclosures about my father, having searched Mo-Mo's telephone book for an address and a number.

"Then we must phone them right away and let them know that you're safely with me in Cornwall," she said. "You can say that you're going to celebrate this important birthday with a poor old widow who might even be persuaded to leave the house and take you out to lunch."

THREE

I didn't find that account of our meeting until after she'd passed away. As I say, it was in her writing-desk together with other papers; poems she'd written; newspaper cuttings, letters, a list of wedding guests, concert programmes and the Order of Service for Bruno's funeral in the Cathedral. Maybe she'd forgotten about it, but I like to think she'd have included it in the appropriate place in the memoir.

Reading it, I realize how overjoyed she was to learn that *Dominic* was her son.

'There is so much of Bruno in him,' she said to me more than once. "If only we'd known for sure while he was still alive, - though he always treated him like a son on the occasions that they met. He never met Donal'.

It transpired later that the reason Donal didn't love me was not so much that he suspected that I wasn't his: he saw me as living proof that Cecilia was *his* mother because I looked so like her! He and Mom split ten years ago after all this came out; and he went to Australia and hasn't been heard of since, though I think my brother and sister keep in touch with him. The two 'boys', as Cecilia called them, had gotten less close to each other as long ago as 1975 when Frances went to the States to join Domino, and Don 'stole her right from under his nose'. Sadly, Mom and my real father have never gotten together, but I have great hopes. But all that can be told another time; this story is Cecilia's.

Her funeral, which took place in Porthwenna Church, was a solemn, beautiful and poignant occasion. She left instructions specifically that 'the old Service' should be used *(none of those sanitized new versions; find an elderly parson who knows how things used to be done)* The music included 'Brother James's Air', *Recordare* from the Mozart Requiem, 'How Lovely are Thy Dwellings Fair' from Brahms's German Requiem, 'Thou knowest, Lord, the secrets of our hearts' by Purcell – the one in the Croft Burial Service - and a setting by Bruno himself of 'Weeping may endure for a night, but joy cometh in the morning'. I was familiar with some of these from the times I'd attended the Anglican Grace Cathedral at home. (Although I usually went to the Catholic Church, I preferred the music there and sang in the Special Choir.) The hymns were 'For all the Saints' and the one that ends: 'Holy, heavenly love', a childhood favourite. She had already arranged a choral group, soloists, instrumentalists - the lot – to be on stand-by for when 'it' happened; even ordered a 'real Cornish tea' in the new Village Hall afterwards. An old friend of hers from long ago, Paul Davies, now eighty years of age, played the organ and really made it 'speak'. I met some of her other old friends also, all of whom said I was the living image of her. (I guess there was no need for the DNA tests we had done the year after I arrived).

Instead of burial, however, she wished to be cremated so that her ashes can be scattered, in a private, family ceremony, around

St Elowen's Well, where Bruno's ashes have already been strewn. This is to take place next year on their Wedding Anniversary, June 3 2012. Her Letter of Wishes ended thus: *My dearest wish is that all my family should be present and that there should be reconciliation between those members who have been at odds with each other for too long. "Love one another."*

My task now is to ensure that each member of the family receives a copy of this manuscript on that day. After that, I may thread my loom again and weave another tapestry exploring the Magdalene connection.

EPILOGUE

A lone *of the little company assembling here today, Maddie knows that the spirit of Cecilia already inhabits this place. She comes often, the old Labrador at her heels, to lean against the ancient tree and shed quiet tears. But each time, after a while, she feels herself to be enfolded by soft wings, and is comforted by the assurance that love does indeed survive beyond death.*

And here they come to gather in front of the Well: Edmund, Agnes and Lizzie with their families, the youngest child trailing a teddy-bear called Rosie; Frances supporting her mother, Moira; Tom Fahy, looking old and frail now; Dominic carrying the ashes in a roughly carved wooden box made by Petroc at school; and Maddie, wearing the dress of deep gold silk that her grandmother wore on her wedding day, the deep rose-magenta of Cecilia's beloved foxgloves providing an intense contrast.

The little ceremony is about to begin when there are two late-comers. One has travelled all the way from Australia, via Ireland, to pay his last respects; the other, a still beautiful, petite, white-haired woman, is his mother, Bridie.

ACKNOWLEDGEMENTS

My sincere thanks to all the friends and family who have encouraged me in the writing of this novel, particularly to Jo Vernon, who allowed me the tranquillity of her French farmhouse in which to write some of it, and who read and commented on the first draft; also to my good friends, Terry Dennison and Sue Aplin and my sister, Bridget Bailey, for their interest throughout the writing of it and for assuring me that seventy-two was not too old to start writing. Affectionate thanks also to the late Mike Aplin who offered a copy of his very latest painting to be used as a cover for this book.

I acknowledge the tolerance of my late husband, Ian, who put up with my absence in 'the room upstairs' for much of each day and did not allow me to feel guilty for my neglect of many domestic chores!

Thanks are also due to John Heaton, my publishing consultant, for his most thorough and encouraging appraisal of this, my first novel, and the advice he has given me since I first submitted it to him.

I owe a debt of great gratitude to my parents, if I may thank them posthumously: to my mother, who left a handwritten memoir, starting with her family history and giving an account of her childhood, teenage years and young womanhood up until the day of her marriage to my father, who was twenty two years her senior. Editing this gave me the idea of starting with a fictitious memoir. My father was responsible for the Irish connection, his mother being a cousin of Douglas Hyde, the academic who became first President of the Irish Republic - in spite of his being a Protestant. In 1962 my father gave me, as a wedding present, a small cottage in S.W.Cork, to which I retreated at least three times a year. (Even now, I still support Ireland's Rugby team – even when they play my native land!)

Lastly, I must thank the writers of the books which helped with my background knowledge of the Industrial School to which the two boys were sent. I will list them as follows:-

THE GOD SQUAD   Paddy Doyle

FEAR OF THE COLLAR   Patrick Touher

SCARS THAT RUN DEEP   "   "

SUFFER THE LITTLE CHILDREN Mary Rafferty and Eoin O'Sullivan

DVD: SONG FOR A RAGGY BOY is a heart-rending story of life in an Industrial Reformatory

DVD: THE MAGDALENE SISTERS tells the story of three unmarried mothers in a Magdalene Laundry.

December 2014

ABOUT THE AUTHOR

Alice Lee Thornton was born in Ely, Cambridgeshire, in 1938. Her father was Precentor of the Cathedral, and Thornton was raised in a clerical household that lived, at various times, in Devon, Cornwall, Shropshire, and Somerset.

Educated at Christ's Hospital Girls' School in Hertford and the College of St. Matthias, Bristol, Thornton pursued a teaching career, specializing in English and music. After retiring from her last school post in 1985, she provided piano lessons to up to fifty students a week and ran a bed and breakfast from her home, Holly Lodge, with her second husband.

Married three times, she has three children with her first husband and four delightful grandchildren. She stays in touch with two sets of stepchildren.

Thornton began writing at age seventy-two, transcribing and editing her mother's handwritten memoir. A holiday in Cadgwith, Cornwall, inspired *Angel, Sinner, Mermaid, Saint*.